CW00498027

Tom Haward
The Path of Chaos

Published by: Cinnabar Moth Publishing LLC
Santa Fe, New Mexico

Cover Design by: Ira Geneve

ISBN-13: 978-1-953971-82-1
Library of Congress Control Number: 2023931196

The Path of Chaos

TOM HAWARD

Content Notes:

Thetfv deals with many difficult topics that may be triggering for some readers.

Drug use (explicit)
Explicit language
Child abuse (non-sexual, explicit)
Medical trauma (explicit)
Genitalia mutilation (implied)
Homophobia (explicit)

Chapter 1

Britannia 2030

London

The nail hit an artery, and blood splattered Max's face. It didn't disgust him; it gave him a hard-on. Before the arterial spray got out of control Max hammered the nail in further, which acted as a plug and controlled the bleeding. He wiped his brow but still had one more nail to do. He stood up and cricked his neck; it clicked in a couple of places.

Max walked around to the other side and picked up the final nail. He weighted it in his hand. With all the advancements in technology over the last 2000 years, the good old-fashioned nail had barely changed, and crucifixion was still as reliable as ever. Guess some things reach perfection quicker than others. He looked down at Olivia (my god, she looked like his ex, Lucy). She was barely conscious. The pain had caused her to pass out a couple of times, and he'd had to up the dosage of saline fluid to ensure she was hydrated. That was one improvement the Romans had made to the crucifixion process: hooking the victims up to saline made the process last even longer and prolonged the agony. Max checked the saline feed was still in place properly. He wasn't going to lose this one early.

He licked her face, but Olivia barely responded and Max worried she wasn't going to last even another hour. He reached into his pocket and pulled out smelling salts. He undid the bottle, bent over and placed the vial under Olivia's nose. She jerked awake from the pungent smell and opened her eyes. She went from docile to distressed in seconds, and terror washed over her face like a thing of beauty to Max.

"Hi darling. Glad you're with us again. Thought we'd lost you for a second."

Olivia let out a noise that came from deep within her gut. It was animalistic.

Max felt his trousers twitch at the sound. He wished he could stick it to her again. He also wished he could have done a double crucifixion with his ex, Lucy.

"Now, now, love, don't get yourself in a tizzy. No point using up all that energy before the fun has truly begun. I've got another nail to do still."

Olivia closed her eyes.

Max slapped her face.

She opened her eyes again and mumbled that she was sorry.

"Good girl. You know I like to look in your eyes while I do it."

Max placed the nail over Olivia's left wrist, positioning it between the ulna and radius bones. He still got annoyed at the depictions of the God-Carpenter's crucifixion because no-one would have been stupid enough to put nails through a person's hands. Those nails would have ripped right through the soft tissue and the God-Carpenter would have fallen off that cross within minutes. But if people were dumb enough to believe the God-Carpenter was some sort of deity after dying so quickly on a cross, then they weren't going to be too concerned about the accuracy of his crucifixion depictions. Max imagined what it would have been like to kill the God-Carpenter, and felt his trousers twitch again.

Focus on the here and now. You can't keep lovely Olivia waiting.

Max fumbled behind him for the hammer and felt an empty space where the hammer should have been. He looked over to his left, assuming he had left the hammer next to Olivia's right arm, but it wasn't there either.

Max muttered to himself that he would forget his head if it wasn't attached to his body. At that moment, his head was almost removed from his body by the force of the blow that connected with his skull. The hammer he had been looking for hit his right temple with such violence it sent splintered bone into his brain. He let out a guttural sound that made Olivia's seem like a cute little squeak. Max felt moisture splatter his face like the arterial spray from moments before – it was spit from his attacker.

"Piece of Roman shit," the attacker said, and spat once more in Max's crumpled, bleeding, distorted face. "And that's for my brother."

The attacker stared at the dying Roman and hoped he was experiencing fear of death as his synapses fired for the last time.

In actuality, Max was wondering if he had left his window open for his cat to get in his quarters. She would be hungry and wouldn't be able to eat otherwise. What the hell was her name? It didn't occur to him that having his skull crushed in would cause his brain to focus on such random and banal things as it fought to survive. He thought he was being a right numpty for being unable to remember the name of his cat. He would have a good laugh about this when he finally remembered.

Snowflake? Nope.

Sooty? No, that's a shit name.

Lucy?

No.

Shit, he missed Lucy. Why did she have to leave? Fucking bitch. Wow. No. He didn't mean that. She's not a bitch. Maybe Lucy would arrive and help him to hospital? Maybe she loved him still?

Lucy. Lucy. Lucy.

"What's he saying?"

"Fuck knows. His brain is mush. They reckon when you die your brain expels random thoughts."

"Who's Lucy?"

"Probably his mum or something," said the attacker.

"Wouldn't he just say, 'Mum' if it was?"

"Seriously, Tobias? You're analyzing his final thoughts before he kicks the bucket? Why don't we put him on a couch and do some counselling? Ask him if he got enough tit as a baby? Find out if he wants to kill his dad and fuck his mum?"

Tobias looked hurt. "I'm just curious, that's all. No need to be a dick about it, Mav."

Mav sighed. "Really? You're going to sulk? What did I say that was so out of line?"

"It's not what you said, it's the way you said it."

"I'm very sorry, petal, do you want me to kiss your hurt feelings better after we finish murdering someone and trying to save Olivia's life?"

"Well okay then. As long as you kiss me like you mean it for once."

"You're proper special, you know that, right?" said Mav.

"You proposed to me, remember?" said Tobias and winked at

his fiancé. Mav grumbled something under his breath but before he had another reason to berate his lover, Tobias was already doing what was necessary to save the crucified victim from her nightmare.

"Olivia? Olivia? Can you hear me? We're going to get you out of here, but I'm not gonna lie, freeing you from the crucifix is gonna hurt like a bitch. I need you to nod or blink that you can hear me?"

Olivia nodded.

Tobias and Mav went to work. After exchanging words on how they would minimize Olivia's agony and not mess things up and accidentally kill her in the process, they went about their task like old pros. To be fair to them, they were old pros. That had in excess of three hundred rescues from the Roman crucifix under their belt. 306 to be exact. Olivia would be 307.

With barely another word spoken to each other, Tobias and Mav carefully removed the nails from Olivia's wrist and feet and plugged the bleeding. Her shoulder had been dislocated (which was common) but that would have to be fixed back at base. Within twenty minutes, Olivia was cradled in Tobias's arms.

"Is he dead yet?"

Maverick glanced over at Max's body and could see his lips were still moving, "Nope, he's still on his way out. Any luck, he'll be alive long enough for the crows to come and pluck his eyes out. Let's go."

"What do you think Boatman will say?"

"He'll say, 'what took you idiots so long?' And I'll say that my dipshit boyfriend got all sensitive in the middle of a rescue mission because I hurt his feelings.'"

"For a gay Black man you're really offensive, you know that?"

"Shut up, and don't drop Olivia. Hurt feelings would be the least of your troubles"

"I'm not scared of Boatman," said Tobias.

Mav let out a booming laugh that echoed off Southwark's cobbled streets and close-knit terraced houses. "Just don't drop Boatman's wife, and we'll forget what you said."

Mav and Tobias walked in silence for a few minutes, and then Mav looked at Tobias and said, "You are an over-sensitive idiot. You know that, right?"

Tobias opened his mouth to protest, but before he could defend himself—he wouldn't see the irony—Mav cut him off and said, "But you're my over-sensitive idiot and I love you very much."

Tobias went the color of the surrounding brickwork and walked with a bounce in his step. Olivia whimpered in his arms but was stable. The two figures somehow managed to disappear into the night, leaving behind them row upon row of crucified bodies and the twitching, dying body of the emperor's son.

Chapter 2

"How is she doing?" asked Boatman, frowning at the bed where his wife dozed.

"She was lucky to have been saved when she was."

"I'm not sure I would use the word lucky, Doc, but I understand your sentiment," said Boatman. Boatman was an intimidating figure, and one sentence could fluster most men as it had done to Doctor Silverman. The doctor's face flushed and he stammered his way through his analysis of Olivia's condition, overstating his optimism for a full recovery. Boatman's intelligence was immense. He cut the doctor off during the cheery prognosis. "Doc, don't talk to me like an idiot or a sensitive schmuck. Olivia was in the middle of being crucified by those Roman fuckers – the fact that Tobias and Mav found her, let alone saved her, is something to praise the gods for. I've resigned myself to thinking she's not going to make it, so it's up to you to prove me wrong."

If Silverman had flushed before, it was nothing compared to the loss of color from his cheeks now.

Boatman turned his attention away from the nervous doctor (who had dropped his clipboard and was struggling to keep his composure) and addressed the large black man in the room, "How did you find her?"

Maverick had been watching the exchange between Boatman and Silverman with mild amusement but went somber and said, "I would like to say we were being smart, but it feels more like blind luck to be honest."

"I would suggest you're being unusually modest, Maverick. What happened? I can handle the truth. I'm a big boy," said Boatman.

"We guessed the Empire was intending on making Olivia a bit of a show for the world to see, knowing who she was and what she means to you. We knew London Bridge would be a rather high-profile spot."

"Because it's the only bridge left that people can walk across," said Boatman. It wasn't a question.

"And she needed to be crucified at a time with maximum exposure," observed Mav.

"And?"

Mav wasn't usually of a nervous disposition, but Boatman had a way of making even an 18-stone muscle mountain look at his shoes.

"And?" repeated Boatman.

"They used Nero's son to do the job."

Maverick had read a poem once which described a loud silence. He'd never really understood, but he did now because Boatman's silence was deafening. Maverick decided to fill the void. "It's uncertain why Max was used, as it was huge risk to his safety."

"He's Nero's son, that's all the explanation needed." Boatman's face dropped when he also came to another realization, "So he raped her?"

"We think so, yes."

"You killed him?"

"We left him for dead," said Maverick, barely able to look at Boatman having seen what Max had done to Olivia.

"So you're not certain Max is dead?"

"No-one could survive a hammer to the side of the head from me," said Maverick, unconsciously puffing his chest.

"Let's hope you're right. Otherwise you left a witness."

"He was bleeding out and his brain was mush. Even if he did survive, he'll be shitting himself in diapers and dribbling for the rest of his life."

Boatman asked Mav a few more questions about Max and anything else that could be useful for their continued war against the Empire. Boatman asked Maverick one last question: "Are we losing?"

"We're not winning."

"We will be. And when Centurion Faust gets home it will feel more like we're winning. You and Tobias best get moving. And remember, I just want you observing."

"I'm still confused by that. All that work to find out where he lives and we just 'observe?'"

"Trust me."

Maverick nodded and left his boss to his thoughts. Boatman asked everyone else to leave the room. Silverman thought about objecting as Olivia needed constant attention but from Boatman's demeanor wisely kept his objections to himself. Boatman seemed to read the doctor's mind and said, "Don't worry, Doc, I'm not stupid enough to leave her in danger, I've done that once already. Any changes and I will call you back in. Just give me a moment with my wife, will you?"

Silverman nodded and scurried out of the room.

Once Boatman was alone with the still figure of Olivia, his

shoulders dropped and he momentarily leaned against the wall.

"I'm sorry, my love. I'm so sorry. Forgive me. Please."

Boatman almost felt unable to look at his wife. He felt ashamed he had failed to protect her. He looked at his rough hands, which Olivia always said made her feel safe when he held her close, and wondered how he had messed up so, so badly?

He was far from a giant in height, but the Empire's propaganda had depicted him as a mythical behemoth. Boatman was infamous for his brutal strength and his brutal rage. Boatman was almost a walking contradiction, though. His eyes were hazel and soft. When he looked at people, they felt comforted, not afraid. Olivia said she'd loved his eyes before she loved him. She'd said that his eyes made her feel safe and protected. She'd said his eyes were almost as gentle as a puppy's. He'd laughed when she said this because it was sweet and also because those eyes had been looking into the eyes of a dying man only hours before. They were the eyes of a wolf then.

That duality was what made Boatman so unnerving. He looked at Olivia with such delicate love and affection, it was easy to think he was unable to even squash a mosquito on his arm. Out of Olivia's presence and in the presence of men (and women) who tried to usurp him, those eyes blazed with vengeance and his hands acted out his wrath.

Maverick commented to Tobias, when whispering in bed once, that Boatman scared him more than the thought of crucifixion. Tobias called his boyfriend a wimp but smiled as his lover hugged him tighter.

Rage was Boatman's close companion from the day he was born. Boatman was conceived out of rage. Boatman's mother was the victim of Roman rage and therefore her son was destined to exhibit the same brutality as the man who had terrorized her. It was common for soldiers to rape plebians. If a victim was with child because of the rape, the Empire believed it 'honorable' to support that child. There was dishonor in producing a bastard, so the soldier would be contractually obliged to marry the victim and raise the child (if it was a boy). The problem was, most victims were far too scared to pursue the incident and identify their attacker. Even so, the uncertainty of a witness coming forward to potentially leech money off the Empire was not favorable. The unofficial (and preferred) rule was that every soldier has urges and they need to be sated. It is therefore wise to dispose of the woman after the act – like you would a condom. The Empire saw murder as a form of contraception.

Boatman's mother had been attacked while cleaning up the blood of a torture victim. She had been getting the site ready for the next day. A rebel had been whipped within an inch of his life, and it was taking her longer than usual to wash away the blood. She had felt a presence behind her as she was on her hands and knees scrubbing the stainless-steel post used to hold the person in place. She didn't even have to time to react and get to her feet. The soldier had been watching her clean and was already buzzing from the adrenaline of the torture. Seeing her wash away the blood turned him on, and all he could think about was fucking her right where he had shed the blood of rebel scum.

So he did.

Boatman's mother never fully recovered from the brutality of the attack. The soldier's intent had been to adhere to party policy and kill the woman after he came. He beat her skull in on the post and assumed that had been enough. Boatman's mother survived because the soldier assumed the blood of the rebel was her blood, assumed she would bleed out in matter of minutes.

She hadn't.

She was found by Joseph, a priest, who carried her to his temple and kept her alive. She had asked Joseph to put her out of her misery many times, but Joseph felt spiritually obliged to keep her alive.

So he did.

The seed that grew inside her was a violent, destructive one. It had become the man who stood in a hospital room wondering whether destruction was his destiny.

Boatman rubbed his chin in thought, making his beard bristle. He wasn't sure how Olivia had been found so easily by the Romans, and he wasn't sure what that meant for their safety. He felt guilt bubble in his belly; he also felt dread wrap its arms around him. Dread that his fate was sealed. Dread that the women in his life were cursed as long as they were associated with him. Dread that life was a flat circle and doomed to repeat itself.

Was Olivia's fate simply a repeat of his mother's?

Would Olivia conceive a Roman bastard?

Would that bastard be born of rage?

Would that bastard draw similar fateful circumstances to himself?

"I'm so, so sorry," Boatman said again and again, almost like a prayer.

Olivia stirred at the sound of his words and Boatman rushed over to his wife's side. He held her hand and felt her resist. She had never resisted him before, and it hurt. She opened her eyes and looked at her husband. She asked for some water and once her thirst had been quenched whispered something. Boatman leaned in as he couldn't hear what she croaked.

She repeated her words. "The buzzing has become so loud."

Boatman looked at her, confused, but she said nothing else and closed her eyes again.

Silverman came back into the room and said, "I saw her heart rate spike slightly, is she awake?"

"She spoke to me," he said without looking at the doctor and continuing to stare at his wife.

"What did she say?"

Boatman didn't respond because he wasn't sure himself.

Chapter 3

"Is he dead?"

"No sir. He's alive. Just."

Centurion Faust removed his helmet and ran his hand through his hair, "Scoop him up and get him back to the Castrum as swiftly as possible."

"Yes sir," said the soldier, saluting.

"And soldier?" Faust didn't wait for an acknowledgement of the address. "If he dies, I will personally rip your throat out."

The young soldier gulped and carefully got to work of tending to the injured heir to the throne and getting him back to base.

What a mess. What was Legatus Titus thinking? What the fuck was he doing sending that little prick to the front line? Faust swallowed hard. This was going to be a shit storm and Faust was certain he was going to be splattered from head to toe in proverbial feces. His objections had been noted in the transcripts and he hoped the transcripts had recorded the moment Titus admonished Faust for doubting his authority and judgement. Well everyone was going to doubt the man's judgement now. If Titus finished the week without being nailed to a cross then, by the gods, Faust would eat his – actually, he wasn't going to mock the gods with a wager. He was barely keeping both feet on fate's tightrope as it was.

It was no good pointing the blame at Titus though. They'd all fucked up. Even if Faust believed it much more appropriate to have crucified Boatman's woman in private and then televised it to the world, it didn't change that he'd messed up security big time. He'd underestimated the size of Boatman's balls. He'd also underestimated the impressive efficiency of Boatman's top officers.

Faust started walking to the end of London Bridge. The cobbled streets were spattered in blood. Some of the blood was from the dead/dying criminals hanging on the crosses on either side of the Centurion but a lot of it was blood of Faust's own men. He stopped for a moment and looked up to his left. The River Thames was snaking off to the east. There were a number of vessels sailing along the river carrying early morning supplies to other parts of the city and some were steaming further afield. Faust momentarily wished he was on one of those boats steaming over to the Aquitania region. Sunshine, wine and cheese were preferable to this god-forsaken, gray shit hole of a city.

Career prospects? Faust laughed to himself. What career prospects? He was meant to be enjoying residing over a Legion of Peace, fucking alabaster-skinned girls and eating oysters until he burst.

But here he was.

Fighting an enemy that refused to surrender and seemed invincible.

He averted his gaze from the boats floating to paradise and looked up at one of the criminals slowly dying. He was one of Boatman's followers, the screen at the foot of the cross indicated so. In spite of his injuries (Boatman's soldiers got a few extra lashings before crucifixion) the criminal was conscious and staring straight at Faust. They locked gazes for a few seconds. To Faust's surprise, the criminal was smiling. Faust moved closer, never breaking eye contact. The criminal was suspended roughly seven feet off the ground so Faust had to look up.

"What's your name?"

"Mattius."

"Why are you smiling, Mattius?" asked Faust.

The criminal's breathing was labored, and he tried to gulp some air before speaking, "I enjoyed watching my friends fuck over your soldiers." The criminal tried to laugh but it came out as a rasping cough. It was gruesome to see as it was like a cross between agony and ecstasy and Faust nearly looked away.

Mattius had indeed enjoyed seeing his friends Maverick and Tobias go to town on the group of soldiers employed as security that evening. Mattius hadn't been on the cross for very long so had even able to let out the odd cheer when Maverick or Tobias caved in a soldier's skull. He didn't cheer so much after he called for his buddies to get him down from this mother fucking cross and they said they couldn't.

Why not?

Boatman's orders are to get Olivia and only Olivia.

Mother fuckers.

Sorry buddy.

Don't sorry buddy me, you pricks.

No need for insults, Matty Boy.

Insults? I'm pissed off! I'm nailed to a fucking cross and you're not going to save me because you're too busy sucking each other's cocks.

Not really making us want to get you down right now.

You utter wankers.

Chin up, Matty Boy.

That some sort of sick joke you piece of shit?

Yup.

Go screw yourselves.

We're planning on it Matty, we're planning on it.

Tell Boatman I didn't reveal anything to those Roman fuckers.

Will do.

Also tell him it has been an honor to fight alongside him.

We will Mattius, we will.

And guys?

Yeah?

I love you.

See you in the next life. Take care, Matty.

"I could ease your suffering if you give me information about your friends."

The criminal looked down at Faust and without breaking eye contact pushed himself up from his nailed feet and held himself there. Faust knew the pain such an act would cause and admired the man's strength and shuddered at his pain tolerance. It almost seemed as if the criminal was enjoying the pain.

"Your soldiers tortured me and didn't get anything out of me," croaked the criminal, "I actually asked them to burn me again." Mattius's face formed his ghoulish grin again and he coughed up blood.

"You're a sick bastard, Mattius."

"I'm not the one who wears a toilet brush on his head. You might want to reassess your view of what makes people sick." His breathing was extremely labored and his words came out as rasping croaks.

"Last chance saloon. I can put you out of your misery and save you from a few more hours of agony. Think about that. You could be up there for a few more hours or you have a golden ticket out of that prospect."

He appeared to consider Faust's words. "Okay," he said.

"Okay?"

A cough. A bit more blood. "Yeah, okay. I'll show you mine if you show me yours."

"I don't follow," said Faust.

"I'll give up some information if you do one thing for me."

"Not entirely sure you're in the position to negotiate."

Mattius smiled sardonically, "I clearly don't have a decent negotiating position. I'm asking out of mercy and grace, which a man of your stature can surely bestow. At the end of this day it won't make any real difference to me as I will be dead."

Faust liked this man. "I guess I have nothing to lose. It's not like you can come down from that cross and hurt me. What can I do for you?"

Mattius was struggling to breathe and had to compose himself to be able to utter his next sentence. "Well it goes like this. It's rumored you pure-bred Romans, and it appears you're one, have cocks of epic proportions. So it would be great if you could whip your giant dong out and then go and fuck yourself."

Silence hung in the air for a moment as Mattius's words settled. Faust then laughed and laughed. If this rebel was a reflection of the demographic of Boatman's recruits, then no wonder they were hard to beat. Here's a man with nails driven through his wrists and feet. Here's a man who has been tortured with steel and flame. Here's a man gasping for his last breath, and he still finds the capacity to take the piss out of a high-ranking Roman soldier when his pain could be swiftly ended. Mattius had a far bigger set of balls than Faust, that was for sure.

Faust walked away from Mattius and inspected the bloodbath at the end of the bridge. No wonder the criminal said he'd enjoyed watching his friends at work. They had obliterated a dozen soldiers with what appeared to be such brutal ease Faust wondered if these men were even human and not forged by Jupiter himself.

He glanced over at the hanging figure of Mattius and, for a confusing moment, envied him.

"Fear the gods, this is a shit show if ever I saw it," sighed Faust to no-one in particular. He pulled out a cigarette and puffed on it while surveying the scene. How did two men manage such carnage on their own? He must have said this out loud as a voice behind him answered.

"No idea, but they've made us look weak."

Faust turned to face the familiar voice. "You've wandered into the wrong jurisdiction, Atticus."

"I would think you need all the help you can get, Centurion."

The two men locked arms and briefly hugged.

"It looks like the eternal Empire sunshine hasn't been caressing your skin in recent weeks," said Faust, looking his compatriot up and down.

Atticus was from southern Italy and usually olive-skinned and fresh-faced. He looked almost gray, and his lanky frame had lost some of the usual taut muscle definition.

"This dreadful city sucks the color out of your cheeks."

Faust murmured in agreement, dragged on his cigarette and flicked it away. "So, what brings you to my calamity?"

"I would say to gloat at your misfortune but some of my men were casualties of your rebel fighters, so I wanted to ask you what the hell happened?"

"Boatman happened."

Atticus spat on the floor in disgust. "May the gods strike that bastard down."

"I wonder if he has a deal with the gods. He's a phantom."

"His wife isn't."

"But his soldiers are. Look at what they did," said Faust waving his hand in the direction of the bloodied soldiers beside them.

"I find it hard to believe two men did this."

"By the gods, I think we're missing something."

"Have you watched the footage?"

"I'd rather watch my wife kiss another man than watch my soldiers being fucked up by a couple of rebel scum."

"You need to watch it," said Atticus, "It's quite astounding."

"You sound like you admire them."

"We're masters of execution, so I do admire their efficiency."

"How have you seen the footage before me? In my jurisdiction?"

"Right place, right time back at the Castrum. You had already left, and I needed to see it because of my men being caught in the storm."

"Protocol means shit nowadays," grumbled Faust.

"I noticed you were talking to one of the rebels. Anything useful exchanged?"

"Oh, you know, the usual. I asked what the view was like from up there and he told me to go fuck myself."

Atticus glanced over at the dying figure of Mattius, smiled and said, "British humor at its finest. Before I stabbed a British rebel through the heart, he said pasta was like that friend you forget to invite to a party but always turns up – bland and terribly annoying. I laughed a lot as I stabbed him to death."

Faust guessed Atticus was talking bullshit but didn't have the energy to question yet another one of his anecdotes. He surveyed the scene and grimaced at the sight. There had been no mercy. Not only had there been no mercy, but it appeared some of the soldiers had experienced pretty sadistic ends to their lives.

He walked over to a sprawled body of a soldier and crouched down to investigate the bloody remains.

"Futuo," said Faust under his breath. "What the hell did they do?"

"They clearly had a lot of fun, that's what they did," said Atticus, standing over Faust.

"How is that even possible?"

The dead soldier was on his back, his left leg bent and hooked beneath his right. His arms were splayed out beside his body and were soaked in blood like someone had poured a bucket of the stuff over him. The excessive amount of blood was not disturbing to Faust. It was the soldier's face that chilled him and confused him. The soldier's eyes were wide open, and if the eyes are a window to the soul then his soul had been filled with horror.

Faust said it again. "How is this even possible?"

The soldier had died from having his jaw almost cleanly torn from his face. There was a pool of blood sitting in the remnants of his mouth, still and shiny. Faust felt a temptation to disturb the blood with his finger. He stood up but didn't look away from bloody mess of the soldier in front of him.

"How is it possible to rip a man's jaw off?" Faust didn't care that he was repeating himself, he was flabbergasted. It wasn't the brutality of the act that shocked him. His hands had been soaked in the blood of dozens of people. He was finding it hard to process the strength it would have taken to do it.

"Clearly with brute determination. Whoever did it is a beast."

"*The* Beast."

"Boatman's second in command?"

"It would make sense," said Faust. "He's like the storms of

Jupiter in his rage."

"Ever been face to face with him?"

"No. I saw him once at the Colosseum and that was intimidating enough. I don't know if you've had to deal with it in your legion, but I have heard of plenty of instances where soldiers speak of The Beast like they're telling a ghost story to shit each other up."

"Yeah, the pussies, he's just a man who I'd fuck up if I had the chance."

'Well, a dozen soldiers had the chance and either had their jaws torn off, their eyes popped out or their necks snapped like twigs. I would think your confidence is misplaced."

Atticus bristled. "I've seen the footage. They caught your men napping; they wouldn't have had such an easy time with me. By the strength of Mars, I would have gutted them last night if I had been here."

"You don't need to get into a dick measuring contest with me, Atticus."

Atticus puffed his chest, but Faust continued to speak. "These men are astonishingly good at killing and we've been underestimating them time after time. With every rebel I have crucified, Boatman and The Beast have exacted retribution and a rescue. This is the worst I have seen though, and easily the most savage."

"We took Boatman's wife. They were going to come at us hard."

"It feels like more than that. It feels like a message or an indicator."

"The message is pretty clear to me. An aerial shot would probably show the soldiers laid out to spell 'fuck you'."

Faust put another cigarette in his mouth, lit it and closed his eyes for a moment. He tried to focus on the finer details he was taking in and filter out the raw savagery.

"I'll leave you to your usual overthinking and go back to the Castra and file my report. I've seen enough to know this was simple savagery," said Atticus.

Faust grunted a goodbye but didn't open his eyes. He had taken in the scene and was now trying to play it out in his head. Before he could survey the scene with his mind palace, he was disturbed by a soldier calling his name.

"What is it?" asked Faust as he walked in the direction of the voice, stepping over a body.

"Sir, you need to see this."

"See what?" Faust was still a few meters away from the soldier.

"It's a message. A message for you."

"What in gods are you talking abo—" Faust stopped talking as he reached the soldier and looked where the young Roman was looking.

A dead soldier had been positioned so that he was lying on his back, legs crossed at the ankles, and holding a sign in both hands across his chest. His eyes had been removed and placed on his stomach. For some reason Faust thought of the saying *your eyes are bigger than your belly* that his mother said to him when he was young.

"What the hell?"

Faust stared at the chalkboard sign and wanted to know how his home address was on it.

Chapter 4

"Hello darling, you okay?"

"I need you to leave the house, Alypia. Now."

"Why? What's wrong?"

"I haven't got time to explain but please, trust me, just go outside and tell the guards to take you to the Castrum and I'll meet you there," said Faust.

"You're scaring me, Augustus."

"Good. Now get a fucking move on. And don't hang up the phone. I need to see you approach the guards and for them to escort you away from home."

Faust saw her explain to the guards what needed to happen, and within minutes Alypia was being whisked away in a chariot to the safety of the Castrum.

Without saying goodbye, Alypia ended the call. Faust mentally rolled his eyes at his wife's oversensitivity.

"Soldier Gallus and Soldier Marius, I need you to accompany me to my home." Both soldiers saluted and followed Faust to his chariot. Faust climbed on and sat down at the rear. Gallus remained standing whilst Marius fired the engine. The bulletproof glass roof closed over the soldiers' heads and sealed the chariot. They sped off away from London Bridge going south to Augustus Park where Faust's house was situated.

Within fifteen minutes Faust was striding through his front door, gun drawn and Gallus and Marius flanking. The town house had three floors, six bedrooms in total and an airy, open-plan ground floor. Each soldier took a floor and searched. They quickly cleared the rooms, finding no-one present and nothing out of the ordinary to report.

They convened in the kitchen, and Faust holstered his gun.

"Maybe we beat them to it?" said Marius.

Faust grunted and didn't bother to respond. He knew something wasn't right in the house but could quite place it. He needed to walk through and check it off. He'd only searched the ground floor but something didn't make sense.

"I need you both to stand guard outside. Anyone so much as approaches the house suspiciously I want you to shoot them. If anyone is allowed access to the house without my permission, I will crucify you both upside down. Understand?"

Both men nodded and saluted and left the house to take sentry out the front.

Faust pulled a bottle of Chianti from the kitchen wine rack, opened it and poured a glass. He gulped it, wiped the wine from his beard and closed his eyes. He needed to walk through his mind palace and ascertain what was wrong in thc house. His senses had picked up on something, and it was time to pin it down. He mentally entered his mind palace and approached his house. He floated up the porch stairs and entered the hallway. He moved through the lounge meticulously checking off what he had seen and referencing it with the images of the lounge he had stored in his palace.

Halfway through mentally walking the lounge, his suspicions were confirmed.

Faust opened his eyes and walked into the lounge and over to where his trophy sword was kept. It was inside a glass cabinet on a two-meter-long white dresser. Flanking either side of the cabinet were Ming vases, a gift from the Empire for his dedicated service. He found their intricate artwork hypnotizing and they were worth a fortune, so it seemed absurd to not have them on show. He would sometimes sit and have a drink and examine their detail, trying to absorb the intellect it took to create them. Something was off with the vases. The vases had swapped places. Faust slowly approached the dresser. His first thought was a booby trap, but he couldn't see any wires or explosives rigged up. He carefully peeked inside each vase, and they were empty. He checked a second time behind them, without touching them, to see if any devices had been planted but there was nothing at all. Faust scratched his head.

He stared at the vases for a little longer and then made the decision to pick them up to see if they had been tampered with. To be extra careful he checked all around them again without touching them to be sure he wasn't about to have his face blown off by a hidden bomb. He picked up the vase to his left and breathed out when nothing happened. He peered inside it and saw there was definitely nothing inside. He turned it round in his hands and found nothing out of the ordinary. Faust sighed in confusion and was about to place the vase back when he realized he hadn't checked the bottom. He turned the vase over and there was a note taped to the bottom:

Look up

Faust looked up.

We watched you and Alypia sleep the other night.

The words were written in large black letters on the ceiling of the lounge. Being such high ceilings meant he probably wouldn't have noticed the writing for days.

"Futuo."

Faust placed the vase back on the dresser and called his bodyguards back into the house. He instructed them to seal the house off and scour the premises for any further evidence of intruders. He said he didn't care how long it would take and their lives wouldn't be worth shit if they found nothing at all. He expected a report to indicate fingerprints had been found, and evidence of who the intruders were. He said he expected them to be able to have something solid to bring a swift resolution to the fact that some motherfuckers had trespassed on his property and threatened the life of his wife. The soldiers saluted and promised an efficient and fruitful investigation. Their faces betrayed them. Faust noted Marius, in particular, looked like he was considering the option of crucifixion as a more agreeable direction for his life.

Faust turned on his heels and left the house. He climbed onto his chariot and sped off in the direction of the Castrum to brief Titus and also see how long he would be in the doghouse with Alypia. He guessed it would be a long time when she discovered intruders had watched her sleep last night and he had failed to wake up.

Maverick and Tobias watched the Centurion disappear into the distance but remained lying on their fronts on the rooftop of the house opposite.

"What do you think?"

"About what?"

"Should we have killed them?"

"It's not what Boatman wanted," said Mav.

"But why?"

"Fuck knows."

"What's his plan then?"

"Unless you seem to think I have the power to read minds or some shit like that, then I know as much as you."

"You're cranky today," said Tobias.

"You make me cranky."

"And by cranky you mean happy."

"If you don't shut up, then punching you will make me happy."

"Pretty sure you need to work on your anger issues, Mav."

"I'm not angry, Tobias, I'm very calm. And I'm calmly telling you to shut the hell up."

"You're very handsome when you scowl."

Maverick's scowl turned into a slight smirk, "Let's go and report back to Boatman. Hopefully he'll fill us in on what the hell's going on and why we let a Centurion live."

Chapter 5

Maverick and Tobias briefed Boatman on what they had seen and asked the question why their mission was to spook the Centurion and not kill him.

"Sometimes making an ego like Faust know he's vulnerable can be enough for him to make some big mistakes."

And that was it, that was the end of the meeting. Boatman never used more words than he deemed necessary, and this was no exception. Maverick and Tobias shrugged their shoulders and left.

Back in their room, holding each other, Tobias kissed his lover hard on the lips. They stared at each other for a moment, Tobias still feeling butterflies after all these years.

"I'm going to sleep. Don't be a weirdo and stare at me for hours," said Maverick.

"Why would I want to look at that ugly mug more than necessary?"

Maverick kissed Tobias and then rolled over and was asleep in seconds.

Maverick was right though; Tobias watched his lover sleep and felt the heaviness of gratitude in his chest, to be loved by this brute of a man. He also felt gratitude that they had become lovers and his skull hadn't been caved in by the giant hands of Maverick. Tobias had killed many people, but it didn't stop him from still believing in the promise of eternal life after this one. He had a small altar devoted to the God-Carpenter Jesus and believed this dark world wasn't the only world. He believed Maverick was destined to be in his life and that is why their paths crossed like they did and meant love was born instead of death. Tobias was certain because of their entwined fates they had never been in a position of having to fight to the death.

They had met because they were both gladiators, captured as children by the Romans and raised with one purpose in life – to kill or be killed for the entertainment of the masses. For centuries, gladiators were a mixture of slaves, volunteers propelled by ego and the prospects of riches and fame, and the odd senator or even emperor trying to prove his superior fighting skills. In the early 1800s, when there was a mass revolt by the Northern African countries, trying to overthrow the Empire and become independent, the Romans realized many nations were training their children as future rebel soldiers. Underground propaganda was being given to young people, teaching them an alternative narrative to that of Empire approved education.

Roman spies flooded the continent to try and discover the sources of the propaganda and quickly deduced that plugging the source wasn't necessarily the solution. Taking away the receptor seemed much more effective and destructive to rebel morale. Romans ransacked towns and villages and took away children to be trained as gladiators and 'teach' rebels that their best efforts to bring down the Empire were futile.

Mothers wailed as their children were ripped from their arms and this, in turn, tore families apart, breaking the hope and rebellious spirit of many groups. Men felt shame at being unable to protect their families, and women felt resentment toward their husbands, fathers and brothers for putting children at risk. The Romans tore the heart out of homes. In 1821, Emperor Pius II declared an end to the Rebel Propaganda War and hosted a series of worldwide games in which many of the captured children had to fight to the death. It was horrific and gained little public support, but Pius's aim was not public entertainment: it was a fierce warning that rebellion was never going to be tolerated.

After the child gladiator massacre of 1821 Pius decreed that children be trained over many years and made into superior fighting machines, with fame and fortune awaiting the best of the best. It was technically true that the thousands of children in captivity could eventually become revered, as there were many gladiators who were celebrities around the world. But those celebrity fighters were usually in the favor of senators and Centurions and never really given any combats that risked death. Of course, death was always a possibility but only stupidity was the real threat to life. Many of the children being trained would end up fighting to the death against three opponents and possibly a lion thrown into the mix and the only armor they had was their bare skin. Celebrity gladiators though, they had one-on-one matches and were so armored up a sword's blow was like a wasp sting.

Tobias and Maverick were products of this original regime, which Pius's successors continued to follow through with, and were torn from the arms of their mothers when they were barely able to walk. Emperor Augustus II, in 1980, ordered his soldiers to sweep through countries to find worthy future gladiators, as he wanted to find someone special he could use as a poster boy to celebrate Nero's birth. Maverick and Tobias were casualties of this. Maverick was taken from the small town of Jinja in southern Uganda, whereas Tobias was captured in Kefalos on the Greek Island of Kos.

Maverick was sent to a training camp in Nairobi, Kenya, where he quickly grew in physical stature and by the age of 14 was already 15 stone, muscular and vicious. He was sent to the Aestii region, ruled by Bjorn Aska, to train with the elites as his fighting skills, strength and sheer brutality meant grown adults were scared of him. By the age of 20 Maverick was feared, revered and respected. Rome adored him. He annihilated people in the arena, and it became difficult to find anyone worthy enough to fight him.

Maverick understood what his role was though and entertained the crowds. He could kill a man within thirty seconds but knew people were paying big money to watch him. Maverick would therefore drag the fight out, making it appear he might (just might) lose this time and maybe had finally met his match. The opponent would lick his lips with glee, hurriedly move in for a killer blow, and Maverick would take advantage of the arrogance and tear the opponent apart.

In one particular event, Maverick was faced off against six gladiators. In order to stand a chance, Maverick dispatched three of them within moments. His favorite weapon was a type of Gladius sword, which was double edged, but he had one specially adapted to also have a grip and hilt for protection. The traditional Gladius swords didn't have a protective hilt, which Maverick always saw as a weakness with its design. The double edge meant whichever way he swung his sword it was going to make a clean cut. And the first three gladiators experienced very clean cuts.

One particular mistake many fighters made was to queue up

to fight him. Their egos said they could get the glory for killing Maverick. This instance was no different and three fighters lined up to fight, whilst the other three stood back hoping they would get a chance. Maverick wasted no time and rushed at the first man who was surprised at Maverick's speed and half raised his sword in-between attack and defense. Maverick sliced through the fighter's belly, pirouetted and simultaneously ducked as the steel of another blade whizzed above his head. As his spun, his sword spiraled, slicing the feet of the fighter clean off. His body came back to the midday position, with his sword outstretched, Maverick adjusted his grip and plunged the sword through the throat of the third fighter, who had been watching the onslaught with a mixture of fear and adoration.

It's possible the man died happy to have been killed by such an exquisite fighter.

Maverick had stood up and braced himself for the next three men but watched curiously as one of the fighters cut down two of the men from behind. The cowardly fighter (and that's what he was for killing two men from behind, thought Maverick) then squared off about ten meters away. He was holding a Claymore, a large sword traditionally used by Scottish rebels which, to Maverick, appeared a bit too clumsy a weapon choice. Not that it mattered what weapon he had, he was going to die anyway.

Maverick's opponent was tall and wiry but clearly very strong because even if the sword was a clumsy choice, he wielded it with ease and the weight appeared not to bother him. Even so, this opponent wasn't going to last long, and Maverick patiently waited in the standoff, staying silent and not moving. One of Maverick's strengths was drawing out frustration. By not speaking or moving the opponent would feel obliged to make the first move for fear of appearing unsure or afraid to attack. Maverick was the master of the counter-attack and reveled in seeing men hastily lunge trying to catch him off guard.

This time was no different. "I'm going to split your head open and scoop your brains out."

"If you manage to get that close to me it's only because I'll be choking the life out of you," said Maverick.

"That's a smart mouth you've get there."

"Well there needs to be someone smart in this arena." The wiry man rushed at Maverick, swinging his sword in wide arcs.

Wiry man moved with more speed than Maverick anticipated, and he had to adjust his stance and parry a few blows with less time than he'd originally thought he had. He wasn't overly concerned but felt stupid for his miscalculation. In between the clashing of the swords the roar of the crowd could be heard, and the wiry man grinned at the attention, swinging more wildly. This was his undoing – the thought of adoration before the job was done.

He swung the sword from waist height hoping to chop Maverick clean in half, and exerted a lot of energy in the process. Maverick brought his own sword down in a vertical position, blocking the attack. Wiry man's attentions were so focused on a final, killer blow he had both hands on the sword and before the chimes of the colliding swords had stopped ringing, wiry man found a giant black hand wrapped around his throat. Maverick squeezed wiry man's jugular causing him to choke and drop his sword.

"I told you I would choke the life out of you, but I've changed my mind," said Maverick, "I think I might scoop your dumb ass brains out instead."

Wiry man tried to plead for his life. Maverick ignored him and put him out of his misery.

The crowd erupted in cheers and chants of Maverick's nickname, "The Beast! The Beast! The Beast!" Maverick bowed and did the obligatory victory lap of the arena. In truth though, he was using this time to mentally finalize his escape route. He had been planning his escape for over a year, and today was the day he could do it. It was his 500th kill and therefore he was going to be pampered and praised and security was going to be slack because of the celebrations of Maverick's dominance.

This was the day he managed to be free.

Tobias's route to freedom was much more fortuitous, coming down to blind luck and the wonder of Maverick's planning. They did not know each other and, in fact, were scheduled to fight in a few days. Tobias was considered an elite fighter and obliterated his opponents with his speed and skill. He was still no match for Maverick, but it was deemed they would have a longer fight than Maverick was used to, and it was billed as a Titanic match up. Luckily for Tobias, it was a match that never transpired. And luckily for Tobias he happened to be in the right place at the right time and find himself escaping with The Beast even though they should never have met.

For Tobias, it meant he was able to muse on how fate had brought him and Maverick together. Instead of clashing swords in an arena Tobias was able to share a bed with a man who he loved with a fiery passion. He stared at his lover and loved every part of the man. He reached out to trace his fingers down the vertical scar running down Maverick's face but resisted. Mav was sleeping soundly and would not be impressed with being woken because Tobias was feeling soppy.

Tobias said a prayer of thanks to the God-Carpenter for being alive and for the love of Maverick and eventually drifted into a fairly contented sleep. The only thing to disturb it was a dream of being hounded by Phobos, the Roman god of fear. In the morning, Tobias had forgotten the specifics of the dream but still felt unsettled and hoped it wasn't a warning from the God-Carpenter.

Chapter 6

The next morning, Maverick met Boatman in his office. Boatman sipped a coffee, staring at a picture of Olivia on his desk. Maverick decided to break the silence:

"How is she?"

"Like she's been nailed to a cross."

"Good to know sarcasm is the dominant reaction around here," said Maverick. He got up and poured himself a coffee. Boatman carried on staring at the photo of his wife.

"You weren't to know," said Maverick.

"I should have."

"How?"

"We got sloppy. We made it easy for them to figure it out. I should have known they would work out she was my wife."

"But *they* didn't. He did. I don't know how, but he did."

Boatman put his coffee down and leant back in his chair, "At least you put a stop to his sleuthing permanently."

Maverick thought about the twitching body of Max. "It's the least I could do."

"Even though it never gave you the chance to find out about Damba?"

"My brother's dead."

"You don't know that."

"Max is, sorry, *was* a sadist. Damba's dead."

"You can't be certain. You survived Augustus and Nero for years. I know it's been three years since your brother was abducted, but remember you were in captivity from childhood and here you are."

"Augustus and Nero weren't fascinated with eugenics."

Boatman considered this, "Maverick, the Empire has always been fascinated with eugenics."

"Maybe, but Max's tastes even make his father's look vanilla."

"Not anymore." Boatman smiled.

"No, I guess not. But even if Damba is alive, Nero will kill him out of revenge."

"Maybe. Maybe not. I hate to say, Maverick, but knowing Nero like I do, he is more likely to use Damba as bait to draw us out."

Maverick dropped his head, "My brother's better off dead."

Boatman let that sentence hang in the air, because if Damba had somehow survived Max's sadistic experiments, then the pain he would have to endure owing to Nero's rage was unthinkable.

Maverick raised his head and looked at Boatman, "Part of me wishes I had followed Damba to Rome instead of coming to London to find you."

Boatman sympathized. It had been three years since Maverick had smuggled himself into London, seeking Boatman's help, and Damba was either dead or still being held captive by the Romans. Truth be told, Boatman never quite understood why Maverick sought him out. Yes, Boatman's aim was to see Rome burn like an ironic homage to Nero's namesake 2000 years before, but he was barely making a dent on Nero's grip on London. He couldn't even think about Rome at the moment.

As if reading Boatman's mind Maverick said, "I guess you shouldn't believe everything you read. I remember reading about the mythical Boatman King who was tearing the heart out of the Empire. I watched that footage of you that looked like it was out of a movie. It didn't seem real."

"I could say the same about you. I've watched your fights."

Maverick squinted, "You know it's not the same. You don't need to massage my ego. You would have destroyed me in the arena. But that's not the point. I thought—"

"You thought I would have been more successful in beating Nero and finding a way to get your brother back."

"Yes. I remember when I was posted in the Slavic province of Aestii training in extremely cold conditions and your name floated around that camp like a ghost story. It was hard to know what was a story and what was fact."

"You were in the Aestii province?"

"For nine months," said Maverick. "That's where my scar came from."

"I'm amazed someone managed to get close enough to you to give you that."

"Me too."

"I'm sorry we haven't been able to get your brother back. We'll find a way."

"I hope so," said Maverick.

Maverick appreciated Boatman's effort (he wasn't one to justify his actions very often) but it did little to ease his fears about his little brother. He thought about the moment he and Tobias had to find a way to help Damba, and he had decided to find Boatman three years ago. Tobias had been stunned to learn his partner was actually scared of someone. Tobias was a cynical man and eyed Boatman with suspicion and felt Maverick's desperation to save his brother made him naive. Tobias wasn't keen at all to go back to Rome but viewed it as the only option to save Damba. Maverick saw it differently and was adamant they smuggle their way to Britannia to find Boatman. Tobias didn't think he was a jealous man, but the way Maverick almost revered Boatman made his eyes have a twinge of green. Besides, Tobias hadn't even heard of Boatman, so was trying to work out how this stranger was the only man to have ever made Maverick 'The Beast' Kirabo seem vulnerable.

"How do we even know you're for real? I still see an Empire, and I still see dozens of motherfuckers crucified across London," said Tobias when he first met Boatman.

"What's your name?"

"Tobias. With a T."

"Very droll," said Boatman. He looked at Maverick and said, "Keep your dog on a lead, will you?" Tobias reacted and lunged at Boatman. He was a skilled fighter and rarely misplaced his attacks. This time though, Tobias felt like he was a toddler wildly swinging his arms, hoping something might land. From Maverick's perspective it seemed as if every punch Tobias tried to throw was repelled by an invisible force. It was strange to watch but hypnotic in how Boatman appeared to be expending no energy in defending himself from Tobias's attack. And then in an almost lethargic move Boatman struck Tobias on the chest, sending him flying backwards. Tobias landed on his back, winded and struggling to catch his breath.

Tobias got to one knee, looking ready to try again. Maverick stepped over to his partner and put a hand on his shoulder, "Tobias, don't be an idiot."

Tobias looked up, "Thanks for your help."

"You're a big boy. And besides, sometimes you need your ass kicked."

"And there I was thinking you loved me."

Maverick helped Tobias to his feet and turned to Boatman, "My boyfriend is very suspicious of anyone who chooses to live in a climate where rain is a main topic of conversation."

Tobias said, "Still not your husband, I noticed."

"Really? You want to have this conversation right now?"

"We wouldn't have to have this conversation if you had sorted the wedding by now."

"Sometimes I wish the first time we met was in the gladiator arena."

"I would've kicked that beautiful ass."

Boatman cleared his throat. "As much as I hate to interrupt whatever this is, what is it you want from me? You sought me out, after all."

"Considering how hard it is finding allies across the Empire, I thought you might be one."

"Quite honestly, when the whispers across the Webspace indicated The Beast was on his way to England, I was hoping you were trying to find me. Which is why it didn't take you much effort to track me down."

Tobias said, "So I'm guessing it's a 'we scratch your back' kind of situation?"

"Yes. Knowing I have The Beast as an ally I might be able to finally cut the head off the Empire. If you can give me some time to draw Nero to London, we could cripple the Empire."

"How long?"

"I can't say for sure."

Maverick sighed, "Time's a big factor for us. It's my brother. Nero's son has abducted him. That's why we came to you. If your name reaches across the Empire, then I figured so did your influence."

Tobias chimed in, "I just want to point out I hadn't heard of you."

Maverick rolled his eyes.

Boatman ignored Tobias's remark, "I can try to get some information from Rome about your brother, but until I get more strength here in London, I'm afraid there's not much I can do."

Maverick considered this, "Well let's entice that mother fucker Nero to London, then."

Three years later and all Boatman had to show for his efforts was his seriously injured wife.

"I think we need to accelerate our plans."

"How?"

"Olivia's capture gives Nero a sense of security. They'll believe we're wounded and will go dark for a while. But—"

"But, like when I was in the ring, when you're wounded you step forward, not back, and it throws your opponent off guard."

Boatman nodded.

"We can't underestimate how he'll respond to Max's death," said Maverick.

"He'll want to watch the city burn. We're going to push forward with the timeframe. I need you and Tobias to prepare earlier than expected." Boatman explained the next steps and what an acceleration of timescales looked like. Maverick listened, asked tactical questions and noted down key elements. He listened stoney-faced, but inside, his stomach knotted in anxiety at the size of the task ahead.

When Maverick had finished his meeting with Boatman, he told Tobias the plan. Tobias listened and asked if Boatman had finally gone insane. "He's joking, right?"

"When has Boatman ever been joking?"

"But he doesn't actually think we can achieve what he's suggesting?"

"He wouldn't ask if he didn't."

"We have a few weeks of planning to try and make sure we don't die straight away," said Maverick.

"I guess we should be flattered," said Tobias.

"About?"

"Well, it's a batshit crazy idea and he seems to think we're the only people alive who can pull it off."

"Or he hates us and knows we'll fail miserably and he won't have to put up with us again."

"We should probably bicker less in front of him."

"Based on what we're assigned to do, I doubt we'll ever bicker again."

"Because we'll be proud of each other?"

"No," said Tobias, "because we'll be dead."

Chapter 7

"Is he going to die?"

"I am quietly confident we can save him."

"How confident?"

"Confident enough I won't find myself on a cross," said the doctor.

"That's good enough for me," said Titus.

The doctor was standing by Max's bedside. "You're absolutely sure a man did this to him?"

"It's hard to believe but, yes, a man did this."

"If I didn't know better, I would say either he fell from a great height or he had a head-on collision with an armored chariot."

"He would have been better off if he was hit by an armored chariot," said Titus. "You're absolutely sure you will be able to keep him alive?"

"Keeping him alive won't be a problem. It's whether we can ensure he doesn't spend the rest of his life wearing a diaper and drinking through a straw."

Titus rubbed his eyes, "Doc, I don't even want to think about what that would mean for you if he wakes up like a vegetable."

The Doctor wanted to express his delight if Max did wake up as a vegetable because everything the Doctor had seen of Maximus Nero made him want to remove all the life support and pain relief as soon as possible from the creep. Of course, saying that out loud would mean Titus would take the Doctor and throw him in the Thames so the Doctor said, "I'm hopeful for a full recovery. He'll be chasing women around London in no time."

Titus eyed the Doctor. It was a poorly kept secret about Max's sexual proclivities and the women damaged by his actions. Even though Titus wasn't going to shed any tears over Olivia King, he found Max's added methods of torture disgusting. For his own sake he wanted Max to live, but he hoped the hammer to the skull knocked the deviancy out of the sick bastard. Titus decided to let the Doctor's comments go. There were bigger things to worry about.

"Please keep me updated on his progress."

Titus left the hospital room and walked back to his office. Legatus Titus was the Commander of Britannia. He had the ear of the emperor and the respect of an entire army. Titus wasn't known for his fighting skills; like Faust, he was known for his tactical nuance and diplomatic intelligence. The British, although viewed by the world as one nation, were a group of rather different nations who tentatively cooperated. Titus was stationed in Britannia to keep the island of nations at peace. A foreign invader ruling over three very different cultures created the real possibility of mass uprisings. Titus though, knew how to charm and equally subdue the influencers and thereby keep the masses placated. Well, for the most part. Boatman King created a glitch in his otherwise blemish-free diplomatic record.

He had once called a meeting with Boatman. He had hoped he would be able to bribe the rebel leader into giving up his futile effort against the Empire. A promise of riches and fame.

A promise of diplomatic immunity and safe haven for all he was associated with. It was all a lie, of course. Nero wanted to flog and crucify Boatman on live television in front of an audience of millions. When the day of the meeting came, it quickly became apparent Boatman didn't believe a single promise made. Firstly, Boatman never showed for the meeting. Secondly, the soldier sent to escort Boatman to the meeting was found unconscious on the steps of the Castrum with a note reading, 'Fuck You' written in the soldier's blood. Titus wasn't surprised, but Boatman's rebellion generated attention from Rome that he did not need and dirtied his previously perfect persona.

Titus was making his way back to his office and his young advisor was trying to keep in step with the Commander of Britannia. He wasn't doing a great job of it. "Where's Faust?"

"On his way back, Sir. He has news of the rebels."

"Good. Get me some wine."

"Sir, there's something else." The young advisor was breathing hard trying to keep up with the commander, whose long strides made him cover ground quickly. "Tell me after you've got the wine," said Titus.

"But... but Commander... I..."

"Wine!" Titus strode off leaving the young advisor panting and the most recent to join a long list of people who wished they had not gotten out of bed this morning.

"How's my son?" said a voice as Titus entered his office.

Titus felt his throat tighten but tried to hide it. "He's going to live, assures the doctor."

"If he dies, he deserves it. The stupid cunt. You shouldn't have let him go on the front line."

"I had no choice."

"You always have a choice, Titus. You always have a choice."

The man stood up from behind Titus's desk. He absently brushed a non-existent speck of dirt from the front of his suit and then straightened his tie. He adjusted the laurel wreath on his head and stepped out from behind the desk. Titus dropped to one knee, bowed his head and said, "Hail Caesar."

Chapter 8

"Stand up, Titus."

Titus stood but kept his eyes lowered. Looking Caesar in the eye was about as comfortable as colonic irrigation.

"I'm not going to kill you, don't worry. I need you here looking after this miserable excuse for a country. I'm going to be staying here a while to monitor Max's recovery. And I need you alive to help me find the scum who did this to my son. After all, you know how this god-forsaken island works."

Titus nodded and cleared his throat, "We have an idea who did it, sir."

Nero narrowed his eyes, "Look at me, Titus."

Titus hesitated but then looked up at his Caesar. He reminded himself to book that irrigation. He struggled to meet the emperor's eyes. Nero's eyes were almost black and even after so many years Titus still felt terror looking at the man.

Nero waited on Titus to speak.

"We suspect it was Boatman's henchmen Maverick and Tobias. The CCTV is fuzzy, but Maverick is pretty unmistakable."

"If we know who then why are they not in front of me being

held to account?"

"They treat this city like specters. They disappear as easily as they appear. And we didn't think even they would storm London Bridge."

"You failed to have the foresight that they would come for Olivia? The Beast threw a spear at my head once when he was a gladiator. He did it to enrage me so I would send my best bodyguard into the arena. The gods were not kind to Julius. They watched on as The Beast tore him apart. No, Titus, don't ever try to predict the actions of people like Maverick – he's a chariot pulled by a thousand horses. We can't predict his moves, only hope we can get lucky and put him down."

Titus opened his mouth to speak but Nero hadn't finished. "You failed to protect my son, so I think it's only fair that you should know the pain of being powerless to protect your children. It might focus your attention."

"Caesar, I, uhm, what… what do you mean?" Titus glanced over his shoulder at the doorway. He felt his face flush. "Caesar, my boy, he's only nine. Please, he doesn't need to be punished for my mistakes."

Titus stepped forward, his legs unsteady.

"Caesar?"

Nero was smiling, watching how Titus responded to the threat of danger against his child. "I find it fascinating how I have conquered a planet. Made kings and Queens bow and grovel at my feet. I have created wealth of deific quantities and built an army of fearsome size. I have made you a rich man, Titus, as I have with so many here in London. But still. Still. I am left with people only willing to give me their everything when fear is involved. London doesn't fear me, Titus. London doesn't fear you. You let my son have his head caved in by traitors. They're laughing at me. If they're laughing at me it is because they think I'm soft—"

"They don't think you're soft, Caesar, they adore—"

"Shut the fuck up."

Titus swallowed his words.

"The thing about being seen as soft is it poisons everything. Like pouring bleach into the water supply. It spreads and infects. Soldiers start losing interest in enforcing law. Citizens rebel. It's parasitic. I won't have it."

Nero stared at Titus, unblinking. Titus didn't know whether to hold his gaze or look away. Both choices felt like bad choices. Nero turned around and walked back behind the desk. Titus swallowed some bile. Nero picked up a ceremonial dagger that had been sitting on the desk. A dagger awarded to Titus by Nero for services to the Empire after Titus slaughtered 200 rebels who had, in their small number, brought London to a standstill by blockading a shipping lane and sinking any vessels attempting to enter London's vicinity. Titus had turned one of the rebels, who then planted a bomb and blew them all up. Nero loved it. He loved it so much he sent the dagger to Titus as reward. And reward it was, containing jewels 'donated' by a former monarch of Britannia. Britannia had a strange relationship with monarchies after the Roman Empire were driven away the first time. There was a brief belief in being a republic, but when the Empire left, the majority of the population believed a figurehead was essential to the fortunes of all. So, a Caesar was replaced by Kings and Queens until another Emperor returned. And now a Caesar stood in Titus's office wondering how this backward city had managed to almost kill his son.

Nero walked back over to Titus and told him to kneel. Titus obeyed. Nero grabbed the back of his head by his hair and held the dagger to the Commander's throat. "Do you think I'm soft, Commander?" The blade drew blood.

"No, my Lord." Titus swallowed hard and felt the blade pressing his Adam's Apple.

"I said I wasn't going to kill you, but I'm sure Atticus could do your job."

Titus felt the blade drawing more blood, he knew he had maybe seconds to stay alive, "Atticus is a blunt instrument. He's like the hammer that caved Max's skull in." The blade stopped pressing.

"That's very sneaky of you, Titus. Explain."

Sweat was stinging Titus's eyes, "Atticus would try to quash the rebellion one death at a time, like a blunt instrument. What is needed is a poison to wipe them out. As I showed with those 200 rebels. I can be that poison."

Nero took the blade away from Titus's throat. Not before making sure of another cut to remind Titus he wasn't entirely safe. Not that the Legatus needed any reminding. "Your remarks about poison have given me an idea. We need a way to spread fear through London and cast doubts about Boatman. Meet me at my quarters in a couple of hours."

Nero placed the dagger on the desk and exited the office. As he slammed the door behind him, he called out to Titus to remember to bring wine.

Chapter 9

Caesar Nero II's father, Augustus II, is considered by many historians to be one of the most pragmatic emperors of modern Roman history. His namesake Augustus, the 'First Emperor', who ruled from 63BC until AD14, was a philosopher and praised for the way he brought peace and prosperity to the Roman ruled world. Augustus II wasn't particularly concerned with peace. He knew greed motivated most people, and so as long as he enabled people to prosper he knew rebellions would be sporadic and short-lived as threats to people's potential prosperity.

Augustus viewed Britannia as somewhat of an experiment, seeing what he could do as a marker for the rest of the Empire and possibly use it as a springboard to reach Indigenous America. The British were an interesting nation. They took a stoic approach to oppression. It's not that they rolled over as such, but they tended to shrug their shoulders like they had been given a shitty hand at poker and carry on regardless, hoping the next hand would be better. When Augustus II came flooding into London with his forces in 1968, the opposition was minimal. The British leader of the time, Churchill, had given rousing speeches about fighting the

Romans on the beaches and never surrendering, but a combination of Augustus giving Churchill a choice of 1,000 British troops dying in the middle of the Mediterranean and him blockading London ports so civilians would starve within 6 months or 1,000 British troops dying and Churchill being given very generous compensation if he allowed Roman troops into London whilst giving off an appearance of resistance, meant it wasn't much of a choice. Churchill also didn't really give a fuck about the 1,000 troops as they were "those useless darkies" who had been slaved off when Britannia invaded a group of small Atlantic islands to set up military bases to stave off Roman attack from the West. Churchill used most of the islands' natives as front-line soldiers, as he didn't really care if they lived or died as long as they kept the Romans at bay a little longer.

When Augustus gave Churchill the choice to live and enjoy an endless supply of whisky, courtesy of Rome, Churchill folded faster than a paper house in strong winds. The night that Augustus's troops marched past 10 Downing Street (Augustus thought the British leader's residence was too drab to use as his primary abode), Churchill was gulping whisky to try and drown out the fact his conscience was slightly pricking around the edges, suggesting he had betrayed his country. Augustus was true to his word, and Churchill enjoyed gallons of whisky as his bribe for handing over Britain to the Romans. And as another part to the deal, Augustus instructed the media to write and air rose-tinted platitudes about Churchill's 'Bulldog Spirit' and his sacrifice to the Three Kingdoms. In Augustus's mind, if he created a mythology around Churchill and 'honored' him then the Brits would remain servile.

There was a small uprising of nationalists who fought in the 'spirit of Churchill' who believed Churchill was acting under duress, but this was quashed embarrassingly quickly; especially when the nationalists watched as a recording of Churchill's self-serving deal with Augustus was plastered on every giant screen London had, accompanied by his words, "I'd rather fight for your award-winning whisky than those idiots on the beaches." And when it became apparent how Roman rule brought the benefits of the Roman economy, many people stepped in line. When Augustus became ill, he decided to step down and Nero became emperor. At this point, London had become almost a forgotten part of the Empire's maneuvers.

Nero's advisors declared it no longer a major concern for rebellion and only mentioned it when they needed to import their next ton of oysters. "I don't know what those Brits do, but their oysters are phenomenal," said Nero after he had eaten about three dozen one evening. "Probably the only good thing to come out of Britannia," he laughed as he guzzled on a bivalve. Oysters and politeness seemed to be the best of Britannia, so Nero became complacent about any threat coming out of London. He believed terror kept the masses in line, and terror wasn't expensive. Nero didn't want to share the wealth, and terrified people tended not to question you about their lack of money; they were happy just to be alive. That was true for many parts of the Empire's reach, but Britannia was more shoulder-shrugging in their oppression.

The general consensus among many Brits was that although they didn't like Roman rule, they guessed it was better to brush themselves off and make the best of a bad situation. After all, as long as they were still allowed to have a pint or two after work then who cared whether it was a corrupt politician or Roman emperor calling the shots? With this in mind, Nero eased off the terror to a degree. Yes, he still crucified people on the streets, because it was easier than worrying about trials, but he found the British were quite happy to plod along without trying to make too much fuss. This made him happy as he didn't have to spend too much time or energy on thinking about Britannia.

Everything had changed though. Everything had changed when Boatman stepped into the limelight. Boatman challenged the status quo and inspired rebellion. He was the catalyst of a very un-British uprising against a very ruthless and terrifying emperor. Nero II obliterated anyone who even dared speak against him. He despised criticism and found it offensive that someone would ever see his rule as anything but majestic. Augustus had warned Nero that to try to obliterate Boatman was futile. He needed to reach out to the rebel leader. Nero dismissed his father's advice as the ramblings of a dying man. The only way to live was to respect the authority of the emperor. To criticize was a sin.

One of Augustus's closest advisors learned this the hard way when he carried on his duties as wise counsellor to Nero II after the death of Augustus. The advisor, Jonas, was commissioned by Augustus to be the voice of honesty and integrity, no matter how harsh that voice might be. Augustus had become so enraged by a country's unwillingness to surrender or even negotiate how Roman rule might apply that he dispatched half of his total troops to the country and annihilated the residents on the borders. The villages had nothing even remotely resembling military defenses, being mainly farming communities. The full might of Roman invasion with orders to kill on sight were excessive and brutal. Jonas berated his emperor. "Caesar, you have committed a war crime. You have shamed the name you carry and lost my respect. Rome has ruled for over two millennia because men like you have had the wisdom, blessings and courage to march forward when all hope is lost. A small country being defiant is not something to lose hope over or engage in devastating retaliation. If you wanted to prove the size of your penis, you should have asked me to find you a bigger chariot instead of killing thousands of innocents." Jonas never filtered his words with Caesar, and Augustus had enjoyed being reminded of his own fallibility. As a result of Jonas's berating, Augustus decreed that every resident of Poland receive 100 gold coins annually for the rest of their lives.

Jonas was assured by Nero that the same honesty and integrity would benefit his rule and leadership when the young emperor came to power, and Jonas tentatively offered his wise counsel to the new leader. Jonas had watched Nero grow from a petulant, rage-filled, small-animal-killing boy into a sociopath. He knew his honesty had to be tempered with wisdom so he wasn't made redundant through crucifixion, disembowelment or whatever imaginative form of execution Nero had thought of that particular week.

The first six months of Nero's reign had been surprisingly pleasant in Jonas's mind, and Nero's humorous, light-hearted nature made Jonas wonder if his belief Nero was the devil was misplaced. Actually, Jonas knew Nero was evil, but he was surprised by the young man's ability to lead with a pragmatism reflective of his father's. Nero may have enjoyed rather strange and dark deviances in private but seemed to rule in public with a professionalism Augustus would have been proud of. With this objectivity being displayed, Jonas had entered Nero's chamber one Monday morning confident he could finally stop kissing the emperor's ass so much and be honest about a few of the young man's decisions in recent days.

"My Lord, I was hoping to offer some advice in regard to recent events erupting in the city's suburbs," said Jonas while walking and bowing. Jonas was pretty sure Nero made people walk and bow just to make them look like idiots.

Nero wiped his mouth of stray beer froth that had clung to his wispy beard. No-one dared tell him the fluff sprouting erratically from his face was bettered by most sixteen-year-olds. "Erupting?"

"Yes, my Lord. There's been an alarming rise in child deaths, which culminated on the weekend when a mother placed her dead baby on the steps to Centurion Quinnus's base headquarters."

"That's hardly an eruption. One dead baby. A dead slum baby."

"With all due respect, Caesar, one dead baby is an eruption because we're the richest city in the world. We shouldn't have any babies dying on the streets."

"And that's my fault?" Nero had another swig of beer. It was only 9am and he was already half drunk.

"Well, no. Not exactly. I… erm…" Jonas stuttered.

"Not exactly? So I'm partially responsible for killing a child?"

Jonas felt the conversation running away from him, "It's not as simple as that, my Lord. It's down to the socio-economic impact of recent events."

"Socio-economic?" Nero said the words slowly. Rolling them around on his tongue.

"Yes, sir. We're starving the citizens in the slums because we've cut ninety percent of welfare."

"We've cut welfare because they're working instead."

"Again, with all due respect my Lord, but a handful of hours a week isn't enough for many families."

"Well then they need to work two jobs."

"It's not as simple as that." Jonas let his voice raise a touch, frustrated.

"And I'm not educated enough in socio-economics to understand?"

"I didn't say that, sir."

"You didn't have to."

"You misunderstand me, my Lord."

Nero stood up making everyone in the room stand. It was to make the point he was still the powerful one in the room. "So I'm uneducated and slow, am I?" Nero laughed. The room followed suit. "And there's me thinking I was the divine emperor of the fucking planet."

Nero stepped toward Jonas.

Jonas felt like a fool. He had walked into a mind trap. In a few sentences he had been painted as disrespectful to Caesar. He had spent months nursing Nero's ego to gain his trust, forgetting that Nero didn't want trust, he only wanted drooling servants.

"Tell me, Jonas," Nero had stepped close to the advisor, invading personal space, "Am I a dullard or am I divine?"

"You are divinely appointed, my Lord."

Nero's beer breath was starting to trigger Jonas's gag reflex, "I didn't ask that."

Jonas realized he had a choice. He realized all have a choice. Integrity or survival. He liked to think he was a brave and honorable man. He liked to think all the years he advised Augustus and gave his brutally honest opinions was because he was brave and non-conformist. He wasn't fazed by a person's position or power; he was driven by only truth. This, Jonas was comprehending very quickly, was bullshit. Augustus enjoyed Jonas's 'honesty' because it made him feel like he was engaging with mortals. Augustus was amused by Jonas and followed his dire warnings because it helped with his public persona. Listen to the little people (or one who represents them) and they are much easier to control. It dawned on the advisor that Nero couldn't care less about public opinion and wasn't interested in honesty from an old man. Nero wanted adoration. It was that simple. So Jonas had a choice: adore his emperor, or be honest with his emperor; he thought Nero as divine as a rabid dog.

"Apologies, Caesar, I misspoke. I meant you are divine. Which is obvious. My opinion though is of irrelevance as your divinity towers above us all." Jonas's gag reflex wanted to kick in again but this time at his own ass kissing.

Nero stayed standing uncomfortably close to Jonas, staring down at him. Jonas kept his eyes to the floor. Eventually Nero stepped away, "Thank you, Jonas, for those kind words. I wonder though, if your opinion is irrelevant, why do I employ you? Looking at you, I would say the only redeeming quality you have are your opinions and they're not particularly earth shattering."

"My Lord, I have failed to make myself clear—"

"Again," interrupted Nero. "For a man my father praised as an orator without equal, your skills are rather underwhelming. This morning you decided to get the balls to tell me what you really think and all that happened is you tripped over your words."

"Apologies, Caesar. I will ensure my words are at the same level of eloquence your father found indispensable."

"Hmmm, that's very sneaky Jonas." Nero smirked. He was back on his throne and sipping his beer. "Mentioning my father to evoke a sense of nostalgia? Placing yourself alongside my father to boost my view of you?"

Jonas briefly raised his gaze to meet Nero's. "No, my Lord, I am simply proud of the service I provided to your father and want to do the same for you."

"Okay, well I do have a dilemma I need your help with."

"I am honored to help," Jonas said.

"I bet you are." Nero had another swig of beer, "I'm in a

quandary that appears to have no true answer."

"I believe truth is an objective thing, Master Nero, so there will always be a right answer. I'm happy to try to help you find what that truth is."

"That's good to know. So my quandary is this: do I let you live or do I kill you?"

Jonas's face went pale.

"Because I feel both options leave me lacking," continued Nero.

"My Lord, I—"

Nero held his hand up. Jonas went quiet.

"If I let you live, then people will think you're pulling the strings, like you did with my father. I hear the rumors."

Jonas interrupted, "I strongly disagree with that sentiment. I was—"

"Shut. The fuck. Up."

Jonas obliged.

"If I kill you, then it could cause civil unrest. I've seen the polls and your popularity is baffling. I can't even fire you as that will be unjust in people's eyes."

Nero wasn't exaggerating. Jonas was a very, very popular public figure. He was dubbed Cicero 2.0 because of his oratory skills and the work he did, in his spare time, to help the most vulnerable in society. Nero used Jonas's work to improve his public profile so knew he had to ensure whatever happened to Jonas didn't come back to bite him later.

"So, Jonas, what do I do?"

Jonas was asking himself the same question. He thought he heard a distant scream of someone most likely being crucified and almost envied the bastard.

"I have served your family with integrity, Caesar. I don't

understand why this conversation is even happening. I can serve you for many years to come helping you shape policy and honor your father's legacy."

"What about my legacy?"

"Sorry?"

"My legacy. What about my legacy, Jonas?"

"I'm not sure where you're going with this."

"It's basically the common theme of this morning. You don't understand anything I'm saying and yet you are the 'Cicero of the 21st Century.'" Nero even used air quotes. "You," Nero pointed, "you, Jonas, blather on about my father's legacy and honoring it and yet there seems to be no concern about my legacy. Did my father sustain peace in southern Europe as quickly as I have? Did my father quash the uprising of those savages in Japan? No. I did. Did my father build the largest army in our Empire's history? No. I did. So you will get on your fucking knees and honor my legacy."

Nero was red-faced, spittle on his lips. He was off his throne again and invading Jonas's personal space. He punched Jonas hard in the face. Jonas clutched his face and the old man dropped to his knees. Nero was still holding his beer glass and he brought it down on Jonas's head. The thick glass made a dull thud but didn't break. The advisor sprawled on the floor and went still.

Nero stared at Jonas for a few seconds, the hall silent. Even Nero's bodyguard, Aloysius was stunned that Nero had just killed Rome's longest-serving advisor. Aloysius wasn't surprised by much of what Nero did anymore, but bludgeoning to death a faithful servant of Rome crossed a line, even if that line was very faint and hard to define.

The emperor mumbled for someone to clear up the mess and get him another beer, which he would take in his chambers. He left the hall without even looking back at the body of the man he had killed.

Chapter 10

Nero had Jonas's body dumped outside the city and burned. He filled media channels with a fake account of the advisor's demise, stating heart attack. Jonas was 83 after all, so the public weren't suspicious. Nero even commissioned a documentary about the legacy of the man. He hated doing it and resented the fact he had to spend large amounts of money ensuring Jonas's death appeared legitimate, but insurrection was a much bigger price to pay.

At Jonas's funeral, Nero used it like a political rally, stating the time for unrest was over, the time for division was over and like any good citizen, even those who disagreed ought to step in line for the common good. No-one dared criticize the emperor for barely mentioning Jonas at the funeral, because Champagne at the wake was far more appealing the having nails hammered through both wrists.

Boatman, Olivia, Tobias, Maverick and a few others had watched the televised funeral. It was a few months after Maverick and Tobias had arrived in London. "Look at the ginger prick," said Tobias nodding at the screen.

"He's got a better beard than you," observed Maverick.

"Like hell he has. My ass has better hair growth than the fluff on his face."

"Your ass has better hair growth than a gorilla."

"Keeps me warm in winter." Tobias moved the conversation away from his hair growth. "You think it's legit?"

Boatman carried on staring at the screen, "What? The funeral?"

"No, the cause of death."

"Why?"

"Not sure, but it stinks of something dodgy."

"Everything to do with Nero stinks." Boatman looked at Tobias. "What's not right?"

"To be honest, I don't know, but my gut tells me something is wrong."

The room went silent as they watched the funeral. The casket was being taken from the Rome Basilica to Nero Palace, where it would be burnt on a pyre. The procession had thousands of people lining the streets. Nero commented in private how he was confused why so many people loved Jonas. Nero never comprehended that when a man spends every day he has off work tending to the poor, feeding the hungry and even going so far as learning medicine and getting qualified so he can lawfully administer life-saving treatments, that man's name will soar through communities. Fear makes a man in history books. Respect makes a man in hearts.

Maverick picked up on Tobias's skepticism. "It's too bombastic."

Boatman glanced at Tobias, Tobias shrugged like he had no idea where his partner was going with his theory or what bombastic meant. "Go on."

"Nero hated what Jonas did in his spare time. He's barely mentioned Jonas in his eulogy and yet he has made the funeral as big as what he did for his father. It's overkill."

"Almost like the way a guy buys a massive chariot to compensate for having a small dick," said Tobias.

"That explains a lot of your life then," said Maverick.

"Sometimes I wonder what's worse, being a gladiator or putting up with your shit."

"You were a crap gladiator, I helped you out."

Boatman tried to move the conversation back to Jonas. "Nero has a small dick complex in general. The funeral might be a simple extension of that."

Maverick shook his head, "It's rumored Jonas wrote once how he believed absolute power corrupted even the best of men, so a man like Nero receiving power was like giving a toddler a gun and being surprised when he shot someone in the face. It was an underground piece, and Jonas made sure his name was never associated with it, but everyone knew the emperor's top advisor had penned it."

"That's where we find out anything to do with his funeral – the underground. We have contacts in Rome we can use," said Boatman.

"I can call Isabelle," said Mav.

Boatman put his hand on Mav's shoulder. "Yes please. Let's do some digging and see if we can unearth anything rotten."

"It's Nero," said Tobias. "Everything about him is rotten."

"If there's something about Jonas's death we can use against Nero, then we need to know it." Boatman went to turn off the television when a voice behind him told him to leave it on.

"I want to see if the camera focuses on Sandra." Olivia put her hands on Boatman's shoulder's and kissed his cheek.

"Do you know her?"

"No, but if you're wanting to get some insight into Jonas's death, how the wife is behaving is probably a good place to start." Olivia looked away from the screen toward Boatman, "It's amazing how much easier a man's life could be if he paid attention to how his wife was behaving." She smiled and looked back at the screen. Olivia continued, "Jonas was publicly a very healthy man, but if he had severe heart problems that they were keeping from public view then she won't be shocked at his death. If something else is behind his death, then Sandra's demeanor and behavior might give you a clue."

Boatman wasn't convinced, "But some brief shots of her on camera won't give us that insight."

"Have you ever grieved?"

Boatman bristled at his wife, "You know I have." His face went dark.

Olivia cupped her husband's cheek, "Sorry," she stroked his face, "That was more a generic question to the room."

Tobias cleared his throat, "When I was a gladiator, I never knew anyone long enough to grieve them. And I was usually killing them. Seemed a bit hypocritical crying over the guy I had just decapitated."

"Helpful as always, Tobias," said Maverick.

"I don't remember you grieving much in the arena. You were usually gloating at how awesome you were."

"Because I was awesome. I grieve having met you sometimes."

"Maybe I've met someone else and am just finding the right time to tell you so you truly know what grief is."

"I doubt anyone would put up with your snoring, and if they did they would have extreme grief over the days of a good night's sleep."

"Are they always like this?" said Olivia

"I switched off weeks ago." Boatman studied the screen for a bit as Nero waffled on.

Olivia continued, "Extreme grief manifests itself in complex ways, but I would hazard a guess that her reaction," Olivia was pointing at the screen, "shows a woman completely unprepared for her husband's death and also a woman who is very afraid." The camera had stopped on Sandra. She was ghostly white, visibly shaking and trying (unsuccessfully) to stem the flow of tears. Olivia addressed her husband. "I deal with scared people everyday, Boatman, and she is terrified. That's not what she should be feeling at her husband's funeral."

Boatman muted the television and paused the coverage when it focused on Sandra again. "Mav, I need any information you can get from Isabelle. Quickly."

"I'll try my best." Maverick and Tobias turned to leave but Maverick stopped, "What if Jonas was murdered by Nero? What are we going to do with that info?"

Boatman shrugged, "I don't know, but it could be useful. Anything that has potential to hurt Nero is useful."

The two men left the room, with Tobias confirming they would be in touch as soon as they found anything out. What they did find out later that week from their contact in Rome was that Jonas had indeed been murdered and his body dumped outside the city gates. No-one was willing to act on that information, though. Fear had too strong a grip on the Senate to convince any senator to try and avenge Jonas's death. The senators were shocked Nero had killed Jonas so casually and feared for their lives every single day. Nero had castrated the Senate's courage.

Boatman stared at the paused image for a while and then broke the silence, "What's your opinion of Nero?"

"He's insane."

"And you charge how much for your expert opinion?"

"I have to charge a lot, my husband is a jobless bum."

"He sounds like a dick, I'd get rid of him."

"I'm thinking about it," smiled Olivia. She kissed Boatman. "To give you your money's worth, I believe Nero is a sociopath with a narcissistic personality disorder."

"Which means?"

"Which means he is dangerous, unpredictable and you'll wish you had signed that treaty with Augustus before he died."

Boatman grunted. "It wasn't a treaty, it was a surrender."

"All compromise involves surrender. It feels worse because the ego gets in the way."

"I'm not so sure Augustus was providing compromise."

"Well, it's too late to know now."

Boatman grunted again. He didn't like his wife pointing out the truth, even if it was what he needed to hear. Augustus had, in his dying days, offered a peace treaty. It wasn't perfect and it wasn't London's liberation from Rome, but it was an olive branch and it was a step forward. Boatman had thought it was a trap and refused to meet anyone. Nero took this as confirmation everyone, like Boatman, needed to be annihilated. "I think Jonas's allies in London will start to disappear. You should distance yourself from them."

"I don't have any allies connected to Jonas."

"Don't bullshit me, Olivia. I know you know Sandra. I don't understand why you've kept it from me, but you need to step away from anything to do with her. You'll be exposed."

"I think your imagination needs to chill out a bit." Olivia started to leave the room.

"Seriously Olivia, it's not a game. You play with Nero and he could burn everything you have to the ground."

Olivia stopped and turned to her husband. "Fuck you, Boatman. Seriously, fuck you. I spend every day counselling Roman soldiers and Senate politicians. I'm a widow, which means they think it gives them the permission to send me dick pics or ask me for a drink hoping the myth about psychiatrists is true and we're all a bit fucked up and horny the majority of the time. Game? I risk my life for you all the time, you arrogant prick. If I do have something I decide to keep from you, it's because I'm protecting you."

Boatman tried to backtrack. He underestimated his wife too often, "I'm sorry, I just—"

"Boatman, you think you're an organized, insurmountable force, but you're not."

Boatman bristled. "I've organized all this." He waved his hands at their surroundings.

Olivia looked at their underground media room and said, "Exactly. We live underground. We live in the shadows. I'm always looking over my shoulder."

"We're getting closer to beating them. We're on the right path. Trust me."

Olivia scoffed, "The right path? Our lives are consumed by blood and violence. That's not organized. That's a path of chaos."

"Chaos that I can protect you from, if you let me. If you listen to me. You need to cut your contacts with Jonas's allies."

Olivia stormed out, telling Boatman he could go fuck himself, leaving the room filled with the sound of the Empire's Anthem being played at the funeral of the murdered Jonas.

Chapter 11

Boatman sat by Olivia's bedside and regretted every fight they had ever had. He'd regretted talking to her like she was inferior. She was the most intelligent person he had ever met, and he was only alive still because of her. He'd allowed his arrogance to step to the forefront and patronize her, and she'd made sure he knew what he could do with that arrogance. It involved shoving it somewhere the sun didn't shine.

Olivia slept. She sometimes pretended to sleep so she didn't have to talk to Boatman but most of the time she was too sedated to know he was even in her presence. Today though, today she was lucid and wanted to talk.

"Can I have a drink please?"

Boatman was jolted from his thoughts and grabbed the glass of water at Olivia's bedside for her. She gulped it keenly. "How are you feeling?"

"Like I've been crucified. You should try it," she said.

"I'll pass, thanks."

"You're missing out." Olivia tried to laugh but a wince was the best she could manage.

The beeping machines and sterile smells were making Boatman feel claustrophobic or maybe reminding him how his wife being here was entirely his fault.

Olivia either had the ability to read minds or the situation meant they would inevitably think the same thing. "I do blame you for being here, Boatman."

Boatman had fallen in love with Olivia partly because of her candor, but he wasn't enjoying her honesty right now. "I know it's a poor answer, but I don't know what to say."

She frowned. "I'm pleased you don't know what to say, I don't want your clever answers. Your crusade got me nailed up by a pervert. It's pretty simple."

"I have always tried to keep you safe and protected from those monsters."

She frowned again. She looked angry but it almost hurt too much to have any extreme emotional responses. "It's weird, I never took you to be stupid, but you're showing it now."

"I don't understand?"

"You always talk about protecting me, but Max found me because you weren't paying attention to me. Your tunnel vision has always been your weakness and such a selfish part of who you are." Boatman opened his mouth to say sorry, but Olivia stopped him. "It's pretty pointless saying sorry."

Much to Boatman's relief, one of his messengers came through the door insisting on his attention. "What is it?"

"Nero is about to make an announcement. All channels are counting down to the broadcast."

Olivia wondered whether Boatman had instructed his young errand boy to come into the room after a certain time period just to ease the atmosphere. She would have been angry if that was the case but, in her equally hypocritical mindset, she actually felt relief Boatman might be leaving. Again it seemed like Boatman was reading her thoughts. "I think I need to leave you alone for a bit."

"I'm tired, I just need to sleep."

Boatman nodded and went to kiss Olivia on the lips. She moved her face slightly away, just enough to tell him she wasn't ready for that. Boatman bowed his head in disappointment and left the room.

Olivia was tired, but she wasn't going to sleep anytime soon. She needed to try and make sense of the voices. They had gotten worse since the crucifixion, and even the morphine wasn't dimming their volume and urgency. Voices wasn't accurate though; they were more like *vibrations* moving through her brain. It wasn't painful, or even disturbing, but it was distracting. The vibrations, to Olivia, seemed scared. The night of her abduction, the vibrations had been fearful but they were so faint she had never really picked up on their distress. She had put her unease down to the simple fact she was walking through London streets alone. It always made her uncomfortable.

The voices/vibrations had always been part of Olivia's life. When she was a child, she'd called them her 'bumblebees' because, to her, the vibrations sounded like bees buzzing. As she grew up, the bees had been quieter until she barely noticed them when she hit her twenties. The bees buzzed a little louder when something bad was going to happen, but until now had Olivia never made the connection. Listening to the bees throughout her childhood meant she assumed it was normal and everyone else did the same.

As a child, she had learned quickly about danger and self-preservation because of the bees in her head. She discerned lies, and she understood pain from a very early age. People would note she had a huge amount of empathy but, for her, she knew empathy was only part of the story. Yes, she ached for others when she saw them ache. She understood grief at an age when death should not even be on a human's radar.

But.

Olivia didn't only empathize; she lived their experience, feeling what they feel and absorbing their pain.

Chapter 12

Boatman was sitting at his desk staring blankly at his laptop when a popup announced the Roman News Channel had a breaking story. The screen was filled with a live stream of Emperor Nero announcing a special day in London in a year's time. What the emperor was saying confirmed he was a true sociopath. Boatman called Maverick and said there was a change to their plans. Lying low wasn't an option anymore because they needed to try and stop Nero dead. Maverick agreed, hung up the phone and wondered if any more chaos could inhabit his life.

Chapter 13

When the video first emerged Gary took to social media to establish its veracity. Sites were inundated with posts claiming its authenticity but Gary was skeptical. It was only a Post-Me, after all. As the name suggested, it was a site used for narcissistic mind vomit. But, three months later and many, many videos and posts by Nero himself proved the video was authentic and therefore a get-out clause for Gary. He laughed to himself at the thought of showing up to work tomorrow after what would happen later today. He was forming a few witty one-liners he would use with his work colleagues. That would show the bores who never seemed to laugh at his jokes. God, they were so dumb, they never understood any of his jokes. Stupid twats.

Gary assumed his work colleagues needed humor transplants or were too prude, but he didn't possess any emotional intelligence or the self-awareness to pick up on the fact most of his equals believed him to be the only twat. Reasons for this view varied throughout the office, ranging from him being that guy who laughs at his own jokes to him being that guy who has always done twice what you have done. You just bought a new shed for your garden? Gary will declare he bought two sheds. Been in hospital for appendicitis? Gary had his spleen removed. Met a celebrity? Gary slept with one.

The top of the list for Gary's unpopularity was his self-declared superiority as an entrepreneur, even though his current status as a trend-setting businessman was trying to sell copies of his badly mixed house music. "All you need is one hit that goes viral and you're sorted for life." Maybe Gary was right; all you did need was that one hit, but so far a hundred streaming listens (mainly by his mom) was probably closest he had yet gotten on his quest to be a superstar, one-hit wonder DJ. Oh, and he'd also met Fatboy Slim at a club twenty years ago, who allegedly said he was good enough to make it as a DJ. When asked how Fatboy Slim had such an intuitive mind to know this about a coked-up guy he'd never met before, Gary always responded with, "True talent knows other true talent when in each other's presence." Nevertheless, Gary was unperturbed by his slow journey to success and, he thought pragmatically, the older he gets the less money his one-hit wonder would have to make to sort him until he died.

Just one viral video. That's all he needed.

So Gary sat at home scrolling through Post-Me feeling angry at his lack of viral attention while others were posting garbage and getting famous for it. Gary's wife rolled her eyes (figuratively and literally at times) at her husband's obsession with fame (or perceived fame) and regularly called him gullible for believing it would happen. Gary declared he wasn't gullible at all, but judging by his long list of saved links and likes of conspiracy theories (the earth is flat, the Romans are Lizards, Churchill was still alive and secretly ruling Britannia) she wasn't so sure.

When the video emerged three months ago Gary had felt torn between hoping the video was fake and wondering whether it was his get out of jail free card. Literally his get out of jail free card, judging by what he was watching. But if it was real, then that also terrified him because in a few months there would be one of the most horrific days in history. Gary felt his skin tingle in fear, but… but… there was a massive upside to this after all. Maybe he was finally going to be a viral sensation? Maybe this was the doorway in?

He had to be clever about it, though. He had to be one of the best. He watched the video again to check the terms and conditions. It stated that from sunrise on the fourth of July next year, the acts were permissible. But if he did it before then, and then posted his video of the act at sunrise, would anyone notice? Would they question the legality? Doubtful. They would be scrambling to deal with the aftermath of people killing each other. Hell, you could easily argue your watch was fast and plead ignorance to it being before the allotted time. Gary grinned – this could be the solution to his woes.

Gary had two primary woes. First, lack of viral fame. Second, his wife. Woe would be a massive understatement, he thought, more like a gargantuan thorn in his fucking side. Tracy had become a bitch. It was as simple as that. They had been together for twelve years (engaged for eight), and Gary had eventually caved in and agreed to adding a wedding band to the engagement ring on her third finger. When he'd asked her to marry him, he hadn't really meant it, he just knew she would go all gooey over the prospect of marriage and be able to show off her ring to her friends who were all bitter women: pregnant, young, and critical of most men. Gary proposing so quickly into the relationship made him seem like, 'one of the good ones' and helped Tracy feel smug that she had landed a decent man who wasn't afraid of commitment.

She did think Gary could have spent a bit more on the ring.

The diamond was a bit small and looked like it wanted to sparkle but didn't have the energy. She'd secretly had it valued and thought Gary was a bit of a tightwad. But he had devoted himself to her so she shouldn't complain. She told herself that maybe he was going to upgrade the ring at a later date. Some men did that, like the first ring was a promise ring and the real ring was around the corner.

Eight years later, and still no big ring or big wedding, and Tracy (and her friends) decided Gary wasn't one of the good ones but just the same as everyone else. Tracy telling him this on more than one occasion finally made him book the registry office. The quick wedding with a function at the local community hall matched the cheap ring. There was no exotic honeymoon either. Tracy had hoped it was going to be a surprise gift (why else would he go so cheap on the wedding?) along with a massive diamond. Three years after the wedding, and still no ring and still no honeymoon.

Gary didn't know but Tracy had recently and more than once caught him jerking off to some slut on Post-Me, so she resigned herself to accepting the reality that Gary was more in love with his mobile phone than with her.

That's when she started making more effort with her appearance. She thought Gary wouldn't notice, but he did. Well, he didn't notice at first; his mate Johnno did. "Tracy's looking a bit of alright lately, mate."

"Is she?" Gary sipped his beer trying to picture Tracy not in her uniform or dressing gown.

"Yeah, she looked amazing when I saw her the other day. I did a double take to be sure it was her."

"You're sure it was her? We haven't been out since Valentine's."

"Positive. She waved at me, which was weird because I know she thinks I'm a prick."

"You are a prick."

"I know, but she thinks I'm an actual prick."

"You are an actual prick," said Gary with no irony.

"Well, anyway," Johnno continued, unperturbed by the prick status consensus, "Tracy all dolled up like that means only one thing."

"Does it?"

Johnno looked at his mate in animated bewilderment like he was the keeper of ultimate knowledge and his mate was an ignorant pleb. "Yes, it does! She's sleeping around. When your missus starts taking pride in her appearance, after this many years, it means someone else is banging her. A lot."

Gary stopped drinking, his pint stuck to his lips, the penny dropping. No, not the penny, a whole fucking ton of pennies dropping. "The fucking bitch."

So Gary was sitting in front of his computer grinning as he watched the video because this was his get-out clause. No divorce. No awkward dividing of goods. No screaming matches. This psycho Emperor Nero had actually put his nutty brain to good use and given Gary a new start in life. All he needed to do was work out the best way to kill his wife.

The video was titled 'EYE FOR AN EYE DAY' and had Emperor Nero II declaring that at sunrise on July 4th, 2031, all citizens of Britain were legally permitted to follow the mantra of an eye for an eye. If someone had wronged you, you were legally entitled to take vengeance on that person. Once you had done it, you were required to post a video of your act on the Empire's specially made website to prove it. Nero smiled all the while declaring this news, making Gary wonder at the pure psychopathy of the man.

Gary looked at the time, 9am. Tracy would be home from her

nightshift at 11am. That gave him plenty of time to find some rat poison and lace her food. Fuck it, he would shove it in everything. Her health drinks, her fruit, everything. He'd even offer to cook her brunch and sprinkle shit loads on her scrambled eggs. That would teach the cheating bitch. Then he would freeze her body and bring it out on the declared day. He was sure he could find a way to manipulate the dates and times on the footage. Anything could be hacked, right?

Gary rubbed his hands together like a criminal mastermind. If any of his work colleagues had seen him do this, they would have unequivocally decided Gary needed to be sectioned.

Gary heard the front door open and close and looked at the time. 9:15? Why was Tracy already home? He swiveled round on his chair, and she was standing in the doorway to his study. Well, study was a rather generous term to give to the spare bedroom, a small cluttered room with a tiny desk emerging from the mess like a pathetic altar to Gary's social media gods. Tracy glanced at the floor and noticed he wasn't even attempting to hide his 'special' socks anymore.

"You're back early."

"I wasn't working," said Tracy, leaning against the door frame.

It was only then Gary noticed she wasn't in her work clothes but a tight-fitting black dress and a rather over the top push-up bra. Gary, on the other hand, was in his boxer shorts and a T-shirt that had the words 'RELAX' on it and a mysterious stain underneath the X. Guess his T-shirts are cum wipers now, Tracy thought.

"Why are you all dressed up?"

"I've been out all night. With Paul." Tracy was balancing a pair of black heels in her left hand. Rocking them by their straps.

"Paul?"

"Yeah, the guy I'm fucking."

"You're what?"

"Fucking," repeated Tracy. She said it slowly like she was using the words as a knife and twisting it into Gary's chest.

Gary had an epiphany at this moment. Minutes before he was all pumped up and ready to kill his slag of a wife, but now that she was standing there, confidently admitting her betrayal, he realized he was a complete coward. He wasn't going to be able to kill her. Hell, he wasn't even able to get out of his office chair to confront her. He just wanted her to go away so he could fantasize about killing her and have a wank over some photos on Post-Me. It was way too much effort to actually do the act.

That had been Gary's problem over the years – everything was way too much effort to actually do. Talking about it was fine. Ask him anything, and he'd done it. He was always lying, but he watched enough videos to be an expert on anything and make it seem like he'd done it. That's what he'd do today – he'd make out he'd killed Tracy (she'd agree if it meant she could run away with 'Paul,' and surely they wouldn't actually check the validity of the videos?) post a video on the day and then brag about it at work. He couldn't believe Nero would genuinely check if the videos were real. This was probably some elaborate propaganda anyway. There would be a ton of fake videos hours after that sunrise.

"Fucking?" Gary asked. He'd never been good with pithy comebacks.

"Is that all you can say? No questions about why? What that means for our marriage? You know I have never worked nights on Tuesdays, and you didn't even question why I was working them for the past month?"

Gary sat silently. He really didn't have anything to say. He had some posts forming in his mind that would be zingers though. He smiled at the thought.

"But you can sit there smiling like some cretin?" Tracy's face had flushed red. Anger had burst forth from her like it had ruptured through her body. A pressure pipe bursting. "*I don't know why I ever married you!*" She screamed the words.

Tracy felt as though the next few moments were in slow motion. Extreme moments cause the brain to process events at a subjectively slower speed. Maybe it was a way for the mind to truly take in what was happening. Maybe human minds are shocked by what happens and can't process the information properly, like a high-definition video buffering. The rage Tracy felt seemed unnatural to her. For the past 12 years with Gary, the majority of Tracy's emotions had been indifference, boredom and disappointment. And, more recently, disgust. But rage wasn't one of them. Gary's complete lack of effort with her – one holiday in three years and that was only to go camping – had almost become a tired joke in her mind. A crappy knock-knock joke that doesn't even earn a smile but you accept it's a joke for some reason.

But as he sat there in his stained T-shirt smiling at her as she declared her infidelity, the rage consumed her. It was true, rage was all-consuming. It was like a virus and overtook her in seconds. She screamed at Gary again, and still he smiled. She screamed for him to stop smiling and he smiled more. She said she would make him stop smiling, and that's when he laughed. She, in that moment, decided to make his laughter stop and in a split second his mouth turned from a laugh into a shocked 'O'. A single line of blood traversed Gary's cheek, reached his top lip and pooled. Tracy stepped away from her husband as he sat there, motionless, his mouth in an 'O' and one of her heels lodged in his right eye socket.

Tracy went viral for the live footage of her killing her husband and in minutes soldiers were at her door taking her away. Gary also went viral, but the stiletto through his eye meant he was never going to know the satisfaction of all those views.

Chapter 14

Nero watched the video of Tracy stabbing Gary through the eye with her shoe and stifled a giggle. It was a beautiful sight. How could anyone not find the positives in his new National Holiday? It was a shame for Tracy that she acted out the new national holiday too early. This Gary (the poster boy for the apathetic side of British culture – overweight, lazy and ignorant) was a waste of time. The wife killing him was an act of mercy for his pathetic life. He wasn't adding anything to society. Maybe he would pardon her misdemeanor for the entertainment of what she'd done.

Nero always did things for multiple reasons. He had been like that ever since he was a child. He planted the seed of 'Eye for an Eye Day' to see if anyone would do a Tracy and kill Boatman out of anger at the rebel's behavior. He didn't think something was worth doing unless there were layers of outcomes and possible solutions. He believed he could flush Boatman out. He was always thinking of how to manipulate people, ever since he was a young child.

When he was only seven years of age, he'd had a dog. It was a beautiful puppy with big floppy ears and followed him everywhere. It would sleep on his bed at night and protected him from anyone he sensed wasn't right. Nero felt great affection for the dog (love would be too strong a word because Nero had no capacity for such an emotion), like a person feels affinity to a prized possession.

Nero saw a flaw in his relationship with man's best friend, though. He noticed how people found Nero to be 'cute' and 'sweet' because his dog was 'cute' and 'sweet'. Even at the age of seven, Nero knew he was divine and that people should fear him. A fluffy sidekick wasn't going to achieve that. If he got rid of the dog though, people would think him a strange child and not fear him as they should.

Nero regularly attended Senate meetings and listened to the wisdom of Cicero's distant relative. Nero learnt that legends were born from whispers. From words uttered fearfully in another's ear. His namesake had not been feared for simply burning cities to the ground; words had floated through the breeze from town to town of Nero I's cruelty and sadism. Those who never met him believed him to be a double-headed beast or a seven-foot giant. Whatever the whispers were, Nero I became a legend associated with fear because words can be more powerful than the might of an army if used correctly.

Young Nero II decided people needed to start to whisper about him. But they also needed to adore him as the child he was. As an adult, Nero had a more complex understanding of this desire. Fill people with both fear and love, and the confusion keeps them submissive.

One afternoon, seven-year-old Nero walked to the kitchen where six staff were busy preparing lunch for the emperor and his family, including Nero. All the staff stopped working because the young heir had never entered their workspace before. They stood silently, slightly bowed, unsure what to say or do. Nero eyed them with a slight smile, walked over to a worktop where one of the staff and been dicing onions and reached up to grab the chef's knife. The chef, whose knife it was, went to object but the look from the young boy caused the chef's mouth to shut quickly. The chef would later recall how he didn't believe in the Roman gods or any gods for that matter, but he now believed the Devil was real because the Devil lived in that boy.

Nero's fluffy friend was standing next to him, wagging his tail, head slightly tilted. Without even a warning Nero grabbed the dog by the scruff and plunged the knife into the dog's chest. The dog's scream would haunt the dreams of all the staff into their old age. And the blood. The blood was everywhere. How could such a small animal produce so much blood?

Nero waited for the dog to die, which seemed like an eternity, then looked at the staff and said, "Don't tell my daddy." Nero then ran from the kitchen screaming bloody murder, crying hysterically and producing those big, blobby tears that children can cry.

Here's where layers of outcome manifested. The official story that Nero told to his distraught parents was that Romulus (the dog) ran into the kitchen because he smelled something tasty, and scared the chef, who dropped his knife in fright. In a freak accident, the knife stabbed Romulus and killed him. From that tragedy, the obvious sympathy and love was poured out on Nero. The general public were instructed to send gifts of condolences. Unofficially, the whispers were carried in the wind. The whispers danced. From kitchen to kitchen. Home to home. Barrack to barrack. Young Nero had butchered that dog and enjoyed it. Young Nero was a monster. Young Nero was the Devil. Don't ever say it aloud, though. Never. He will find you in your sleep and slit your throat. Adore him, love him, praise him. Fear him. Fucking fear him. If a seven-year-old can do that, imagine what adult Nero will do.

So now Nero sat at his computer contemplating how anything he did has layers, disappointed when this did not produce what he expected. He had declared the day to instill fear in the Londoners. They had grown complacent. But what he really wanted was for it to smoke out Boatman. Surely there were rebels who resented Boatman's cause, who would use the day to stop Boatman's crusade? There must be family members of crucified rebels who hate Boatman for sending their loved ones to death, who want retribution for having their husband, son, father violently torn from them?

Nero watched the video of Tracy killing her husband again, amused by its pathetic protagonists. Dying while in stained underwear was surely as pathetic as any man could be. He was about to close the window and find a boy to distract him when a live video started with the title, 'FOR NERO II'. Nero clicked play and the live stream buffered into action. A brief pixilated image smoothed into an image of Boatman with a knife to the throat of a young solider. If Nero was shocked to see one of his soldiers in a life-threatening situation, he hid it well, Boatman thought.

"Hello Caesar."

Nero didn't respond.

"Wow, it's not often you're lost for words, considering you love the sound of your own voice."

Nero smirked, but it looked more like a sneer. "That's rich coming from you, Boatman."

"Takes a narcissist to know a narcissist, I guess."

"For the first time ever I would have to agree with you," said Nero and this time his smirk didn't make him appear aggrieved.

The young soldier looked bemused at the rather civil interaction between the two men and squirmed in Boatman's grip. Boatman pressed the knife slightly harder, and the squirming abruptly ceased. Nero noticed a trickle of blood on the soldier's neck. "You think threatening one of my soldiers is going to intimidate me? You think I will suddenly walk away from hunting you because you have a hostage?"

"A hostage?" Boatman made a mock quizzical frown. "More like a legion." The camera jerked as it was removed from what Nero assumed to be a tripod. The person behind the camera walked past Boatman and the solider and walked through a doorway, turned left down a hallway and then entered through a metal door on the right. The room was slightly dim, and the camera adjusted to the light. It revealed a bare room and sitting on the floor were approximately 80 soldiers from Nero's quick estimation, which meant Boatman had somehow ambushed and caught an entire Century without killing anyone. They weren't bound or gagged, which seemed strange, but they were sitting deadly still and kept their heads bowed even when the cameraman walked into the room. The camera did one last sweep and then left the room again and regained its original position with Boatman and the solider.

Nero spoke first. "I'm impressed – you managing to capture an entire Century without killing any of them is quite an achievement. You're more ignorant than I first believed if you think it will force my hand." Nero paused, thinking. "I'm not sure what you think you will be able to influence me on, anyhow. You know I won't suddenly remove my forces from London. What, you want me to stop hunting you?" Nero laughed, his black eyes glistening, "I will never stop hunting you, you cunt."

"Your father should have loved you more as a child because that's one hell of a potty mouth." Boatman eyed the soldier. "I know you won't stop hunting me but if I slit the throat of Kevin here – yeah, I know his name – that would warn you I have another eighty throats I can slit, too." Kevin's eyes widened. His eyes welling in fear. "I swiped eighty of your soldiers without breaking a sweat, Nero. The great, *fearsome* Nero."

Those final words were enough to bring the rage forth. "I couldn't give a fuck if you slit that idiot's throat and then skull fucked him. You kill one solider and I will send a hundred to replace him. *You kill eighty and I will send eight thousand! I have endless resources and wealth! You ignorant, primate! They're replaceable commodities."*

"Hey, Kevin, have you ever met your emperor before?"

The soldier shook his head.

"You ever been thanked for your service?"

The soldier shook his head.

"You ever heard him say he doesn't give a fuck if you die?"

The solider glanced at the camera and back at Boatman. Kevin was clever enough to realize whatever his response now, it didn't really matter as he was screwed either way, so nodded. Boatman took the knife away from the soldier's throat. "It's entirely up to you, but you're no use to me as a hostage because your Caesar finds you worthless, so you can carry on serving him, or you can work with me instead."

For a moment Boatman thought Nero's jaw was actually going to drop.

"Oh, my *Lord,* you should be aware the rest of the Century have heard everything as we linked speakers into their room."

Nero never showed his true hand and if his mask ever slipped, like it just had, he was adept at getting the mask back very quickly. "Eighty extra rebels added to your numbers will have little impact on my dominion. Whereas I will wipe you out at some point soon. By the way, how's the wife?"

Boatman resisted throwing the camera through a window and said, "She's fine. How's your son? Head still caved in?"

Nero cut the call. Throwing the computer across the room, screaming the word *fuck* and pacing like a caged animal. Nero felt like he was in a vulnerable position. Since the day he'd gutted his dog, he had always had control and power, but at this moment, he didn't have full control. He had eighty soldiers who appeared to have defected, after Boatman had somehow managed to capture them with utter ease. Boatman was mocking his comatose son simply because he could. No-one, absolutely no-one, had ever spoken to him with such disrespect the way Boatman had, and it infuriated him. He called in his bodyguard. "Aloysius, I need your advice."

Aloysius was surprised. He was a personal guard, employed to keep the emperor safe. He wasn't known for his sage advice. His personal life typified that. None of his friends would ever think of him as the go-to person for advice on anything but how to drink a pint in under 10 seconds. He was pretty sure Nero wasn't looking for advice on how to get shitfaced, though. "Happy to help, my Lord."

"How long have you been my bodyguard?"

"740 days, my Lord."

"Really? So, that would mean you've kept me safe from harm for two years?"

"Yes, my Lord."

"And, have you ever been in a position where you have had to draw your weapon to protect me, Aloysius?"

"Twice, Caesar. Both false alarms."

"So if I do this," Nero drew a gun from inside his suit jacket and pointed it squarely at Aloysius, "Would you draw your weapon?"

Aloysius didn't flinch. "No, Caesar, I would never draw a

weapon on you."

"Not even to protect yourself?" Nero fired the gun. The bullet stuck in the wall behind Aloysius's head. Aloysius instinctively reached for his sidearm whilst crouching slightly and in one swift moment the gun was aimed at Nero's head.

Nero laughed. "Your training is your instinct, isn't it Aloysius?"

The guard straightened up and holstered his gun. "Apologies, Caesar, you're trained to react before your brain has time to think."

Nero waved the gun in a dismissive motion. "There's no need to apologize. I was intrigued by your training. I shouldn't have fired my gun. That was rude of me."

"You are the emperor, you can do anything you want. I'm not worthy to even listen to your explanation."

Nero lowered the gun and laughed. "It's funny, I honestly thought hearing your worshipful words would make me feel better after being disrespected by that scum, Boatman. But it's simply confirmed people tell me what I want to hear. Ironically, Boatman is the only person who speaks honestly to me."

Aloysius stayed silent. He wasn't sure Nero knew the true meaning of irony; but he wasn't prepared to quibble grammar with a psychopath holding a gun. He'd been guarding the Caesar long enough to know the danger of speaking at the wrong time. He was cursing himself for even speaking at all, feeling it was too much. This he found truly ironic because his ex-girlfriend regularly told him he didn't speak enough and that she didn't know what he was thinking. He would have told her, if she was in ear shot, that his current thoughts were he wished he had pulled a sickie today as his psychotic boss had the look in his eye that he wanted to kill someone. And he would have told her how speaking too much tended to get you nailed to a cross or whipped within an inch of your life, so it was better to shut the fuck up.

Of course, she would have said it's pretty bloody different speaking dissent to the leader of the entire planet and sharing if you're feeling okay, emotionally, to your girlfriend. Although Aloysius wasn't convinced by this, as the last time he allowed himself to open up emotionally his dad called him a pussy. Although that was twenty years ago, the condemnation dripping from his father's tongue still hurt.

Aloysius needed a way to leave the room. He was watching Nero pacing the room, babbling about Boatman while waving the gun. Aloysius was the bodyguard of the emperor of the modern world because he had training in psychology, too. He had to be able to discern potential threats to Nero's safety from the way people behaved in close vicinity, but he also had to be sensitive to Nero's behavior. If Nero was erratic, his bodyguard needed to be able to react to that and create sufficient protocols to try and cover eventualities from the Caesar's outbursts. Aloysius grimaced at the bitter irony coming in swathes in a very short space of time because he was an expert in profiling the leader of the world and his enemies, but his ex broke up with him because he never picked up on when she was feeling upset or vulnerable. The problem with analyzing everyone for danger was that there was no room in his head for basic empathy.

The only thing filling the bodyguard's mind right now was a sense of danger and the risk of his boss shooting him in the face. Nero was still raging about Boatman. "…He has the audacity to use my city – my power grid, my amenities – to rebel against me! And then he says to me, the emperor…" and so it carried on.

Aloysius decided to do the opposite of what he would advise others and interrupted Nero. "My Lord, apologies, I need to perform my scheduled security checks. Especially now Boatman has been in contact." Caesar stopped pacing, his finger still far too close to the trigger for Aloysius's comfort. He held his breath. Nero's back was to the guard. He was staring out over the courtyard. "That's fine. Go keep me safe." Aloysius breathed out and backed out the room.

As Aloysius walked down the hallway, he heard a gun discharge. He turned and ran back to Nero's quarters. He burst into the room, his own firearm in his hands. Nero was still standing by the window, facing the courtyard. The window was now open and the gun still in the emperor's left hand.

"My Lord," Aloysius spoke firmly but at low volume. "Are you okay? Are you hurt?"

Nero turned around, walked over to his desk and put the gun down. "I'm fine. I'm going to get a drink."

Nero left the room and Aloysius walked over to the window. A soldier was lying on the floor, face down. A bloody hole in his back. Another casualty of Nero's rage toward Boatman. Maybe Nero would always find someone to rage against, but in the short-term Aloysius knew he needed to find Boatman and kill him.

Maybe a sacrificed Boatman would appease the devil. Or at least make the devil avert his gaze from the bodyguard.

Chapter 15

Boatman took the phone apart, snapped the sim in two and threw everything into the fire. "So, what do you say?"

"Do I have a choice?"

"You always have a choice."

"And how's that a comfort? Last year I had food poisoning. It was awful. I was vomiting everywhere. At one point I had the choice to puke in my bedside drawer or on my girlfriend's pile of clothes. I had a choice, but the choice was ridiculous and I wish I had neither options. So, when you say there's always a choice, it's bullshit. It's not black and white and you're being a patronizing asshole."

Boatman looked at Kevin, the soldier, the way bacteria was analyzed under a microscope; robotic, unfeeling. That was one of the surprising things about Boatman, his detachment. He was immensely organized and a chief delegator – able to organize people to co-ordinate a very successful rebellion. He was never viewed as a charismatic leader, though. Violent. Yes. Persuasive. Yes. Passionate. Yes. Empathetic? Questionable. Boatman knew how people worked like a scientist knows the laws of physics; raw emotions were reserved for those who mattered. Kevin was a pawn – emotion wasn't needed. "Okay, I'll give you that, it's not black and white at all. I apologize. I assume to be a soldier for Nero means you leave your brain in a jar at home."

"Go fuck yourself."

Maverick and Tobias were in the room and glanced at each other. Telling Boatman to go fuck himself didn't tend to end well for the person saying it. Mav admired the young soldier for his balls, though.

Boatman seemed unfazed. Pissing off the emperor of the world probably put things in a bit of perspective. "So, what is it, Kevin? You hate me for taking you out of the army, serving the emperor, or you hate me because I'm rebel scum?"

Kevin's answer was quick, "Neither. You've dragged me out of a stable job and now my girlfriend and young boy are in danger. You've painted me as traitor; they'll kill my family." His words seemed to punch him in the gut and he crouched as if trying to catch his breath.

Mav and Tobias looked at each other again and Tobias mouthed the word, "Shit." Boatman's expression didn't change, but he took his time to respond. "We'll save them."

Kevin laughed. There was little humor in the sound. "I don't want them to have to be saved." He ran his hands over his head in frustration, "Jesus Christ," he said it to himself. "I had a pension. London was an easy gig. People just want to get on with their lives. They don't want to rebel. You…" he was now pointing at Boatman, "…You make the job dangerous. You make London dangerous."

Boatman showed a bit of emotion at Kevin's words, "Then you're brainwashed. London is being held by terror. But how would you know? You're part of the terror."

"Londoners don't show any terror when I meet them."

"Fear isn't always visible. Conformity is a symptom of fear."

"That goes both ways. You might not be the liberator you think you are."

Boatman stepped toward Kevin. It was a small step, but it was enough to make the soldier flinch.

"Those people who I pulled down from crosses would beg to differ. They'd suggest London is very dangerous."

Kevin went to speak again but Boatman's demeanor made him think twice. Boatman stepped back. "Say what you're thinking."

Kevin took his time, his words came out measured, the quiver barely noticeable because if he was honest the look in Boatman's eyes made him wonder if he was getting out of the situation alive. His girlfriend, Sam, crossed his mind and his quiver settled. "I resent you and what you do. My girlfriend and my son aren't being liberated by you, they're going to be murdered because of you."

That seemed to knock Boatman back.

But he doubled down, nevertheless. "We'll save them."

Kevin slumped against the wall, his energy sapped from him and began to sob.

Chapter 16

Kevin's girlfriend, Sam, called for Molly to come downstairs as lunch was nearly ready. Molly didn't answer. Not necessarily unusual, because the ten-year-old frequently had her head in a book and blocked the outside world out. Sam called upstairs again, but still no response so she climbed the stairs to go find Molly who was more than likely sitting in her reading chair in her bedroom. Sam frowned; Molly's bedroom door was closed. Sam couldn't remember the last time that door was ever closed. The primal part of Sam's brain, right at the back, fired. That was the part of the brain that some would call a sixth sense but basically acted as a warning sign when something wasn't right and possible danger loomed. Being the civilized animals humans are, that warning sign has been dampened down from one generation to the next, so Sam only felt a tiny niggle in her stomach that something could be wrong. Her primeval ancestor would have stopped before opening the bedroom door and considered preparing to fight or fly. When Sam did open the door expecting to see Molly immersed in a novel she was confronted with a very different sight.

Molly was not in her chair but standing in the middle of her bedroom. The hand over her mouth to stop her making a sound belonged to a short, tubby man. Molly was struggling not to gag, not because she was scared but because the tubby man's hand was sweaty and smelled foul. Molly wondered if he could sense her revulsion because he gripped her a little harder on her shoulder with his other hand.

"Who are you?" asked Sam.

"I think the better question would be, why am I here?"

"I don't care why you're here, I just want you to take your hands off my daughter and leave."

"I can't do that."

"Yes, you can. My husband is a soldier here in the city. He will be home soon and will kill you for being here and scaring his family."

The man laughed but it sounded raspy, like he smoked. "Kevin won't be home; that I'm sure of. And he's not a soldier anymore."

"I – I don't understand."

"Your boyfriend is a traitor and the emperor has personally ordered his treachery to be made an example of. And you will be used for promoting Eye for an Eye Day."

Sam grimaced. "We would never get involved with that."

"Well, it's lucky I'm here then, isn't it?"

The man didn't wait for Sam to reply or even attempt to understand what he was talking about. He pulled out a gun and pressed it to Molly's temple. Sam screamed for him to stop, to leave her baby alonc, to point the gun at her. She lunged forward to try and help her child, the man lithely avoided her lunging arms and his agile movements seemed alien considering his physique. He spun with Molly seemingly attached to him given the ease with which he moved. Now the man was standing with his back to the door and Sam facing him. Sam was trapped, the man had blocked her escape route.

He now had his gun aimed at Sam. "This isn't a situation you have any control over. I'm not here for you to try and convince me to stop what I'm doing. I can shoot you first or I can shoot your daughter first. That's the only element that has an option."

Molly was trembling, too young to understand the looming possibility of death but old enough to know this situation was bad. Very bad. Mommy was crying, which Molly had never seen before and never wanted to see again. The man's hand was gripping her jaw; his fingers smelled rotten, making her want to gag. It made her cry and scared her.

"Please, don't do this. Not this. There must be some mistake. Kevin isn't a traitor. He's not. I don't believe it."

"It doesn't matter what you believe, you stupid woman. You should feel honored; the emperor personally ordered this visit."

"I – I…"

"I – I…" The man mimicked Sam and laughed his raspy laugh. He flicked the off the gun's safety and aimed squarely at Sam. "Hail to Emperor Nero," he said.

The roar of the gun made Molly's ears ring. Blood spattered her face, the man's hand loosened its grip on her mouth, and Molly screamed. As the man fell down, Molly screamed again as she saw half of his head missing and a bloody mess where his face had once been. Molly ran to her mother who was staring dumbfounded at the dead man in her daughter's bedroom. Sam looked to the doorway where the origin of the gun roar came from, and a giant black man was standing there, calmly surveying the desecration of Molly's innocence.

Mav lowered the gun and said, "I know you're in shock but it's important you listen to me. We need to leave now."

"Leave? Leave for where? I don't know you. You have murdered a man in my house!"

"I wouldn't go so far as calling that sack of shit a man, but I understand the shock." Maverick put his gun away, "Your boyfriend is safe with us, but you are not safe if you stay here."

Sam was staring at the body. "How do I know you're not sent by the emperor?"

"No offense, but me shooting the face off a colleague just to fool a woman and her child into thinking I'm a friend when I'm not is a messed up way to go about it. I'll carry you both out if I have to, but we need to leave."

Molly took hold of her mom's hand and said, "I think he will look after us."

"Out of the mouths of babes," said Mav.

Molly guided her mom out of the bedroom with Maverick already going down the stairs checking no-one had been instructed to arrive a few minutes after the dead man as a precaution.

Mav led Sam and Molly through the back garden and out on to the street where Tobias was waiting. "You took your time," said Tobias.

"The man was shooting his mouth off."

Tobias and Maverick led Molly and her mom away from the house to where the dead man's chariot was parked. Sam and Molly climbed on board and sat at the rear with Maverick and Tobias at the front. The chariot grunted into life and they sped away. Sam had to raise her voice to be heard. "I'm confused!"

Mav looked over his shoulder, questioning. "If we're stealing this chariot to get away, how did you get to us in the first place?" Maverick grinned and turned to face the front again without answering.

Sam didn't have the energy to ask again. She felt the shock

of seeing a man die creep through her body like a poison and hugged Molly close to her, hoping her little girl's innocence would somehow infuse into her and help her forget what she had seen. Molly buried her head into her mother's arms not even slightly excited by her first ever ride on a chariot.

Chapter 17

The chariot stopped under a railway arch. Tobias jumped out and jogged over to a homeless man sitting under the archway. The homeless man had a fluffy, little black-and-white cockapoo as his companion, which wagged its tail at Tobias. It jumped on to its hind legs and rested its front paws on Tobias's legs, hoping for a chin scratch. Tobias obliged while letting the dog know he was a good boy.

"How's it going, Mikey?"

"Living the dream, Tobias, living the dream."

Tobias slipped Mikey a couple of gold coins and a pack of cigarettes, spun on his heels and jogged back to the chariot.

"All good?" Mav asked.

"Yup, all good," replied Tobias.

Mav nodded in approval and proceeded to help Molly and Sam from the chariot. "Okay," he said, "Follow us."

They walked about halfway up the pathway under the arch on the opposite side of Mikey and faced the wall. Mav looked left and Tobias looked right, scanning for any unwelcome visitors. Satisfied they were alone, they stepped forward and placed their left hands on the wall. It looked random and Sam believed she really had been abducted by a couple of delusional lunatics. In fairness to Sam, many would consider Mav and Tobias to be lunatics.

Mav and Tobias removed their hands from the wall, and Sam gasped as the wall parted to reveal an entrance. In fact, the wall hadn't actually parted but a set of double doors had opened. They were camouflaged to look like a wall and only a very, very keen observer would even notice doors were there. But a keen observer would struggle to spend enough time examining a random wall under an archway because before they could Mikey would be badgering them for spare change or Gordon the dog would be humping their leg. Not many people wanted to stick around for that so the archway tended to be avoided as much as possible or people scurried through as fast as they could.

Even local solider patrols tended to steer clear; Mikey and Gordon were part of the landscape but a smelly, keep-at-arm's-length, part of the landscape. Which was very handy for Mav and Tobias at this particular time considering they were betting on Mikey sending any soldiers looking for a stolen chariot in a very, very wrong direction.

Mikey was about to do just that.

Tobias had fired up the chariot and guided it under the archway, bumped it up the curb and through the invisible entrance. Mav, Sam and Molly were waiting in the gloom of the entrance. Once the wheels disappeared from Mikey's sight, the doors shut, leaving the wall looking like any other wall.

Mikey unwrapped the cigarettes, pulled one out of the packet and sparked up. He took a deep drag and sighed a happy, smoky sigh. Gordon popped his head up and tilted it, listening for something in the distance. Mikey scratched the dog behind his ear, "It's okay, Bubs, just the usual patrol." Gordon seemed to understand, rested his head on Mikey's lap again and sighed too.

Two chariots entered the archway from the opposite end Mav and Tobias had and rolled to a stop next to Mikey. There were two soldiers in each chariot. Both drivers shut down their engines and Mikey felt his stomach drop. They never usually shut down their engines. A short, brown soldier stepped off the chariot and stood over Mikey and Gordon. Gordon opened his eyes and glanced up, sighed again and tried to go back to sleep. *Thanks a bunch, Gord,* thought Mikey. His usual routine of humping anyone who came near seemed to be forgotten. Mikey put the cigarette to his mouth and noticed a slight tremor in his hand so took a quick drag and flicked the cigarette away.

The soldier turned his head to watch the cigarette hit the tarmac and its embers scatter. He turned back to Mikey, "Hi Mikey."

"Hello, sir." The sir came out strained.

The soldier glanced in the direction of the cigarette again and asked, "Where'd you get the cigarettes from?"

Mikey glanced left and then back at the soldier, "A kind passerby."

The soldier smiled. His eyes didn't match his mouth, though. "That's very kind."

"Gordon always makes people feel charitable."

As if on cue Gordon looked at the solider and wagged his tail. The soldier's smile reached his eyes, and Mikey thanked the gods the soldier liked dogs.

"What did they look like?"

"Who?"

"The cigarette Samaritans."

"Erm, like normal people."

"People? I thought it was a kind passerby on their own?"

Gordon, hump his damn leg and start barking, for god's sake, Mikey desperately thought. "Well, yeah, it was a kind person who gave me the smokes, but he was with a friend."

The soldier eyed Mikey, as if looking for a lie. "So what did they look like?"

Mikey thought of Tobias and Mav and described two people who looked the opposite. Just as the soldier opened his mouth to ask another question about the cigarette Samaritans, a voice called from the chariot called, "Oi, Zac, we couldn't give a fuck about Mikey's smoking habit. Unless they were in a chariot! Mikey? Someone has stolen a chariot from the emperor. Have you seen anything?"

"No, sorry. Not much happens this way. That's why I camp here."

"Well if you see anything." The voice trailed off, not needing to say much more.

The soldier, Zac, turned to the source of the voice to complain as he had been just about to get to asking Mikey about the chariot; his partner needed to always stop undermining him. To support the soldier's sense of being undermined and not being taken seriously, Gordon got to his feet, sniffed Zac's leg and proceeded to start humping it. Zac started to shake his leg to get rid of Gordon, which only encouraged Gordon and increased the speed of his humping. Zac flailed around in circles, hopping and flapping while Gordon became more vigorous with his thrusting. The soldiers in the chariots simply laughed hearty laughs. Zac managed to escape the dog and scrambled back on to the chariot. One of the soldiers said he'd told him not to get off the chariot as the dog would do that, so it's his own fault. Zac went a very dark shade of red.

A voice from one of the chariot's shouted out to Mikey, "For the love of the gods either get that dog's balls cut off or find him a shag." The chariots fired up and sped off. The laughing echoed under the archway.

Chapter 18

Maverick, Tobias and their new wards had been watching the scene from behind the camouflaged doors. The doors had a one-way screen so no-one could see in but observers could see out. Satisfied and amused by Mikey and Gordon's ability to get the soldiers moved on, they turned away and made their way through the tunnel they were standing in. The tunnel had motion sensors so as they walked the ceiling lights blinked on.

The tunnel was about 20 feet wide and ten feet high. Their footsteps echoed as they walked, and it made Molly hug into Sam as they walked. Sam looked at the two large men, questioning where they were.

"The Romans think they're the masters of everything, including construction. What they forget is, they're the masters of slavery and the construction experts are the slaves they round up. Before the Romans arrived on our shores, many great architects and builders got together and built this tunnel system in preparation for resisting Roman rule."

They got to the end of the tunnel and boarded an elevator waiting for them. The elevator descended and when the doors opened Sam gasped. In front of her was what looked like a temple. The gigantic room was 30 feet high, 100 feet long and probably similar in width. On the wall facing her and to her left and right she saw a total of six large tunnel entrances with massive archways. Above each archway were stained glass windows depicting various scenes of a religious nature, which were backlit by spotlights. Sam only scanned them, but it appeared the windows had pictures of Roman gods, the God-Carpenter and other characters she didn't recognize.

Sam looked at Mav and Tobias and they simply looked back at her and then guided her toward a tunnel on the far right of the room. As they got closer to the entrance Sam admired the window above the archway and noticed it was of a mansion with the words *In my house are many rooms* underneath. When they entered the tunnel, the *clip-clop* of their shoes went silent and Sam enjoyed the softness of a plush carpet running the entire length. The tunnel curved to the left and then a number of tunnels were adjoined to the main one, showing doorways roughly spaced apart by ten feet. After walking past four tunnels leading off, they turned right down a tunnel and reached the second door on the right. Mav opened it and it revealed a living space.

Kevin was sitting on the sofa and jumped up when he saw Sam and Molly standing there. They rushed to each other and had a three-way hug. Relief washed over them, and they ended up kneeling and hugging and crying. Mav stepped out of the room and closed the door. "We'll leave them to it."

"Boatman said what he wants from Kevin yet?"

"Not yet, but I imagine Kevin won't like it."

"Doesn't it seem a bit strange?"

"What?"

"Kidnapping a grunt seems pretty pointless if we're trying to get to Nero," said Tobias.

"And Nero knows the grunt is with us now, so there's no element of surprise."

"Well whatever he's planning for Kevin, it won't be subtle."

Maverick snorted, "Subtle? I don't think he knows what subtle is. Look at us, for instance."

Tobias conceded the point.

As they walked away from the reunited family's room, Tobias felt a tinge of pity because if they were part of a plan concocted by Boatman it probably wouldn't end well for that young family.

Chapter 19

Maverick and Tobias went back to their room to freshen up. They jumped in the shower and Tobias noticed a deep frown on his partner's face, the water dripping off his graying beard. "What's on your mind?"

Mav grunted and wiped his face, moving aside so Tobias could get some of the shower stream, "I have a bad feeling in my gut."

"About?"

"Whatever is going to happen next."

"You're talking about the instructions from Boatman?"

Maverick murmured a positive. "Everything is happening very quickly. Spying on a Centurion and then ambushing a Century would usually happen over—"

"A three-month period," Tobias interrupted.

"But we did it like a knee-jerk reaction," Mav finished. "Which means the plan is imminent."

It was Tobias's turn to grunt.

They finished showering in silence and dressed in silence too.

Maverick received a text from Boatman to meet him straight away, so they walked out of the living area, across the main temple area and entered the tunnel, which had a stained glass window showing the Roman god Mars with his foot on the throat of a dragon.

They reached a metal door being guarded by two women wearing Kevlar and carrying tasers. "Hi boys," the guard on the left said.

"Evening, ladies," said Tobias. "How have the residents been?"

"Annoyingly cooperative. Haven't had to use the taser once."

"Yeah, it's been dull as hell," said the other guard.

"Wow, you two need a hobby or something," said Tobias

The women smirked, opened the door and stepped aside.

The men walked in and Boatman was talking to Kevin. Boatman waved them over. Tobias swept his gaze across the room. The hostage soldiers were sitting with their backs to the wall or in the middle—huddled, handcuffs off, and many of them hugging mugs of tea and chatting. It was all very, very relaxed for a hostage situation.

"How are you both doing?"

"We're fine, thanks, Boatman." Mav looked at Kevin. "How are Sam and Molly?"

Kevin hesitated, seemingly surprised at the question. "They're… erm… they're fine. A bit shaken up but thankful to you for saving their lives." He glanced around the room, almost subconsciously. "And they're very surprised at their new accommodation."

Boatman smiled. "We're rebel scum, not savages."

Kevin managed to laugh.

Tobias looked confused, "You're much more relaxed than when we last saw you."

Kevin shrugged, "My family are safe and in a place Nero won't find."

Tobias squinted, unconvinced by the answer, but Boatman spoke before Tobias could press Kevin further.

"We're going to push forward with our plan and green light it for Saturday night."

"Saturday?" Mav didn't attempt to hide his surprise.

"I know it seems quick, but we have Nero on the back foot. Kevin? You're sure you want to do this?"

The man nodded.

"Do what?" Maverick asked.

"He's the bait."

"Bait?

Boatman dismissed the question, "Kevin, you're clear about what needs to happen?"

The man nodded again, not looking quite as relaxed as before, Tobias noted.

"How exactly are you going to be bait?" Maverick asked him.

"I'll stand outside Faust's home."

"And our threats to Centurion Faust will mean he will be the first to arrive on the scene hoping to make amends."

Boatman nodded.

"But what's with this lot?" Tobias jerked his thumb at the 80 soldiers in the room.

"They're the reinforcements and distraction."

Maverick thought about it. "Which is where our part comes in."

Boatman nodded. "You think you can do it?"

Maverick looked at Boatman, hard, looked at Tobias and then looked back. "Honestly? I think that there's a very good chance either Tobias or myself will be sleeping alone on Sunday night."

Chapter 20

Thursday was spent finalizing the plans. Boatman spent a few hours with the soldiers cementing what they were meant to be doing. It had taken little effort to convince them to be loyal to the cause. He played them the recording of Nero's tantrum exclaiming his indifference to his subjects being slaughtered and also gave them monetary incentives. With a (heavily guarded) tour of the expansive underground town, plus an insight into Boatman's ideology and a reminder of the money they would make as rebels, it was very easy to get them to share in the vision. Nero recruited through fear; Boatman believed he recruited through passion.

Boatman spent the rest of the day with Kevin, Sam and Molly, reassuring Sam that Kevin would be okay and running through Kevin's role. The plan was dangerous, yes, but Boatman would keep Kevin under close guard. It did little to ease Sam's fears.

Maverick and Tobias used their short amount of time for planning to work out how to reduce the chance of them being killed from 100 percent to about 80 percent. They scoured the plans on the table in front of them, debating the most effective tactics and putting together a chronological plan they would commit to memory. They knew their plan had a lot of flaws, but they also knew they were very gifted at plugging those holes on the cuff.

Friday was used for rest and relaxation. Boatman believed in rest before any operation in order to truly absorb the plans made. It was also important to appreciate the people around you, just in case things went wrong, because as confident in his abilities as he was, Boatman had seen enough death to know it wasn't certain he or his loved ones would come back alive.

Which is why, on this rest and relaxation day, he sat by Olivia's bed regretting how he had allowed her to be so horrifically injured. Olivia stirred and asked Boatman for a drink. He put the glass and straw near her mouth, and she took some little sips. He put the glass down and stroked her hair. She smiled; she always liked it when he stroked her hair.

"Mmmm, that feels nice," she whispered.

"How are you feeling?"

"A bit better," she said. She was speaking truthfully, too. It had been three months since the crucifixion, and she was almost recovered. The physical toll crucifixion had on her body meant she struggled to find energy, though. She was still in the hospital ward and some days slept more than she was awake. If she was honest though, it wasn't only the brutality of the crucifixion that was tiring her out; it was also the vibrations. They were incessant. She assumed her brush with death had somehow opened her mind to greater sensitivity to the vibrations. Those vibrations were like echoes of people's pain, moving through her. It was tiring, and it struck her how many people were in such sadness. There was one vibration though that was prominent. It wasn't a dark vibration; it was an innocent one. Close by.

"I am so sorry, Liv. So desperately sorry." Boatman's voice

moved her consciousness back into the room and away from the innocent vibration.

Olivia looked at Boatman, tired but still with the fierceness that Boatman adored, "Remember when we met?"

"How could I forget? You called me an arrogant prick."

"Because you are."

"You still chose to marry this arrogant prick."

"I thought you were rich."

"And I thought you fell for my good looks and good humor."

"We both know I'm the funny one. I have to be good humored to have married you."

Boatman laughed and it felt good to do it. It felt good for Olivia to be able to make a joke.

"Do you forgive me?"

"It's not your fault."

"I should have kept people watching your office."

"Let's not talk about it. If it's okay, I need to have another sleep."

Boatman nodded and kissed his wife's forehead. "I'll see you soon," he said and hoped he was right. He wasn't going to mention his plans for tomorrow. He prayed he would see his wife again but knew nothing was certain anymore. If there ever was certainty to begin with.

Chapter 21

Maverick and Tobias left the headquarters before dawn and made their way to their destination over an hour before Boatman and his team prepared to leave. They wanted to be in position and ready to move without hesitation.

A light on Tobias's headgear was shining on the building plans in his hands. He shone the light on the door and then looked back at the plans, "Right, this is the way in and puts us on the same floor as the cameras."

"How sure are we?"

"She's as reliable as we're going to get. I trust her."

"There's a chance she sold us out."

"There's always a chance of that."

"Well, we'll know in a second," said Maverick.

The door was sunk into the wall, so it was hidden. There was a handle embedded into the door that had to be pulled out to turn it. Tobias pulled the brass handle out, turned it, cracked the door open an inch. He waited for an alarm to sound but everything remained quiet. Tobias eased the door closed again and turned to face Maverick. "Looks like we're in luck."

"I wouldn't say this situation is something I would call lucky."

They both removed their headlamps, pulled night vision goggles out of their backpacks, checked their equipment and briefly went over the key points to the plan again.

"Ready?"

"Ready."

Tobias turned the door handle, quietly opened the door and rushed through, aiming for the door on the right of the hallway they had entered. He didn't look back, trusting Maverick was close behind. He turned the door handle and the door opened, just like he was told. He glanced back and Maverick was on his shoulder. They entered the room, it was dark, and they quietly closed the door behind them. Maverick put a chair under the handle and turned the lights on. The room was about 30 feet square with oak-paneled walls, intricately carved coving, a garish chandelier in the center of the ceiling. To Maverick, it was needlessly ostentatious.

"How long do we have?" asked Maverick.

Tobias checked the timer on his watch. "Twenty minutes. I only need a couple."

"Just what every man wants to hear."

In front of them was an array of 50 flat screens with CCTV images. They were depicting live feeds of places across London, changing camera feeds every couple of minutes. Tobias pulled a tablet out of his rucksack and found the broadband router on top of the PC controlling all the screens. He found the wifi password on the router and connected his tablet. Next, he booted up the PC and logged in. The password was stuck to a Post-it on the screen of the system viewer. Tobias muttered something about Governments ruling the world but still unable to have up-to-date computer systems and security.

"You are joking, right? You've just accessed the Empire's CCTV for London the way I would log-in at my mum's house." Maverick was bemused.

"It's called arrogance. After all, who would be stupid enough to break into their London headquarters and access their computer system?"

Maverick shook his head; there was a legion of soldiers guarding the building outside, but an empty room, with access to the eyes of London, had no security. "If it stays this easy, I'll suggest to Boatman we should lead the rebellion and he can retire."

"Don't worry, it will all go wrong soon."

Tobias accessed the app for the CCTV. "Can you find his house on the screen and tell me the camera code on bottom right-hand corner?" said Tobias.

Maverick scanned the screens, found the camera and relayed the number. Tobias pulled the image up on the desktop. "All quiet so far." He proceeded to then find the access details for the cameras on the app and entered the details on the same app on his tablet. Within a few seconds the house they wanted was live streaming on his tablet. "Right, I have it, let's move on."

Maverick shook his head again in disbelief and wondered aloud how the Roman Empire was still an empire when it had security at the level of a retiree who believed a rich prince in Nigeria had just left him millions. Tobias told him to get over it, as it made their life a damn sight easier.

They put their night vision goggles back on, turned the lights out and slipped out of the room. They glided along the hallway away from where they emerged out of the tunnel until they reached a narrow staircase to their left. They had their backs to the wall, each of them on either side of the entrance. Maverick pulled out a small extendable mirror and checked the stairway was clear while Tobias kept an eye on any unwelcome visitors coming down the hall. It was still before 6am and in this part of the building it wouldn't see another soul until 8am, but you could never be too careful.

They quietly ascended to the next floor and waited at the top for any signs of activity. Confident they were alone they turned right and crept to the door at the end of the hallway. Tobias drew his handgun with a silencer attached and stepped back, gun drawn and facing the door. Maverick crouched and pulled out a key. It was a skeleton key that unlocked most doors in the building. It was an old building, used for public service before the Romans took it over, and their informant had told them most doors had the same lock because no caretaker could have had that many keys for so many rooms without severe hip problems carrying a key chain that big. The Romans had never felt it necessary to change that logic.

Maverick gently put the key in the lock and slowly turned it, sliding the hidden lock across. To Maverick it sounded like the loudest thing he had ever done. He pulled the door handle down and swung the door open in a crouch position, going with the door, while Tobias followed in close behind. Tobias moved into the room straight ahead into a lounge area sweeping his gun left and right as he went. Maverick had arched to the right moving fast and low. They were in a lounge area, sparsely furnished. They padded across the carpet and reached another door. The door had no lock but they did the same routine again, Maverick crouched low and Tobias slightly back from the door. This time Maverick swung the door open quickly with Tobias rushing into the room and Maverick close behind to his left.

Tobias was on to the bed in under a second as the figure in the bed rolled out, taking the duvet with him. The man under the duvet threw the duvet at Maverick. Maverick swiped it away, but as he did so was shoulder barged. Maverick grunted from the contact but used the momentum of the barge and swiveled away from the attack, causing the figure to stumble forward. Tobias was on top of the figure in an instant but was surprised when the figure went from a stumble into a forward roll into the lounge. Tobias could see the figure would be out the main door in an instant, so he fired his gun. The rubber bullet hit the man in the back and flattened him. Maverick and Tobias were on top of the man pinning him down before he could attempt another escape.

Maverick pulled his knife and put it to the man's throat. If the man had decided to struggle the knife made him rethink that as a viable option. Tobias closed the door.

"So you're Aloysius, I presume?" said Maverick.

"Nice move with the duvet," said Tobias.

Aloysius was breathing hard, winded from the bullet. Maverick put cable ties around the Roman's wrists and ankles, picked him up from underneath his shoulders and tossed him on the sofa. Tobias pulled out his tablet and brought up the live stream. The cameras on the house showed no activity still. He looked at his watch. Any minute now.

Maverick went into the bedroom and grabbed Aloysius's clothes, which had been discarded on the floor. While Tobias trained his gun on their captive, Maverick cut the cable ties, told Aloysius to dress and politely reminded him that his neck would be snapped if he tried anything.

Aloysius had barely said a word but was looking back and forth at his captors with a look of almost wonderment at the shear lunacy of holding the bodyguard of the emperor hostage. Tobias seemed to read his mind. "You think we're nuts, don't you?"

Aloysius was breathing hard from the impact of the rubber bullet. "It had crossed my mind."

"Don't worry, we know we are," said Maverick.

"What do you want?"

"We need you to take us to the emperor."

"Oh! That's all? And there was me thinking you two were fucking deluded and wanted something impossible."

"It's simple, walk us to his quarters, telling anyone who asks what we're doing is none of their damned business, and we kill Nero."

"Apart from the legion guarding his quarters, you are The Beast, you're recognized everywhere." Aloysius was looking at Maverick. "Anyone who sees you will try to arrest or kill you, regardless of my presence."

"Mav, can I have your autograph?"

"Yeah, I'll print my name on your ass with my boot."

"You say the sweetest things," said Tobias.

Aloysius looked at the two men with dismay.

Maverick turned his attention back to the Roman, "We'll worry about the guards, you just need to lead us to Nero. We know only a few people know where the emperor sleeps in this building, with you, the bodyguard, being one." Maverick had his gun drawn again ensuring Aloysius didn't get any ideas. The bodyguard was trained to deal with pain, but even he didn't fancy a rubber bullet to his face at close range. Maverick asked his partner how they were looking.

"It's on, we move in five minutes."

Chapter 22

Boatman and Kevin slipped through the early morning November darkness, avoiding main roads and skirting through alleyways. The reached their destination, breathing hard, the mist from their mouths ballooning and disappearing. They were peering round the side of a house, two doors down from their target. Boatman checked Kevin was happy with the plan, or at least understood it. He doubted happiness came into it. Kevin nodded.

"And remember you need to make sure the CCTV sees your face clearly. There has never been a clear picture of my face, and I don't want today to be the day they get one."

Boatman put his hood back up and indicated for Kevin to stay put until it was clear to follow.

Boatman walked along the pavement, hands in his pockets, looking casual. He reached the house where two soldiers were standing, guarding.

"Excuse me, guys, I'm a bit lost, can you help?"

"Haven't you got a phone? Piss off, mate, we're cold and not tourist guides."

Boatman pulled out his phone. "Can you just tell me where this building is?" Boatman put his phone in front of the cold guard. As the guard squinted at the screen, his eyes adjusting to the brightness in the dark, Boatman Boatman hit the second guard in the throat with his right hand; the guard crumpled, his throat crushed. He barely made a noise because he couldn't. As the cold guard's brain began to register his comrade's demise, Boatman pulled the phone away. The guard instinctively looked up and Boatman head butted him square on the bridge of his nose. A rock-hard forehead verses soft nose cartilage was no contest. The guard was unconscious before he hit the ground.

Boatman waved down the street to let Kevin know it was safe to approach. When Kevin arrived, he glanced back and forth down the street, just as instructed and they walked up the pathway and entered the house.

Within minutes of them being inside, two legions of soldiers arrived at the house. Atticus was leading them both. He instructed one legion to surround the back of the house and the other to form an arch around the front. Atticus shouted into the morning darkness, lights from the chariots silhouetting his form against the house. "Boatman! I assume that's you in there? This is a simple choice. You're going to die, but you can choose if the deserter dies with you, or you let him into our custody where he at least has a chance to live."

The house remained still, no sign of movement.

Atticus pulled his phone out and called the commander of the legion that had moved behind the house. At the back of the house was a large garden, 100 feet long and backed on to a nature reserve, a tributary of the Thames running along the border to the garden. Atticus knew the house well; he knew the grounds well; he had been here many times. Before they had arrived on the scene, Atticus had been watching the CCTV footage of the deserter entering the house just after a hooded figure (Boatman, surely?) floored two soldiers without breaking a sweat. As he swept out of the Castrum, he phoned his legion commander and described the lay of the land they were going to. He told him that at the side of the house there was an entrance into the rear garden, to take that and surround the house with half the legion. The other half were to take the small foot bridge that allowed access into the nature reserve and to flank that, just in case the intruders tried to slip through.

The commander wasn't answering, the phone not seeming to connect. Atticus tried the number again. Nothing. He pulled the phone from his ear, frowning at the screen. He had full signal. Atticus called his other commander over and instructed him to go round the back of the property and to keep his fucking phone switched on. The commander nodded and jogged into the darkness, the lights of the chariot making his shadow dance across the house.

Atticus looked at his phone again and clicked his tongue. He had a bad feeling in the pit of his stomach. It had been a long time since a knot like that had settled in his belly. Blood and fury and noise was what he was used to when facing an enemy. This was quiet. This was eerie. This was how Boatman operated. When he stood on London Bridge surveying the massacre two of Boatman's henchmen had inflicted, the quietness of the death was disturbing. Atticus enjoyed the loudness of death, men shouting and screaming. Men swords clashing and guns firing and bones breaking. Boatman seemed to quietly destroy.

"Futuo," said Atticus and put his phone away. Atticus clicked his tongue against the roof of his mouth again, weighing up his options. He felt stupid, as he had two legions against two men.

Well, against one man. The deserter was hardly a threat and Atticus was going to enjoy putting the nails through his wrists personally. So he had 160 men against one man, one unknown man, and yet he couldn't shake that dread churning in his stomach. Atticus pointed to a cluster of soldiers. "Follow me," he said and strode toward the house. He's just a man, he mumbled under his breath and drew his sword. And this man would bleed.

Atticus marched up the path, his sword's shadow jumping in the chariot's light. Atticus stopped halfway, looked back and instructed the men to draw their guns and kill on sight. He turned to face the house again, and as he stepped forward again a bright light assaulted his eyes. The light was closely followed by an intense heat that melted his eyeballs.

The house exploded, glass shards whizzing through the air, ripping through soldiers' faces. Following the glass shards were nails and bolts, lethal bullets being catapulted at thousands of feet per second. Most of the eighty soldiers were killed instantly by the enormity of the blast. Those who weren't, wished they had been.

Chapter 23

Boatman had heard Atticus shouting, demanding surrender, but hadn't bothered to wait around for whatever bullshit deal he was pretending to offer. He knew there would be no deal. In fact, Boatman wasn't even in the house when Atticus had arrived. He and Kevin were in the back garden. They weren't alone, though; half of Atticus's soldiers were in the garden, but they also weren't alone as they had knives to their throats from the soldiers Boatman had kidnapped and turned into rebels. Boatman had the commander's arm behind his back and his face close to his ear. "You need to tell your guys to not resist and come with us. Trust me, you don't want to stay here." The commander didn't take any convincing, he had seen the London Bridge massacre and knew he was already on borrowed time as he should have been the one responding to the rescue of Boatman's wife.

The commander cleared his throat. "Gentlemen, do not resist. It's not worth the fight."

Any soldier with a gun or sword in his hand dropped their weapons and put their hands in the air. The soldiers now on Boatman's side showed their former colleagues they meant no harm and they all filed out of the garden and made their way across the foot bridge into the nature reserve.

Boatman pulled Bella aside and told her to start leading everyone back to headquarters. He would catch up. As they all dispersed, he turned back to the house and pulled out a burner phone. He unlocked and dialed the only number in the phone. It connected and the house exploded.

He felt the heat from the blast on his face and felt satisfaction. Atticus had been vanquished. He remembered Atticus from the early stages of Boatman's arrival in London. Boatman had found an underground movement limping along in its goal to defeat the Empire. Their subversion of the state amounted to poorly printed literature and occasionally bribing soldiers for inside information. The information was usually pretty weak, and never revealed much more than who a married sergeant's mistress might be. The movement was able to blackmail with this information, but it barely kept the movement solvent and was as much a threat to London's Roman occupation as a fly on someone's shoulder. Barely noticeable.

Boatman believed shock and awe were key to rocking the heels of the Romans, and he had convinced three comrades that they should raid an outpost in the city center. If they were swift and efficient, they could put fear into the Romans and conjure a sense of foreboding. Boatman's plan was to enter the outpost in the early hours of a morning and take out a guard. Then they were to do the same a week later at a different outpost. The result would be soldiers' fear at their vulnerability.

The night they attempted to raid the outpost only ended in shock for Boatman and the rebels, though. One of Boatman's weaknesses when he'd arrived in London (and some would argue still to this day) was his arrogance, his belief that he was stronger and smarter than anyone else. And as it turns out, bribery can go both ways and someone very unhappy with Boatman's forceful arrival on the scene of London's slow-burning rebellion tipped off the outpost of the planned attack.

When Boatman arrived at the outpost, they split into two pairs and went in opposite directions. Boatman and Bella, who had been invested in Boatman's vision from the beginning, took the outside stairs leading to the first floor of the building. They were then going to traverse the corridors and go back down a level to get to the door of the night guard they were going to take out. The night guard should have been awake, watching CCTV and remaining alert to any potential threats, but security was very lackadaisical owing to no-one being stupid enough to attempt to attack a Roman outpost in the capital of the country. Until now.

Boatman and Bella were to guard the door just in case anyone unwittingly stumbled into their path. The other two of the team would enter the room via a window, assassinate the soldier and knock three times when the job was done. Bella and Boatman arrived at the room with no incident but started to grow concerned when they heard no knock after much longer than it should have taken. On the count of three, Boatman opened the door while Bella had her sword drawn; they discovered two dead bodies on the floor with Atticus standing over them, grinning.

"This one," Atticus pointed his sword at one of the bodies, "Made a great joke about me being Italian. Something about pasta and being mundane. I do love your British humor." Atticus was still grinning.

Bella went to move on the Centurion, but Boatman grabbed her arm, "No, Bella, don't."

"What? Why?"

"We need to go. Now."

Boatman, still holding Bella's arm, spun her round, and she quickly followed as Boatman sprinted for the exit. They burst through the main doors and into the night.

Boatman felt himself grinding his teeth as he thought back to that night when Atticus had made him look clueless. The initial burst of adrenalin warming his insides almost as much as the flames from the house were warming his body on the outside started to wane, and he still felt bitterness at how Atticus how outwitted him so easily all those years ago. This booby trap was crass. It did the job, but it was like shooting a fish with a shotgun instead of patiently luring it with bait.

Boatman thought back to Bella's confusion as to why they ran, telling him they had a Roman Centurion almost in their grasp and they ran away like frightened school children.

"Bella, he was in that room on his own. There wasn't another guard, it was just him. Waiting for us."

"I know!"

"Jesus," Boatman rubbed his face in frustration. "Why would a Centurion not have anyone else with him?"

"Because he clearly felt able to handle whoever came in that room, and he fucking showed it."

"Bella, he knew we were coming. Think about it."

"He stepped back further into the room, I thought he was scared, even though he was laughing. Like it was a nervous cover."

"That laugh was genuine," said Boatman.

"He wanted us in that room, close to him."

"Exactly."

"Why?"

"Because Atticus isn't afraid of death. He welcomes it. And he thinks his death will bring him an eternity of wealth and, knowing him, screwing."

"He was going to blow himself up?"

"Someone who thinks they're going to become a martyr is more dangerous than anyone else. And he looked ready to be a martyr."

Bella went quiet in shock and Boatman let her process her thoughts about it all. It was hard to fathom someone would be so willing to commit suicide and take other people in the process. It was a type of murder you couldn't predict or necessarily stop. It was a terrifying method to kill.

Boatman hated that Atticus, even in death by being blown to smithereens, might have still had a fleeting moment where he believed he was a martyr.

"Shit!" Boatman realized Atticus had not only played martyr over the years but had also played decoy. As a man who seemed to fear nothing, he was a great decoy. He was a decoy tonight; this was the last time but Boatman had, yet again, failed to realize that. He had arranged for this house to be booby trapped and for it to lure soldiers to kill or recruit because it would grab the attention of those in the upper echelons of Roman government. It had worked almost perfectly, and he was pleased it had drawn Atticus; revenge is sweet.

But.

Atticus had yet again been a distraction. Even in his death. Boatman had chosen this house, Faust's house, because he had hoped Faust himself would be lured into the trap. Faust was nowhere to be seen. Because Faust had sent Atticus. Because Faust knew it was a decoy. Because Faust knew the plan was something else.

Boatman started running back to headquarters, fumbled his personal phone out of his pocket and tapped on recents in his phone app. He tapped on Maverick's number, begging it to be answered.

It went straight to voicemail.

Boatman kept running. He needed help. In his desire to quickly destroy Faust he had failed to see the lure bobbing. Faust was holding the fishing rod and Maverick and Tobias were about to be hooked.

Chapter 24

Aloysius led Maverick and Tobias through the labyrinth of the Principia. It was colloquially known as the HoC based on what it was used for before the Romans descended upon it. Nero's father, Augustine, was whimsical about the building as a 'powerhouse of democratic debate' and the great Cicero would have adored the pompous bluster of the main debate chamber. Augustine even played clips, to Nero, of famous debates in the HoC and regularly got over-enthused about the wonderful way the Brits so politely debated each other, even if they hated each other. He laughed with fervor when a politician would 'strongly object to what the *right honorable lady* is suggesting,' when that right honorable lady was politely suggesting the right honorable gentlemen was a war criminal.

Nero never understood his father's amusement at such exchanges because he would have had the right honorable lady dragged outside and skinned alive.

Nero also never understood how his father appeared to be enamored with the HoC but wasted no time in expelling all of its members when he conquered London and turning it into the Principia. If he found it to be a shining light on how to govern, he wasted no time in destroying its ability to govern. Now the building was an army barracks and, it seemed, Nero's hotel for the foreseeable future.

Aloysius was walking ahead with Tobias's gun trained on him. Maverick was guarding the rear, ensuring they had no surprises behind them.

"How much further?"

They had walked down two flights of stairs and along yards and yards of hallway. "We're almost at his chamber," said Aloysius.

"Stop there," said Tobias.

Aloysius obliged. They had come to the end of a hallway, which turned only left. Tobias told the prisoner to get on his knees. Tobias pulled out a small extendable mirror and edged it past the wall to see down the hallway. Maverick had his gun trained on Aloysius.

"Is that the door to his quarters?"

Aloysius nodded.

Speaking to Maverick, "There's no-one guarding the door."

"Why's there no-one guarding the door?"

Aloysius shrugged.

Tobias scowled at the Roman and looked at his partner, "What do you think?"

"If no-one's guarding either he isn't there or—" Maverick looked at Nero's bodyguard. "Where's your comms piece?"

"After being ambushed and bundled out of my room I didn't think to pick it up."

Maverick swore.

"What?"

"If there's no-one guarding Nero's room, it most likely means Nero has been moved."

Maverick swore again.

"What?" asked Tobias again.

"If Nero has been moved, that's an emergency and if it's an emergency…"

"Then Nero's bodyguard would have been contacted. And if they weren't able to contact him then…"

"I would have been sent to find him." The voice came from behind Maverick. Maverick spun and pointed his gun at Faust. Faust was unarmed and raised his hands. Tobias put his gun to Aloysius's head. "Surely you wouldn't shoot an unarmed man?"

"Couldn't give a fuck. A dead Roman is a dead Roman."

"I know you're called The Beast, but I'd like to think your brain isn't so primitive and would register my being unarmed is significant."

Maverick hesitated. Faust smiled and then a distant explosion caused the building to tremble.

"I'm rather upset that you have destroyed my house," said Faust.

"I'm upset you weren't in it at the time," said Maverick.

Faust laughed, "I remember a number of years ago you fought a centurion called Romulus. Well, he wasn't actually named Romulus at birth, he gave himself that name. He had some sort of delusion he was a reincarnation of Romulus and therefore immortal. He wanted to fight you to prove you were just a man and he was more than a man. Do you remember him?"

"Romans with delusions of grandeur mingle into one in my mind, if I'm honest."

"I'm pleased to see you haven't lost that sense of humor you had in the ring, Maverick. Romulus screamed he was a god as he swung his sword at you and just before you killed him you said he wasn't a god but a little bitch. I nearly wet myself laughing at that."

"Sorry, am I missing something? Is this the Maverick best bits fan club?" said Tobias.

"Nothing wrong with appreciating an artist in his work."

Tobias looked at Faust, then at Maverick. "Mav, shoot this idiot. He thinks hacking people up in a gladiator ring is art."

Maverick raised his gun at Faust. Faust stopped laughing. "Okay, I see you're not easily flattered. But hear me out."

"Thirty seconds and then I shoot you."

"It was clever breaking into my house and writing that message; it distracted from the bomb you planted. It also distracted from your plan to come here to kill Nero."

"It didn't distract you."

"Well, no. Almost. It was Boatman 'accidentally' revealing his face to the security camera which made me hilsts it was a trap."

Maverick frowned. "If you knew it was a trap, why didn't you warn Atticus?"

Faust shrugged. "There was always a chance it wasn't a trap, and I couldn't deny Atticus the potential glory of apprehending the infamous Boatman."

"Something smells off to me," said Tobias.

Faust shrugged again.

"I'm not hearing any reason to not shoot you."

"I want to meet Boatman. I have a proposal."

It was Maverick's turn to laugh. It boomed around the grand hallway of the HoC. "That's not exactly a cunning plan."

Faust took a step forward. Maverick did the same, with his gun still raised. Faust didn't flinch. "I'm serious. I want to meet Boatman. I have an offer."

The gun didn't waver, "Well obviously that's never going to happen. If you have an offer, then it goes through me."

"Us," said Tobias.

"What?"

"It goes through us."

Maverick kept his gaze on Faust but spoke to his fiancé, "What are you talking about?"

"If he has something to say to Boatman, it goes through his top two commanders."

"That's what I said."

"No, you said 'it goes through me' which means you forgot about me in the process."

"Who cares?"

"I just think you need to remember your partner in how you say things."

"I'm getting tempted to use this gun on you instead."

"I'm just pointing out this relationship is a partnership."

"You really need to find better moments to bring your insecure shit up," said Mav and turned his attention back to Faust. "If you have an offer, then it goes through *us*."

"Thanks darling," said Tobias.

Mav grunted.

Faust glanced back and forth between these two men, confused they were the ruthless killing machines who had caused the carnage on London Bridge. He cleared his throat, "So, anyway, I can't give you that option. I have to speak to Boatman directly."

"For a centurion, you seem a bit slow on the uptake. Or this is a pathetic way to stall me shooting you in the face."

"I can help Boatman get rid of Nero."

Maverick let his gun drop a little. "Sorry, I'm confused, I thought that's why we were here."

"You mean you didn't bring me here for a tour?" said Tobias.

"Your plan was never going to work. You both know it. It was a stretch too far. Even if you had managed it, you would have made him a martyr and Max would ascend to the throne."

"Max is dead."

"No, he's not. He's in a bad way but he will recover."

"Bullshit.

Faust slowly raised his left and said, "I'm going to slowly reach across to my front pocket and pull out my phone. I will just use my forefinger and thumb."

Mav raised his gun again while Faust reached into his pocket and gently pulled out his phone. He raised his eyebrows in a question and Maverick nodded it was fine to proceed. Faust unlocked his phone and swiped a few times before turning his phone around. "This is Max in the hospital. You caved in his skull, but he's still alive."

Mav glanced at the screen. It was Max. Heavily bandaged, his body a cacophony of tubes, but it was definitely him. "I must be getting weaker in my old age."

Faust turned the phone around, studied the photo for a few seconds and then carefully put his phone back in his pocket. "I think a skull as thick as Max's would've taken two blows even from Jupiter himself."

"Okay, I'm listening."

"Like I said, I need to speak to Boatman directly. I've said too much here, in these halls already."

Maverick clicked his tongue. "Where?"

Tobias laughed. "Yeah, good one, Mav."

Maverick didn't respond. He just carried on staring down his barrel at Faust.

"Maverick, I'm not understanding the joke. I mean, you're the straight man in this little duo usually, but I really don't get this joke," said Tobias.

"It's not a joke, Tobias."

"Right, okay. Guess we're through the looking glass now."

"What the hell are you talking about? How is that reference even relevant?"

"I dunno. It sounded appropriate."

Faust cleared his throat.

Mav grunted yet again. "Where?"

"Take my number and text me when you get Boatman to agree, and I will send a location."

Maverick took Faust's number and then ushered him and Aloysius into a room off the hall, closed the door and broke off the handle. Tobias and Maverick made their way out of the building and back underground. When they were clear of the HoC and close to their HQ, Tobias finally spoke, "So let me get this straight, we have agreed to have our leader meet one of Rome's top generals at a location of his choice? And we're fine with that?"

"It seems that way."

"Well okay then."

Chapter 25

Titus hated Britannia. "This fucking country," he said to himself. He had been promoted to Commander of Britannia and believed it would lead to something greater. Believed it would create an opportunity to be commander of so much more. Britannia was, in his mind, a stepping stone. A way to earn favor with the emperor by turning Britannia into an apathetic state, its population like lemmings walking off a cliff of subservience. Unfortunately, for him, the ongoing rebellion coupled with losing Boatman's wife and the emperor's son being turned into a dribbling mess meant greatness was running away. It was a mess.

Titus prided himself on his ability to see things in a calm and measured fashion. Before his promotion to London, he had been stationed in the Middle East. It was a volatile land that the Romans barely kept from imploding. It was a hub of zealotry and animosity. People who believed their destiny was entwined in the very dust of the earth they walked on. With such blind belief in a divine right, many saw the Romans as insignificant and a minor blip on a greater plan. They saw the Romans as imposters who were interfering with something ordained by their gods. Which god had ordained their eternal destiny was up for debate. Ultimately though, many in the Middle East believed their god had chosen them as instruments for Armageddon, and a measly Empire wasn't going to get in the way of that.

Titus had been stationed there in the early 1990s when a rather delicate peace deal was about to expose just how delicate it was. Augustus II had sought out Titus to go there and flay anyone who dared rupture the peace that had tiptoed around violence for decades. Titus though, he saw flaying and fear as short-term solutions to the eternal conflict. For peace to be maintained, all parties needed to envision their willingness to be participants of a peace that would be key to a future paradise. Diplomacy was key, but it had to be diplomacy that massaged egos. Titus found that fluffing an ego achieved far more for him than promising the world on a platter. Within a few years of overseeing the region, the threat of war became a whisper, which became an irrelevance. Admittedly, Titus did have to make some sacrifices and crucify half a dozen of his governors to appease the region's factions. When it came to maintaining peace or replacing governors, the choice was simple.

And now Titus sat at his desk, in overcast London (by the gods, why was the air always so damp in this country?) and grimaced that he was in a situation without peace; he could be facing the same fate as those governors. He was turning his phone over in his hand, mentally flipping a coin as to whether to phone his contact. He was weighing up possible outcomes of the current situation in London and knew each one left him with rather narrow odds of escaping alive. Nero's ego could only be fluffed so much, and Titus had exhausted that option months ago. Nero liked his ego massaged, but Titus noticed it wasn't so much the ego being massaged that

Nero found pleasure in; no, Nero found pleasure in watching people degrade themselves by spouting cringeworthy praise of the emperor in order to stay alive. Nero liked the degradation. Titus was certain there was no amount of ass kissing he could give at this point to alter the course of near-certain death.

Why was he sure death was coming? Nero would never admit his own mistakes or his inability to judge a situation correctly. He believed he was half god, after all. In Nero's mind, the only reason any situation was running away from him was because of the errors of the mere mortals he had to tolerate. Titus was the obvious choice of a mortal who had committed a mortal error by failing to protect the emperor's son.

Sledgehammering his thoughts back into the present were the simultaneous barrage of messages on his phone and his bodyguard bursting through the door blabbering about an explosion at Faust's home. Titus could hear the commotion inside and outside of the Castrum.

"Sir, we need to get you to safety. The Castrum isn't safe."

"I'll be out soon. Get a group together and make your way to Faust's house. He will need everyone."

"What about you, Sir?"

"Don't worry about me. I will be long gone from here by the time you have managed to understand the mess made at Faust's."

The bodyguard stiffened. "I need to stay here with you. And get you to a safe house. I insist."

"You insist? I'm your commanding officer. I'm the bloody Commander of Britannia. I don't have to do anything you *insist* on, soldier."

The soldier nodded and left Titus alone.

For the first time in weeks, Titus felt happy. He felt happy because he saw an opportunity. He could see an endgame. It felt like old times when he didn't feel so impotent. He assumed it was the work of Boatman destroying Faust's house in the aftermath of Eye for an Eye Day announcement. Everyone was stretched, clearing up the mess; some of the population had assumed they could start killing already. Nero had assumed it would somehow flush Boatman out, but all it did was seemingly strengthen Boatman's hand. For the past three months, Titus had been against the event. He didn't believe it served any purpose and also wouldn't expose the rebels. Boatman's followers were too loyal. Faust, though, Faust keenly supported the emperor's plans. Faust seemed to be too keen about the idea. Faust had a big brain, and if he supported the Caesar's plan then he had something up his sleeve. Titus had a big brain too, but couldn't see what was hidden up Faust's sleeve.

Enough of what Faust had planned, though. If Faust was still alive, that was. Reports of the explosion were still frantic. Faust's possible demise only concentrated Nero's rage even tighter on Titus, which was the final element to persuade Titus to try to escape Britannia. Titus was going to use the chaos in the city able to quietly escape from London and, hopefully, transport to the other side of the world. With this in mind, he called his contact. The conversation was brief. The contact told Titus a time and place and the line went dead. The Commander of Britannia took a big swig of his wine and pretended his hands weren't shaking.

Chapter 26

Titus made his way out of the Castrum and instead of taking his chariot hopped on a tram going to the Winding Valley borough of London. The southeast area of the city was in lockdown because of Faust's house, but trams were still running to the northern parts of the city. Even so, the tram was quiet as people quickly scurried home when the explosion was announced. For most people, it wasn't fear of the rebels that caused them to get home and lock their doors; it was, rather, fear of what the Romans might do. With Nero in town, the brutality of his soldiers had risen. Nero believed everyone was in collusion with Boatman, so anyone who even looked slightly 'rebellious' was dragged away and interrogated. It was safer to get home to avoid any risk of a soldier asking awkward questions. Even so, Titus was not alone on the tram and a handful of people were either willing to take the risk, too stupid to know the risk of being out, or hadn't heard about the explosion and were blissfully unaware they might get collared at any moment.

Although Titus was the Commander of Britannia, most people wouldn't have recognized him on the street as someone of such high stature wouldn't have been taking a public tram. And even if someone did recognize him, they certainly weren't going to make it obvious: why would anyone want to disturb the most powerful man in Britannia? And it would certainly not be any of their business to question why the highest-ranking Roman soldier in Britannia was casually riding a tram to Winding Valley.

Titus got off the tram and made his way to a backstreet where there was a rather inconspicuous doorway. He knocked three times, and the door opened. He went inside and was in a small bar with dim, red lights and Titus wondered if his contact was a walking cliché for choosing this place. A hand raised up from the far-left corner of the room and Titus went over. Of the few people sitting in the bar, only the barman even remotely registered Titus's presence.

Titus sat opposite his contact and within seconds a glass of red wine was placed in front of the Commander.

"It's a decent Chianti," said the contact. "Assuming you would like something different to that English shit."

Titus took a swig. Damn, that was really good. The Empire, since ruling Britannia, had a paradoxical ethos of wanting to promote 'purely Britannical goods' even though the country was ruled by an Imperial force. It was actually a clever method of subversion by making the British believe they were somehow superior by only consuming what they produced, even if a lot of it was absolute dog shit. Roman propaganda made the people think they were leagues apart from other nations because of their produce but, in fact, most of it was substandard. The thing is, most of the populous had nothing to compare it to, unless you were very wealthy.

A generation had passed since the British imported lots of goods, so most of the population either had a whimsical memory of certain foods and products or had never experienced them. The Romans had cleverly isolated Britannia by a false sense of superiority and with that, made the British believe they were too superior to travel abroad. They lived in a bubble of apathy and subservience, which made ruling them so easy.

Until Boatman appeared.

Boatman wasn't a thorn in Titus's side; he was a spear. So much so that in a very short space of time, Titus had gone from the almost deific Commander of Britannia to a feeble nonentity. A nonentity who needed to get out of the country before he found himself hanging from a cross on London Bridge. Which is why he was here, drinking an illegal Chianti, opposite a rather dodgy contact.

Titus decided pleasantries weren't needed. "Can you get me out in the next few hours?"

The contact smiled. "What, no foreplay? I just bought you a drink."

"I doubt you bought it."

The contact smirked and brushed his hand over his face, as if wiping away Titus's last comment. "That's no problem." He took a drink and thought for a second. "It's going to be a shit journey for you. No fine wines and no bodyguards."

"I don't care."

"You sure? You might be a Roman, but you have to be a hard bastard when traveling with fishermen."

"Fishermen?"

"Of course." The contact had another sip of his wine. "I can't fly you out of here. You're the most powerful man in Britannia. You need to be smuggled by boat up the coast and then we can fly you via an RIA charter from the top of the Caledonia Kingdom."

Titus felt his hand shaking again. He was deep into enemy territory and was trusting savages to get him to another savage land. He fucking hated boats, too.

The contact picked up on Titus's anxiety. "You can bail out now and try your luck with Nero or rough it for a few days and see what the RIA can offer a very valuable asset of the Roman Empire."

Titus didn't speak for a few minutes. He sipped his wine and considered his options. He had done enough research to know traveling to the RIA would be risky but with his knowledge they would welcome him. They needed as much information as they could get in order to defend against an impending attack from Nero. Every day was moving closer to Nero trying to invade the RIA. Titus mused that Boatman's defiance had been massively impactful on delaying Nero's plans to overtake the other side of the globe. One man had basically halted an Empire.

"I'll take my chances with your fishermen."

"Learn to tie a bowline at least so they don't think you're completely useless."

"Fuck you," said Titus. "I have commanded thousands of soldiers. I can handle a crew of fishermen."

The contact stared hard at Titus. "It's nothing to do with commanding. It's about being at their level. If you appear to be someone they can have a beer with and can casually tie a knot when they're mooring up, they won't hate you so much. It's subtle breaking down of barriers; not everything is about control."

Titus felt stupid but also annoyed. Surely these fishermen would be honored to transport the Commander of Britannia?

The contact was well aware of Roman arrogance about their stature in the world and said, "There's a big difference between respect and fear. Just because people fear you doesn't mean they respect you. These fishermen are allies of the Republic of Indigenous America, so don't view even the mighty Titus as anyone particularly special."

Titus arched his eyebrow. "What on earth do fishermen of Britannia have to offer the RIA?"

"Well, the willingness to transport a prized Roman asset for a start."

Touché.

Titus was done with this meeting. "When and where?"

The contact gave Titus the details and said the fishermen won't wait so he couldn't be late.

"That doesn't give us much time."

"Us?"

"I'm taking my mistress with me."

"Not your wife?"

"She hates the water. And she hates me too."

"You've never mentioned taking someone with you. That's double the price."

"If I'm paying double, then the fishermen can wait a bit longer."

The contact downed his drink, wiped his lips and said, "I don't think you're truly grasping the situation, Commander."

Titus clenched his jaw; he didn't like the way the contact said the word Commander.

The contact continued. "They won't wait for you and your mistress if you're late. You're not important to them, Titus. You're in a whole new reality where you're a fugitive. Your title means nothing. You're potentially going to arrive in the RIA as a refugee. I'm not busting your balls about this, Titus. I'm simply stating the facts of your situation."

Titus rubbed his face in frustration. He wasn't sure what decision was the right one. Maybe he could negotiate his way out of trouble with Nero. Maybe. He'd traversed the nightmare of the

Middle East after all. But was it worth it? Was this shitty country worth his sweat and potential blood? He wasn't so sure. What was his title worth anyway?

"We'll be there on time," said Titus. He downed his wine and left the dim bar. He regretted not taking his chariot now as the tram was going to be a slow trek across town. He checked his watch again. It was going to be tight. Well, it was going to be tight if he collected his mistress. He had plenty of time (and more gold) if he went to the dock alone.

He jumped on a tram that would take him away from his residence and straight to the river where his boat would be waiting. Maybe he would find a way to get his mistress to him at a later point, he thought. Sitting on the tram, he gripped his knees harder to try and stop the shaking as he knew he was lying to himself. Once he was on that boat, his wife and mistress would be dead.

Chapter 27

"Are you okay?"

Maverick glanced at Tobias, and they shared a look indicating they didn't know how to respond as they had never been asked that question before.

"We're… Erm… we're fine." Maverick coughed. "Thanks."

Boatman looked at Maverick and Tobias and said, "How did you get out of the HoC?"

"We basically walked out of the front door," said Tobias.

"The front door?"

"Yup. After Maverick had a nice chat with Centurion Faust," said Tobias.

Boatman looked surprised. "You saw Faust?"

"Saw him? We had a little mother's meeting with him. Pretty sure I know his star sign now."

Maverick sighed. "Tobias, for once in your life can you not be a dick?"

"Oh, I'm sorry, but I distinctly remember you and Faust having a cozy chat about all of us meeting up."

Boatman rarely looked surprised, and this was one of those rare moments. "You arranged to meet with Faust?"

Maverick was six-foot-five, shaved head with a black, bushy beard, and those who met him in a dark alley found the alley darkened by his size blocking out the light; he still managed to blush at Boatman's question. "I weighed the options. It seemed the best move."

"Okay," said Boatman.

"Sorry?"

"I said that's okay. Maverick, I trust your judgement. If you think Faust has something to offer us, then I'll meet him."

Tobias spoke up, "Can I just double check you both haven't taken insanity pills or something. Maybe you've both banged your heads and need medical attention? It's clearly a trap."

"I don't think it is," said Maverick.

"Oh, well that's fine then. I feel all warm and fuzzy now you've said that. This is Faust we're talking about here. Remember him? Remember what he did to Anthony?"

Maverick bristled. "Of course I remember."

And how could Maverick forget?

Anthony had been a young guy who had traveled out of a quiet English village to join the rebellion in London. He had consumed online videos of Boatman's rallying words for people to join him in London and drive the Romans out of the city and the country. Anthony felt inspired. His life wasn't bad where he lived, and he had a fairly serene lifestyle of doing various odd jobs each week to give him enough money to buy a few beers at the weekends. The thing was, he was bored. He was bored of the quiet life and hated how he wasn't making a difference in the world. He believed people should live in actual freedom, not freedom induced by fear. Where he lived there wasn't a sense of visceral fear, but a dark underbelly of it. Everyone in the village got on with their fairly mundane lives in peace, but the fear of the Romans was like a toxin running through people's veins. No-one explicitly showed their fear, but it was whispered not to step out of line because it wasn't worth getting a knock on the door at night and being dragged away for inciting insurrection.

Anthony though, he didn't feel that fear in his veins. Every day when he illegally streamed footage of Boatman, he knew that could be the day his door was smashed in, but it didn't scare him. He enjoyed the adrenaline rush of the risk. In some ways, he didn't really care if he was killed by the Romans. And that's what scared him. It scared him that he had those thoughts. It scared him that he viewed his life as expendable, even worthless. With such a throwaway attitude to his own life, he ventured to London to find Boatman.

Finding Boatman wasn't easy, for obvious reasons, and anyone hoping to join his fight had to pass the ultimate test. The only test truly worthy was, of course, Maverick. After Maverick had scared the life out of Anthony, he quickly ascertained Anthony was genuine. Naively genuine, he thought, but genuine none the less. Even after Maverick threatened to kill him and said Anthony needed to get out of London before having his skull caved in, Anthony stood his ground. This scrawny lad, with his patchy mustache and a nose too big for his face refused to back down against Maverick. Maverick had known gladiators as big as a bus and as solid as a wall who had backed down sooner than Anthony. Either he was very brave or very dumb. Maverick liked him.

Maverick decided he would take this young, dumb kid under his wing and train him. In a matter of weeks, Anthony was an asset to Boatman's cause, especially in regard to the online propaganda they were flooding Roman television with. Anthony, it turned out, was very good at hacking. One weakness the rebellion had was trying to counter the Roman narrative. Their message was getting through, of course (otherwise Anthony wouldn't have risked his journey to London), but the message wasn't loud enough and it wasn't clear enough. Anthony's skillset was definitely increasing the rebellion's volume and clarity.

With that in mind, Boatman asked Anthony to do a specialized task and try to hack Centurion Faust's personal computer. Anthony eagerly agreed, in awe that Boatman would trust him with such an important mission. Maverick agreed to chaperone Anthony and protect him while he carried out his task, as the major danger to the mission was Anthony having to physically access the computer.

Faust worked like a man possessed almost every single day. He rarely went home, and it seemed from the extensive surveillance of his home that he rarely slept. The man was a machine because he *appeared* to never tire. Maverick found the lack of need to sleep confounding as he was a grumpy bastard without enough sleep. Tobias would point out that Maverick was a grumpy bastard regardless of sleeping patterns.

With Faust's neglect of his home life, Maverick assumed it would be fairly simple to access Faust's home and get Anthony access to the computer. Maverick's assumption was right. They got into Faust's home without even a hint of a problem. Maybe Maverick had become complacent, or maybe he hadn't had enough sleep, but for it to be so easy should have rung every alarm bell in his head. It didn't, though. If Maverick had lacked enough sleep, he was making up for it by being asleep on his job as Anthony's protector.

Faust was clever, very clever. He had a photographic memory and was a paranoid man. Faust would counter that it's not paranoia when it's true. Whether it was paranoia or simply being astute, Faust was a step ahead of Maverick and, unfortunately for poor Anthony, about a hundred steps ahead of him. Faust knew he was addicted to his work. He knew because of the neglect he gave to his home it would be an obvious target for Boatman. If it was an obvious target, why not make it seem like an easy target too? Why not bait the trap? Faust had noticed in recent weeks that Boatman's cyber attacks had increased exponentially. He guessed they had recruited someone with the skills to up the tempo, and wondered whether he would be a target. If so, then the hook was baited. If he wasn't a target, then the bait was irrelevant. It mattered little to him either way.

Unfortunately for Anthony, the bait mattered a lot to the one taking it. Maverick gained access to Faust's office without disturbing even a fly and in moments Anthony was tapping away on the Centurion's laptop. Faust was a Roman, through and through. He didn't particularly care about being 'true-blood,' but he was in the tenth generation of Fausts to serve the Empire. He was determined to see an eleventh generation serving at some point. It wasn't only his bloodline that made him a Roman in the truest sense of the word but also his love for the Romans' brutality. He loved the way they killed. Loved it. He loved the bloodiness. He loved the terror. He loved the pain inflicted. He didn't care if that made him a sociopath. He saw how the gods inflicted their pain and terror on humanity every single day through pestilence and natural disasters so, in his mind, he was simply a mouthpiece of the gods. Faust the Prophet. With such a love of brutality, he enjoyed seeing whether Boatman would take the bait at Faust's home.

To Faust's disappointment, Boatman didn't personally attend, but at least one of the rebels' minions did. Anthony had sat in front of Faust's computer, puzzled that it wasn't password protected. Not that it was too suspicious; he knew many people failed to use passwords out of ignorance, laziness or fear of forgetting the bloody thing. Anthony figured Faust was arrogant enough to believe he didn't need a password because, after all, who on earth would try to hack a Roman Centurion's computer? Faust's arrogance would be his downfall, thought Anthony. It was going to be a simple job really: plant a virus in the Roman network and watch their world burn. Before he planted the virus though, he saw a folder entitled FOR BOATMAN. He glanced up from the computer at Maverick who was standing guard and thought for a moment about calling him over, but decided against it. Think of the praise he would get by downloading a personal message from Faust and delivering personally to Boatman? He grinned wide as he double clicked the folder.

When the computer exploded it blew up a USB stick filled with acid. The acid burned Anthony's grin permanently to his face. Maverick didn't tell Tobias that his dreams were haunted by the scream and its accompanying grin. Maverick had spent years in the gladiator ring. He knew lost causes, and as soon as he saw the computer flash and burn and light up Anthony's face, he abandoned the place. He knew Anthony was going to die. If he tried to save him, he would also die. So Maverick disappeared into the night as he had done so many times before, and Anthony's face disappeared under the searing agony of acid.

Maverick tried to wipe away the guilt in his mind about being so complacent about Faust's abilities and wondered whether Faust had duped him again. "Maybe Tobias is right."

Tobias spoke up, "Sorry, did someone get a recording of that?"

Boatman was pacing. "I can't figure out the play. If he saw you coming, the only reason he didn't kill you both is because he wants to do a deal."

"But we're not the prize. You are," said Maverick.

"A deal or revenge? How was he when he realized Atticus had been taken out?"

"He's hard to read. Even when we felt the explosion from so far away, he barely reacted," said Maverick.

"I thought he seemed quite pleased Atticus was dead," said Tobias.

"If he was pleased, then maybe he's thinking of deserting."

"Whatever he's thinking, there's a game involved. We just have to figure out what it is," said Boatman.

Boatman told Maverick and Tobias to get some rest and they'd reconvene in a few hours once he'd pondered Faust's potential offer.

Chapter 28

"Daddy, are you okay?"

"I'm fine, Baby Girl," said Kevin.

Molly wrinkled her nose. Daddy definitely wasn't fine. Daddy was sitting on the sofa, elbows resting on his thighs, and his right leg was twitching up and down. Very quickly. Molly had heard Mommy tell Daddy that he shouldn't bite his nails, as it was a bad habit. Daddy was now doing that bad habit. Mommy was asleep but would tell him off if she saw him. The girl didn't really understand what was happening and why she was in this strange place, but she did understand that the bad man, who'd had his hands covering her mouth, had been going to hurt her and the big man had saved her. She also understood that her daddy wasn't going to be a soldier anymore, and that made her happy because she didn't like him doing that job. It seemed scary. She hoped Daddy would like not having to be a solider anymore, but he seemed scared and she didn't like seeing him scared.

In truth, Kevin was scared. Somehow, he had gone from an unknown soldier to becoming personally known by Emperor Nero. Unfortunately for him, it wasn't a good thing to be known by Nero because Nero wanted to string him up and probably disembowel him. Kevin didn't want to be a hero or a martyr. He didn't want to be a poster boy for soldiers who rebelled against the Empire. He liked being an insignificant soldier. He liked patrolling London, hiding behind the enormity of the Empire. Even Boatman's rebellion had barely made a dent on Kevin's professional or personal life; he always volunteered to patrol areas where he knew the likelihood of bumping into The Beast was slim to none. There was always a mixture of soldiers who wanted to avoid the chance of seeing The Beast and those who thought they might find fame by being the one who took out the fearsome Maverick.

It was all down to ego.

Kevin's ego didn't care about trying to fight a Ugandan giant. He knew he would lose. He cared about doing enough years with the Empire to earn a good pension and be able to enjoy a quiet life with Sam and Molly. Boatman had ruined that. Boatman had ripped him, Molly and Sam out of their quiet existence and thrust them into the sights of the emperor of the world. Kevin was definitely scared and very angry.

"Daddy, it will be okay."

Molly's voice pulled him out of his thoughts. "I know, Baby Girl. We're safe now," he lied.

"I'm going to draw you a picture to make you feel better," said Molly and she disappeared to her bedroom. Kevin wanted cry at the beauty of such innocence. Ruined by Boatman. Here he was, in an underground lair, steamrolled into becoming a rebel. He got up from the sofa and went for the exit.

"Where are you going, Daddy?" Kevin turned to see Molly clutching some colored pencils.

"I'm just having a walk. I won't be long." Molly's face dropped a bit, like she was scared he wasn't coming back. "Don't worry, Molly. I'll be back soon. Make sure you get your picture done for when I'm home." Home. Kevin almost gagged at the falseness of that word.

He left the apartment and made his way toward the grand concourse. His anxiety was ambushing his mind. He felt like his brain was on fire and he needed some fresh air to put the fire out. In the space of a few hours he had gone from almost absently patrolling the streets of London to being enemy number one of Nero. The change in circumstance was decimating his mental health, and his anxiety was edging him ever closer to a panic attack. He needed to get outside and breathe because his chest felt like someone had tied a belt round it and was tightening it, pulling the buckle inward, notch by painful notch.

He got to the concourse, and the giant hall spiked his heart rate even more. He needed to get out of there, so he did. He walked briskly out of the hall and along the corridor that led to the secret entrance he and the other soldiers had come through. Some people have the instinct to fight when trapped. Kevin needed to flee. He said to himself he wasn't running away, but simply getting some air so he didn't hyperventilate. Although the vast tunnel network beneath London was airy and surprisingly bright, he still felt claustrophobic. It was the thought of all that *stuff* above him. All those buildings and roads that could cave in on them at any moment.

He got within a few meters of the doors when a voice behind him stopped him. "Kevin, I wouldn't walk through those doors."

"I just need some air," he said.

"Look up at the monitor above the doors."

Kevin did and saw there were a number of Roman soldiers outside the entrance. "I don't understand, what are they doing there?"

"They're looking for you. They won't find the entrance, it's too well camouflaged, but they're trying to find something to lead them to you. They'll try to press the homeless guy, Mikey, for information. He sees a lot. He won't say anything though."

Kevin stared at the screen. "I know those guys. They're friends. They'll be pleased to see me." His face brightened. "I can probably convince them to join us."

"That won't happen. They're too scared. Nero will annihilate their families. He tried to with yours. Remember?"

Kevin turned to Boatman, "Of course I remember. I seem to remember that it wasn't Nero putting my family in danger, but you."

"Your family is safe."

Kevin snorted. "Oh, what a wonderful life they now have. Living in a tunnel."

Boatman's voice remained even. "We're close to breaking Nero's grip on London."

"It really looks like it," Kevin said, sarcastically, waving his hand at the screen.

He was breathing hard. Short sharp breaths. He was close to a panic attack. "I just need some air."

"You can't go out there, Kevin. You can't reveal this entrance to them. It will cause havoc."

Kevin wasn't thinking clearly. He was in flight mode. "You've caused havoc with my life. Maybe you need a taste of your own medicine." He stepped toward the door release button.

"If you touch that button, I will shoot you." The source of those words wasn't Boatman but Bella. She had silently appeared, and it reminded Boatman why she was his best commander. Even Maverick would agree on that.

Boatman raised his hand to interject. "Bella's not going to

shoot you, Kevin."

"If he tries to touch that button, I will," she said. She had a bow fully drawn, and the arrow was aimed directly at Kevin.

Boatman turned to Bella. "You're not shooting him."

"I'm not having him ruin all the work we've done."

"He won't." Boatman turned back to Kevin. "You're not ruining all the work, are you?"

"Don't patronize me." Kevin spoke to Bella, "You can shoot me, but that door will be open by the time the arrow hits me."

Bella faltered. Usually people backed off with the thought of an arrow pummeling their chest. "You'll die for nothing," she said.

"I have nothing anyway."

"What about Molly and Sam?"

"Now that I have a target on my back, they're better off without me." Kevin stepped closer to the button.

Boatman raised his voice. "Kevin. If you touch that button, you will die. Understand me. It's not an abstract or something vague that occasionally crosses your mind. You will die. And it will be unpleasant."

"Boatman, I don't think you understand. You've put me though massive trauma. My home life destroyed. My family almost killed. Using me as bait to kill a fucking Centurion. You have ruined my life."

Kevin rushed at the button and smacked it. As his hand came away from the button, a knife went through his hand. He cried out in pain. Bella still had her arrow quivering on her bow. She looked at Boatman, who was still in his throwing stance. "I told you that you wouldn't shoot him."

The doors whizzed open, revealing a dozen soldiers looking bewildered. Boatman swore and pulled out a small controller. It had two buttons on it. He pressed them. Six small, controlled blasts went off around the arch of the entrance and the soldiers went from being bewildered to being buried under a pile of rubble as the entrance collapsed. Kevin was buried with them.

Boatman threw the controller across the tunnel. "Fuck!"

Bella stared at the now blocked entrance with dust swirling in the flicker of the emergency lights. She went over to the controller, picked it up, and handed it back to Boatman. "We need to block this tunnel." Boatman stopped pacing, pulled himself together and nodded. They left the tunnel and strange silence following the explosions and pulled a pair of reinforced sliding doors shut.

Boatman rubbed his face in frustration; things were falling apart. "We need to get everyone together and work out what the hell we do next."

"No offense, but I think the first thing we need to do is go see Sam and Molly."

Boatman felt his stomach twist. He had become so used to death he sometimes forgot about what death meant. He hated himself for being so desensitized to it all. "Sorry, Bella, you're right. I'll go see them."

"I'll come with you."

Boatman nodded. They walked away from the massive doors, and Boatman pressed the second button on the controller. It caused another set of controlled blasts that brought the whole tunnel down, stopping any chance of the Romans finding a way through to the rebels' headquarters. As they walked away, trying to formulate what they would say to Kevin's family about his death, rebels ran past them to ensure the reinforced doors were sealed and the rebel headquarters were still safe from Roman penetration. The sprawling network of tunnels underneath London were so vast that the Romans had been confounded in finding the rebels' whereabouts; this explosion possibly ruined years of Boatman's stealthy movements around the city.

Chapter 29

Titus arrived at the marina where he was instructed to meet the fishing boat. The marina was accessed via a number of metal walkways that sloped down to floating pontoons. All manner of boats were moored on the pontoons, from elaborate sailing yachts to small dories and work boats that fished for eels and salmon in the Thames.

The Romans kept a cap on how many vessels could fish in the Thames and how many months a year those vessels could fish. It meant stocks were never depleted and in spawning months the fish were able to reproduce. London adored eels and salmon, so the boats made a good living out of the short season and then most changed their fishing gear over for oyster dredging gear and steamed up the coastline to catch oysters instead. London adored oysters also, and the fishermen made a healthy living out of the mollusk. The cyclical approach to mixed fishing meant the industry was sustainable and profitable.

At the entrance to the marina was an archway with three sets of double gates. The gates were locked with a lone soldier acting as security. People who paid for moorings had access keys to the marina but there was always someone hoping to steal an outboard engine for a quick profit, so a solider was a necessary deterrent.

Titus approached the soldier, who was about the same age, in his fifties. Titus wondered why the soldier was still a Munifex, a basic foot soldier. Was he incompetent? Or did he choose to never advance through the ranks? The soldier eyed Titus, clearly not realizing who he was looking at. Then it clicked, and he stiffened and saluted. "Hail Caesar."

Titus did the obligatory response.

"Legatus, wha… what are you doing here?"

"No need to panic, solider. I'm on a very personal mission for the emperor. I need access to the marina. I'm meeting someone."

"What boat are you going to? I know the marina very well, so can take you to it."

"There's no need, Munifex, thank you. I do need you to do a patrol of the immediate area though, to ensure there's no-one following me or potentially going to cause trouble." If I can get this soldier out the way for long enough, I can escape, thought Titus.

The soldier nodded, opened the marine gate for his commander and went off to look for Titus's imaginary stalkers.

Titus walked through the gate, looked back to make sure the soldier had left, and then hurried down the walkway to the pontoon to find the waiting tender. He found his potential boat to freedom on a berth at the far left corner of the pontoons, a position to create easy access for the fishing boat if it needed to moor up. The fishing boat wasn't there, though; instead, a 16-foot dory with a few fishing nets in and a man and a woman were waiting. The man was young (twenties, Titus thought), blond and clean-shaven. He had a rollup cigarette protruding from his mouth and was sitting on the gunnel of the boat. The woman was of a similar age, also blonde, and holding the tiller of the outboard engine. She spoke first. But not to Titus. "Johan, do you think this one could make it any more obvious he is going AWOL? He could have at least changed into something more subtle than his bloody Commander uniform."

"Mia, I couldn't care less what he's wearing." Johan looked at Titus. "I only care if you have gold."

Titus reached into his inside jacket pocket and pulled out a coin holder. It had 12 gold coins in. He threw it to Johan, who opened it and emotionlessly closed it and put it in his own jacket pocket. He waved the Commander of Britannia onto the boat and Mia started the engine. They were cruising out of the marina in seconds, and Mia skillfully pulled up alongside the fishing vessel that Titus hoped would take him safety.

Titus climbed from the dory onto the larger boat, which was nearly twenty meters in length and was a hive of activity with crew getting the trawler ready to go to work. Waiting for Titus was a heavy-set man with a gray beard, piercing blue eyes and wrinkles on his face so deep it seemed time had etched them. Titus reached to shake the man's hand. The man looked at Titus's hand and briefly pulled a face like it was toxic before deciding it wasn't and shaking it. To Titus, it wasn't shaking hands; it was trying not to cry out in pain at the vice threatening to crush every bone in his hand. The wrinkled man didn't have hands but shovels. To Titus's relief, the man let go quickly. Titus put his hand in his pocket to avoid rubbing his knuckles. He introduced himself as the Commander of Britannia and was met with a disinterested look. When the wrinkled man spoke, his voice was low and gruff. "We need to start things the right way."

Before Titus could respond with a question as to what the wrinkled man meant, he found himself wheezing for air and on his knees. The wrinkled man had punched him in the stomach with such speed and force it had taken the air out of him.

The crew carried on working as if what had just happened was a normal occurrence, which wasn't a comfort to Titus. As he continued to gasp, the wrinkled man spoke again, his low, gruff voice paradoxically very audible. "Now you have paid me the gold and are aboard my ship, you are no longer the Commander of Britannia. You're a traitor to the Empire and, in turn, make me a traitor. You no longer have any power over myself or my crew. That gold doesn't simply give you passage to safety, it also stops me from throwing you overboard."

Titus looked up at the wrinkled man and managed to nod. He didn't get to his position in the Empire by needing to be told twice about anything. He knew if he stepped out of line, there wasn't any amount of gold that would save him. If he was going to get to the RIA, he had to keep his head down.

The wrinkled man was satisfied with the nod. "I'm Captain Fiske Carson. We have a long steam ahead of us, so if I were you I would get some rest as this isn't a pleasure cruise. You will be working to pay for your passage. Like I said, the gold merely stopped me throwing you overboard." Captain Carson left the panting former Commander of Britannia and made his was back to the bridge. Johan reached his hand out to Titus and helped him to his feet. "My father isn't as fierce as he makes out."

"You could have fooled me."

"I thought he was restrained."

"Futuo," was all Titus managed to say before being guided to where he would be sleeping for the next couple of weeks.

Before going below deck, Titus glanced back towards London and wondered if he would see another set of city lights again or his final moments would be looking at the nothingness of the deep blue sea.

Chapter 30

"What do you mean you can't find him?"

Titus's bodyguard swallowed hard. "He's not at home, his mistress's or his office, my Lord."

"You're telling me the Commander of Britannia is missing on the same day The Beast infiltrated the HoC and one of my Centurions was blown to hell by Boatman."

"Yes, sir." The bodyguard wasn't sure he could swallow much harder. He prepared himself for Nero to rage and rant but instead Nero laughed. He laughed and laughed. This reaction scared the bodyguard even more. Nero waved the bodyguard away, and it took the will of the gods for him not to run from Nero's office.

Nero stopped laughing, wiped his eyes and wondered how he could have been so ignorant to Titus being a traitor and spy for Boatman. On Titus's watch, Max was almost murdered; Boatman managed to kill Atticus; and for years no-one had been able to find where Boatman's HQ was. It was bloody obvious now: Titus kept the Empire off the right trail. But it was only bloody obvious now that Titus had disappeared.

He dialed Faust, who answered in two rings. "Good to know not everyone is disappearing or dying. Titus has disappeared, and I think he has betrayed me. I need you to come to my office immediately."

"Of course, my Lord. I will be there in haste."

Faust ended the call and swore. Titus? Betraying the Empire? It didn't seem right. It also messed with Faust's plans to use Titus as a distraction for his own plans. If Titus really was missing, then there was a moving part Faust wasn't able to predict and that made everything much more dangerous. He deleted the message he was about to send to Maverick and made his way to Nero.

Chapter 31

Boatman stood impotently in Sam and Molly's apartment as they both sobbed at the news of Kevin's death. Sam hugged Bella tightly and cried and cried. She hugged Bella because Bella had lied and said Kevin was killed by the Romans. Boatman was surprised and relieved by the lie. He had no idea how he was going to keep them from running away and exposing the location of the rebel HQ if they knew the truth. He considered; he could put them in the prison quarters, but Olivia would have been horrified at such an action, and he couldn't bear the thought of her losing all faith in him.

He felt like a fraud lying to Kevin's family about the real cause of his death, but maybe Bella was right. The Romans deserved no mercy, and they had effectively killed Kevin the day they decided to occupy Britannia. Boatman slipped out of the room, the family's grief so overwhelming his absence would not be noticed.

He made his way to Olivia's hospital room and saw that she was awake. She managed a smile when he walked into her room, and he felt his heart break because of the love he had for her. When they'd met, Olivia hadn't known Boatman was part of the rebellion. Boatman had still been navigating between 'normal' life and distributing anti-Empire propaganda. He had decided to attend a lecture about the tension between Britannic and Roman cultures, hoping to find willing converts to the rebel cause. Armed with leaflets highlighting Roman hypocrisy and deficiency, he had given one to Olivia after the lecture. Instead of her agreeing with everything on the leaflet, she pushed back and asked Boatman very awkward questions. Even before Boatman became the leader feared by so many, he was used to people being enraptured by him and what he had to say. Olivia, though, she was almost indifferent to him and wasn't enraptured by the brooding, rebellious man.

"You're an arrogant prick, you know?"

Boatman almost choked on his drink. "Don't beat around the bush."

"You've waltzed into this event, with poorly produced literature, littered with grammatical mistakes, and think you can charm people into risking their lives," said Olivia.

"It's worth the risk if we can get rid of Roman occupation."

"Who says their 'occupation' is something people want to get rid of?"

"We didn't elect them. We didn't ask for their laws to be our laws."

"Which laws do you particularly hate?"

Boatman squinted. "Sorry?"

"Your leaflets are filled with vague, emotional ideology, but I've noticed there's nothing concrete in them. So, Mister, sorry, what's your name again?"

"Boatman King."

"So, Mr King, what laws do you particularly hate?"

Boatman wasn't flustered. He rarely got flustered. He thought he was in love, though. Olivia had pulled him apart in seconds, and he was enamored because of it. "Off the top of my head, I would say the crucifixions are something no-one would miss."

Olivia laughed. "Okay smart-arse. I was thinking of something less obvious."

Boatman waved a leaflet in the air. "The fact that criticizing Roman rule is illegal. If we can't criticize those who lead us, then we are living as barbarians."

"There's a difference between criticism and encouraging insurrection."

"It's only insurrection if it's against a democracy," said Boatman.

"I think you need to look at the definition of insurrection."

"I'm happy to be helped with that, if you're free later?"

Olivia smiled. "If I were you, I would work on both your grammar and your pickup lines." Before Boatman could respond, Olivia turned on her heels and was gone. It had made Boatman even more besotted.

Now, Boatman looked at his wife as she lay in her hospital bed and hoped that sarcasm she so effortlessly used on him for so many years would return. She said, "Who's the girl who's suffering so much grief?"

Boatman raised his eyebrows. "Who told you about that?"

"Just tell me."

Boatman eyed his wife for a moment. How did she know about Molly so fast? Another thought crept into his mind, but he swatted it away before it could manifest into something dangerous. He answered her question. "Her name's Molly. She's ten."

"Dare I ask why a ten-year-old girl is so upset?"

"Her father died today. He was a soldier of the Empire."

"Did you kill him?"

"No." It wasn't a lie.

"But you played your part."

"Yes."

Olivia sighed. It was a disappointed sigh. The sound hurt Boatman. Even with the sigh, she reached out to hold his hand. "Was it always this brutal?"

"Brutal in what way?"

"Where children were caught in the middle of your war?"

Boatman squeezed his wife's hand and said, "It's not just my war. Honestly, I don't know. Maybe. Maybe I just didn't see it." Boatman bowed his head. He was feeling the weight of it all. "I was trying to do the right thing. I was trying to save Molly and her parents. I was trying to get them out of Nero's shadow."

"Children are smarter than us. Innocence brings a clarity about the world we fail to comprehend. I'm sure she will see your intentions when she's old enough to truly understand."

Boatman appreciated Olivia's words. Not because of their content, but because she was trying to comfort him. He despaired he had lost her love and this moment was a big step toward him finding her forgiveness. "Thanks, Liv."

"Don't thank me, Mr. King, I still think you're an arrogant prick. I need to have a sleep."

"Do you want me get the doctor?"

"No, it's fine. I'm just tired. The doctor said I should be out in a few days, but it will be a while before I don't get so tired."

Boatman leaned in to kiss Olivia's forehead and she guided his mouth to hers. That gentle kiss almost made the man who wanted to topple an Empire topple over in that hospital room.

When Boatman left Olivia alone, she tried to focus on the vibrations of Molly's pain. The vibrations changed in pitch, sounding more like the buzzing she remembered from her childhood. The buzzing seemed to send a message of not only grief but of something else coming from Molly. Olivia tried to slow her breathing and focus on the buzzing. She tried to focus on the emotions vibrating from Molly. After a few moments, Olivia found clarity in the noise.

Distrust.

Lies.

Distrust.

Lies.

She felt her heart quicken. Those words were almost venomous in their tone. Surely they didn't originate from a ten-year-old girl? And if they did? Olivia felt a deep sadness. Fatigue washed over her, and she felt the words *distrust* and *lies* almost serenade her to sleep.

Chapter 32

Faust entered Nero's office and tried not to wrinkle his nose at the smell. Nero had been drinking hard over the weekend, owing to his frustration at how many wins Boatman was having, although Nero didn't need much of an excuse to drink hard. It meant the office smelled of stale alcohol and, Faust noted, fear. He glanced around the office and saw the sofa in the far corner had crimson patches on it. Nero was a sadist. Just as the night always follows day, so too did Nero's sadism follow his drinking.

Faust had heard many stories coming from Rome about the young emperor's grotesque desires. Word traveled fast across an empire, and when someone was as depraved as this Caesar, half the globe already knew about his acts before they were finished. Faust had visited Rome on occasion to attend sycophantic ceremonies where they verbally masturbated over some Centurion's efforts to quash a rebellion. Each time he had visited, though, whispers of Nero's depravity had floated throughout the city. What Faust found fascinating when he heard the rumors wasn't so much what the rumors were about, but the fear that accompanied the rumors. The Empire, in large part, thrived on fear. When in Rome, Faust was usually in a room with dozens of officers who owed their success to fear. Fear promoted them. Fear generated gold. When it came to Nero, though, the fear was a different kind. A visceral kind. An unpredictable kind.

It was that unpredictability that was so powerful for Nero. The Romans did thrive on fear, yes, but that didn't maintain the Empire; the Empire was maintained through order and organization. Nero didn't do order and couldn't be predicted. That scared anyone who was in his presence because even when he smiled and laughed with you, he could be holding a knife behind his back. After all, Nero's murder of Jonas was the worst-kept secret in Rome. If a man believed to be the reincarnation of Cicero wasn't safe, no-one was.

Faust glanced at the bloodied sofas again and wondered how many gold coins it took to convince anyone to be hired by the depraved emperor. Or how naive the men or women were who agreed to entertain the emperor. Faust also mused on whether those people who had occupied this room were even still alive. Faust had no compunctions about killing, but killing with such pleasure and doing it to gain pleasure were feelings he could never understand.

"Any news on Titus?" Nero's words focused Faust back into the room.

"No, my Lord. It's very strange."

"Or maybe it isn't."

"How so?"

"His marks are on every misfortune I have experienced since being in this sewer of a city. By the gods, Faust, I feel like sending you here was a punishment, not a promotion." Nero glanced over at the ruined sofa, smiled, brushed an invisible speck off his shoulder and Nero continued, "But anyway, you do well enough out of it."

"Which I am eternally grateful for, Caesar."

"Hmm, yes, I am sure you are. But so was Titus."

Faust noticed Nero's black eyes had a glint and concluded his blood might soon be on that sofa if he didn't move the conversation to a safer place. "I'm intrigued why you think Titus is behind recent events."

The black-eyed glint went. "When I saw Max's caved-in skull, I thought Titus was negligent. Definitely not incompetent. I saw what he did in the Middle East. That wasn't luck or bluffing. But I didn't think it was deliberately negligent, until now. The Beast infiltrated the HoC when Titus wasn't there, even though I was staying. Too much negligence for a man of such apparent brilliance."

Nero's leaps made no sense to Faust because Titus was a diplomat, not a saboteur. Max got his skull caved in because Titus didn't want to deal with the little prick's tantrums. And The Beast's infiltration definitely wasn't because of Titus. His disappearance was a good distraction though, so Faust fed the paranoia. "Not forgetting that somehow Atticus ended up at my house even though it was outside of his jurisdiction. He must have been sent by Titus."

"It would be very useful for you to have Titus out of the way, wouldn't it? I'm not stupid, Faust, I know you believe you would command this country better than Titus."

Faust chose his next words very carefully, navigating a mine field. "I command nothing, Caesar, only prayerfully serve your intentions."

Even if Nero knew Faust was groveling, the implication that Faust believed Nero to be a god was enough for Nero to feel his ego swell. "Would you like a drink?"

About ten drinks, thought Faust. He said he would, and Nero told Faust to pour them both some wine.

Faust poured the drinks and noticed the emperor hovering near the blood-stained sofas. He had a brief fear he would have to sit on one of them. He breathed out only when Nero sat back behind his desk.

Nero took a swig of wine, and droplets clung to his wispy, ginger moustache. He wiped the wine away with the back of his hand. At times, when alone in his thoughts, Faust would go through his mind palace and analyze people out of sheer interest in their minute details. Their tics, their blemishes, their traits. Faust had spent more hours than was probably healthy picking apart every aspect of his emperor. Faust could have almost said how many hairs were on Nero's head. He found Nero's rather disproportionate face quite fascinating. The squashed nose, which would usually indicate having been in a fight or in battle, but was just a natural occurrence. The chances of Nero willingly having a fair fight with another man were as remote as Jupiter coming down from the heavens.

A beard usually made a man appear more rugged, and even refined if they had a baby face. Faust didn't wear a beard. It made him look too old. Men like Boatman, though, they looked like they had been born with a beard. Nero, in contrast, his beard (for want of a better word) made him look like a teenager desperately trying to prove he was now a man. Nero had the kind of growth that people would joke about all coming off in a strong breeze. One senator did make that joke to Nero after having had too much wine. He wound up being crucified upside down. No. Faust happily observed Nero, but he would never comment on Nero's appearance. Nero's physical appearance, to Faust, made the man seem weak and almost pathetic. He wasn't a presence in any way, yet absolute power was able to make most men bow in fear. Fear was a tool greater than physical strength.

And those eyes.

Faust wasn't a superstitious man. He secretly believed the gods were just a figment of mankind's imagination. But Nero's eyes seemed like they swallowed life itself. If the eyes are a gateway to a person's soul, Nero's eyes were a gateway to hell. If hell existed, Nero was probably its gatekeeper. Faust enjoyed the process of picking apart every detail of a person, but with Nero he did it for his own safety and sanity. If he truly knew the man and his little details, Faust hoped it would give him enough information to stay alive. Which is what prompted him to say his next words. "Do you think it is still safe to be here in London, my Lord?"

Nero took a sip of wine and squinted at Faust. "Do you?"

"I would be more comfortable if you were safely back in Rome."

"More comfortable about my safety, or my absence preventing me from seeing what you're up to?"

"I have nothing to hide, Caesar."

"We all have something to hide, Faust. Even the God-Carpenter had his secrets he hoped no-one would document."

Faust tried changing the subject. "I did't realize you followed the myths of the God-Carpenter."

"Myths are just distorted echoes of a truth. Did you know my namesake killed thousands of men and women who refused to denounce the God-Carpenter?"

Faust nodded.

"And that's the fascinating thing. Nero the First gave these people a chance to live. If they denounced this Jesus, then he would show mercy. They refused to deny their god and were willing to go through a horrific death." Nero laughed, "Even I am a little disturbed at the *imagination* Nero showed in how he killed the Jesus worshippers."

"It was a barbaric time," said Faust.

"But that's the thing. They were willing to die in agony rather than say Nero is Lord. That's more than following a myth. That's pure devotion. Would you do the same for me, Faust?"

"Of course, Caesar."

Nero smiled. "How's Alypia?"

"She's been very upset at the terrorist attack on our house."

"I'm sure she has." Nero paused, as if contemplating something, "You know, the last time I saw Alypia, I'm sure I could smell her cunt." Nero's words seemed to stop time for Faust. Had he heard correctly?

"I'm sorry?"

"Her cunt, Faust, I'm certain I could smell it." Nero licked his top lip, "Smelled like one of the young whores I had earlier. What's the word I'm looking for? I'm sure it will come back to me later, but the word *fresh* will suffice for now."

Faust felt his temper flare at anyone speaking that way about his wife. "That's my wife you're talking about."

Nero put his glass down, "She's actually my wife, Faust. She's my wife, because I own her, like I own you and everyone else in this god-forsaken country. Or what, you think the words of a god are inappropriate?"

Faust felt stunned into silence. He also felt like a fool. He had underestimated Nero.

"Well?" Nero had finished his drink and was playing with the glass. "Maybe you want to question me, like Jonas did before his unfortunate death?"

Both men knew that Nero wouldn't be able to kill Faust in a simple one-on-one fight, so Nero wouldn't be able to attack Faust like he had Jonas. Faust went to get up and leave.

"Sit down." Faust hesitated. "You will sit the fuck down or I will send men to you in the night and they will cut your eyelids off so that you have to watch while they slowly cut up Alypia."

Faust sat down.

"I won't go back to Rome. I will stay here and flush out Boatman like the rat he is. And there are good ways to flush rats out."

Nero dismissed Faust, as if the conversation hadn't taken a diabolical turn. Faust cautiously got up to leave. As he approached the door, Nero spoke. "Faust, remember who I am." Faust nodded and left.

Faust made his way back to his temporary quarters, since his own house had been destroyed. He walked into an empty space. He had half expected it. Alypia had endured upheaval and uncertainty in her time as Faust's wife, but having her house demolished by terrorists was a step too far, he conceded. She hadn't even left a note. He panicked that perhaps Nero had taken her, but Nero would have bragged about doing so. He still felt anxious for her safety, though. She would be safer with him if Nero had his eyes on her.

Faust lit a cigarette as a form of rebellion against his wife's disapproval of smoking indoors. The cigarette tasted bitter; he stubbed it out. He opened a beer, hoping it would drown out the bitterness of the cigarette and the lingering taste of the god-awful wine Nero had served him. But the beer tasted bitter, too. He put it on the dining room table and sat down. He phoned Alypia's best friend in London, who said Alypia was fine but didn't want to talk. Faust knew she was lying and Alypia wasn't there, but he didn't press the issue. Alypia had been with him long enough to make sure no-one knew what she was planing so he couldn't find her through them. He tried the beer again. Still bitter. He hoped that wasn't going to be permanent.

Chapter 33

Alypia keyed the code into the pad from memory. She had repeated it over and over until it became as reflexive as knowing her date of birth. The door swooshed open. Bella was standing there.

"You okay?"

Alypia felt words catch in her throat, so she nodded instead.

Bella gently guided Alypia over the threshold, and the doors swooshed shut.

"You okay?" Bella repeated the question.

"I am now," Alypia said and allowed Bella to pull her in close with a hug.

"It's going to be fine," said Bella.

"I hope so," said Alypia.

"Trust me," said Bella, and then kissed her lover.

Chapter 34

Boatman, Maverick, Tobias and Bella sat in a booth at the hideaway pub they regularly frequented. The owners, Marie and Fletcher, pretended they had no idea who the four were even though Maverick was far from inconspicuous. It was early evening on a Monday, but the pub was buzzing with people unwinding after being elbow deep in fish guts and scales.

The pub was in the Fish borough in east London. The main hub was the Water Gate building, where merchants bought and sold fish to the city and beyond. The Romans were passionate about having a thriving fish market and invested in the infrastructure of the area to ensure trading was as seamless as possible. The Fish borough grew as more people saw the opportunity to make money out of fish and shellfish. Shops, pubs and housing spread throughout the borough and hence, it quickly acquired its name. Visitors to the borough immediately knew where they were because of the smell.

The Fish borough was also like its own village than like other areas of London. It was a hard-working community that revolved around catching, processing and selling fish and shellfish and living as one very large family. Being so close-knit meant it was also very protective of anyone connected to it. Romans tended to avoid the Borough. They claimed it was because of the smell, but the truth was that they were afraid of the fishing community. Soldiers were intimidated because the men and women of the Fish borough had no fear of the Romans and made that lack very clear.

A Roman soldier who had recently arrived in London went to the Fish borough to buy something for dinner and noticed he was charged triple the price of the customer before him, even though they had bought the same thing. He very loudly told the fishmonger that if he wasn't reimbursed, the fishmonger would find himself crucified at the borough gates. That soldier swiftly found out why Roman command rarely interfered with the Fish borough. He was held down and forced to eat the sea bass he had bought. Raw. Whole. The Roman learned that sea bass have an astonishing number of sharp spines on their backs. The soldier returned to Italy soon after, able to eat only soup.

Boatman's family were intimately connected to the fishing industry. His great, great grandfather was also called Boatman and had farmed oysters until the day he died. The Fish borough respected Boatman and generations of fisherman and fishmongers had dealt with Boatman's family, so they protected Boatman and anyone he loved. Because of that, Boatman was able to access the borough through underground tunnels and disappear again.

Fletcher brought over a round of drinks and left the four rebels to it.

"So, where are we at?" Boatman looked tired.

"Feels like a stalemate," said Maverick.

"Why?"

"Well, Nero didn't flush us out, and we didn't flush him out."

"How are people feeling about Faust?"

"Bloody mental," said Tobias.

"I agree," said Bella. "Bloody mental."

"Maverick?"

Maverick puffed his cheeks, "I'm trying to understand the game he's playing, but can't."

Bella spoke up. "The simplest answer is usually the right one. He wants to meet you to kill you."

Tobias made a sweeping gesture with one hand while having a swig of beer, "Exactly. It's a trap."

"But he said he would help me get rid of Nero."

"True. That seemed pretty risky considering the lengths the Romans go to bug the HoC. There's probably a recording," said Maverick.

Bella spoke again. "If he doesn't want to kill you then what does he want? Power?"

"Nero's power?" Tobias answered his own question. "But that's ridiculous."

"It might not be," said Boatman. "I've seen plenty of men have delusions of the power they could obtain. And Faust is unique in his intelligence."

Maverick grunted. "You give him too much credit."

"You don't give him enough credit."

"Maybe," said The Beast and drank some beer.

"Let's work this out pragmatically," said Bella. "If he wants Nero's power, how possible is that?"

"He's just a Centurion," said Tobias, "before getting rid of Nero he needs to get rid of people like Titus."

"Exactly." Boatman pointed his finger at Tobias. "To be anywhere near to being next in line to Nero, Faust would have to remove a large number of people throughout the globe who are more likely to be the next emperor. Just off the top of my head, Brutus or Bjorn would be next in line."

Maverick put his glass down and spoke quietly. "Bjorn would make people miss Nero."

Tobias looked at his partner. "You know him?"

Maverick nodded and absently ran his finger down the scar on his face. "Too well."

"He's a bit of a myth," said Boatman.

"Like the Boatman of Britannia," said Maverick. "Not so much when his axe almost chops your face off." Maverick raised his glass and said to Boatman, "If Faust wants to take out Nero then he will need to be prepared."

"For what?"

Maverick drank his beer and made a point of savoring the flavor. "For feeling a fear he never thought possible if he encounters Bjorn Åska."

"Do you feel that fear?"

"No."

"Why not?"

"Because he's just a man."

"There's also the problem of Max," said Tobias. Maverick kicked Tobias under the table.

"What problem?"

Maverick cleared his throat. "Max is still alive."

"But he'll be eating through a straw for the rest of his life," said Tobias, quickly.

"You sure of that?"

Tobias hesitated and Maverick said, "No. We're not sure of anything with him. He's been shipped back to Rome for treatment."

"How did you find this out?" asked Boatman.

"Faust told me. He showed me a picture of Max in a hospital bed."

"So Max is still alive, but Faust still sees an opportunity to take Nero out. Essentially, if Faust wants to get rid of Nero, then it's an opportunity for us. Why he wants to isn't our concern. For now. And if Max is shitting into diapers, then he can wait." Boatman drummed his fingers on the table, thinking. Weighing up the risk. "Mav, set up a meeting. It's worth the risk."

Maverick said, "He was meant to be in touch today but hasn't. I will get a message to him somehow."

Boatman put some money on the table and said the three of them should have a few drinks and relax; the next few days would probably be hell. He wasn't staying. He needed to get back to Olivia. As Boatman navigated back through the tunnels to HQ, he tried to unpack Faust's motives. The excitement of finding a way to kill Nero dominated his mind. His gut told him this was the moment he was waiting for and maybe, just maybe, he could redeem himself with Olivia.

Chapter 35

Boatman walked into his quarters and was surprised to see Olivia resting on the sofa. "I asked to be discharged," she said.

"Do you feel well enough?" Boatman knelt by her and held her hand.

"I need to be at home."

Boatman squeezed her hand. "I need you at home. It's horrible without you here."

"How's Molly?"

"Who?"

"Molly, the little girl you saved."

"Obviously distraught about her dad. Bella has been checking in on her and her mum."

"Is there something you're not telling me, Boatman?"

"About Molly?"

"Maybe. Or about her dad."

"It was an unfortunate set of events. Kevin was adamant he could reason with the Romans." Boatman tried to tell himself he wasn't lying to his wife, but he conscience told him otherwise.

"I won't push you on it. I haven't got the energy, but if you're keeping something from that little girl and her mother, then that could hurt you down the line."

Boatman bristled. "Liv, I'm dealing with trying to take down the Roman emperor. Winning favor with a little girl isn't on the top of my list."

Olivia sighed, opened her eyes and turned to face Boatman. "Some people are born rotten, like Nero. Their souls are black. Empty. Some people are distorted through the course of their lives as toxic people corrupt them. An innocent little girl can grow into a woman full of resentment and distrust if men in power, like you, deceive and distort what is right and what is good."

"Liv, I'm trying to do what's right. I'm trying to remove the toxin from this country."

"Maybe." Olivia sighed again. "I'm just sensing that Molly knows something isn't right and she will grow to blame you as that seed of distrust grows. And trust me, Boatman, a girl like Molly will grow into a woman who you will want as an ally, not an enemy."

Olivia hadn't let go of Boatman's hand. Her words were hard, but Boatman appreciated the honesty. He needed directness from Olivia. He had enough people blowing smoke up his ass, and she kept him grounded. Even if he had to take a few days to process what she said and understand that, usually, she was right.

It was Boatman's turn to sigh. "I don't know. I should just accept that you're probably right, but I can't help thinking that Molly and her mom will ultimately appreciate being saved and given a safe life here."

"Let's hope so," said Olivia.

They stopped talking. Olivia sat up and swung her legs off the sofa. Boatman stayed crouched in front of her. He couldn't place it, but to Boatman, his wife looked different. It was her eyes. They had something about them when she looked at him. It compelled him to speak. "There is something you should know. Max is still alive."

"I know."

"Who told you?"

"No-one. I just know." Olivia leaned forward and put her forehead against Boatman's. She closed her eyes. "You won't understand, and I don't hold it against you for not understanding what Max did to me. What he put me through. It changed everything. He's a part of me now." Olivia felt Boatman tense. "You have to listen to me. You have to let me say it." Boatman nodded. "When a man does that, when he exerts that power, it alters everything. He takes something away and leaves his dirt behind. I know he's alive because I still feel his dirtiness in me. Like it's going through my veins." Tears began to fall down Olivia's face. "And you know what?" She sniffed and her voice broke. "I feel like I deserved it." Boatman went to speak, to say of course she didn't deserve it, but Olivia stopped him. "I know I don't. I know it's part of the abuse. *I know.* But that little voice. His voice. It whispers horrible things. And that's why I know he's still alive."

Olivia leaned back and wiped her eyes. She tried to breathe. She tried to compartmentalize the darkness.

"I will get him," said Boatman.

"I know you will. The thing is, he'll still be here." Olivia touched her chest. She looked at her husband and saw, for the first time, a man who seemed vulnerable. He didn't know what to say, and his brutal physicality provided no ability to solve something so delicate. She didn't want to admit it, but she wasn't sure what that made her feel about him. "You look tired," she said. "Let's get some sleep." Boatman didn't object. It was late into the night and the thought of having his wife next to him for the first time in months made his heart ache. They went to bed and within minutes Boatman was asleep. Olivia struggled to sleep. She felt Molly's pain. Her grief for Kevin. That wasn't the worst of it. She sensed Max. She sensed his poison. She prayed to the God-Carpenter for some peace, and eventually sleep came.

Chapter 36

Faust was discovering that cigarettes were still bitter. He had barely slept through the night, keeping one eye open and one hand on a sword, waiting for Nero's bodyguard, Aloysius, to creep into his quarters and slit his throat. Aloysius never came, but Faust wasn't feeling safe. Alypia wasn't safe, but had disappeared. Nero was paranoid at the best of times and now, with Titus AWOL, Atticus murdered and the HoC breached, Nero was no longer trusting anyone. And rightly so, thought Faust. It's not paranoia if it's true, and Faust *was* going after Nero.

He needed to throw Nero off the scent, though. He needed Nero to focus his paranoia and rage on someone else. He needed Boatman to stick his head up above the parapet so Nero could take aim. Faust messaged Maverick with a time and place to meet and specified that Boatman had to be there or the deal was off. A message came back almost immediately confirming the meeting and the conditions. He dragged on another cigarette; the bitterness had dissipated slightly.

He closed his eyes and took himself into his mind palace. Certain things had moved into place and other parts were uncertain. Maverick's agreement for Boatman to meet had moved some pieces, and now Faust was seeing a clearer image.

Titus was still a blurry part, and Faust carefully moved through his palace trying to join the pieces of what he knew about Titus and what could have happened. Faust's gut instinct was that Nero had had Titus murdered and was sending out fake news that Titus had deserted. The problem with that was Nero was genuinely confused as to what had happened to Titus. Faust could read people easily and know when they were lying. Nero wasn't lying when he said he didn't know where Titus was, so that meant Titus had either been kidnapped or had deserted.

Faust walked through a set of doors in his mind palace, and it took him to a few months previous when he had spoken to Titus about the Eye for an Eye Day. To Faust it made no sense for Nero to orchestrate something that obvious and brutal. It was never going to flush Boatman out. Boatman was never going to try and stop it from happening, just as no-one would have dared try to kill Boatman. Titus also found the idea dangerous, but for logistical reasons. It would stretch his already vulnerable soldiers. Faust had enthusiastically agreed in front of Nero because dissent wasn't worth the risk but agreed with Titus in private. Titus always gave pragmatic feedback. Faust slowed the conversation down and analyzed Titus's facial tics as he spoke. Something Faust hadn't picked up on at the time, owing to Titus being such a good negotiator and diplomat, was fear. Titus was afraid at the time of the conversation. He had managed to hide it with his easy demeanor, but his pupils were dilated in fear. The eyes never lie. Faust realized that Titus has terrified of something. Knowing Nero and Faust's most recent encounter, Titus was likely afraid for someone else.

Titus was very private about his personal life, but there was a son. Faust was sure Nero would know about the son and maybe a flippant threat was enough to make Titus run. No, Titus had been in the Middle East, where threats to family were common.

Self preservation. That was it. What else did men do when under threat? Try to save themselves. Yes, many a man would say that they would die for their children or partners but most men, instead of nobly standing to fight for their loved ones, would flee to preserve themselves. Faust had seen it time and time again as the Romans marched across the globe. Most people will take the opportunity to save themselves and hope the guilt of leaving others behind isn't all-consuming. And that was it. That was why Titus had disappeared. He could see an endgame, and in that endgame he would be the scapegoat. Nero was potentially facing defeat in London and Titus knew that as Commander of Britannia he would be taking the blame for the defeat. Defeat was by no means a certainty, but Titus was looking at the long game, Faust was sure. Fight or flight. Titus was flying away before having to choose to fight.

Faust moved out of his palace and back into the present. If Titus was really running, then it was possible to use so many resources to search for him that it would weaken the security around Nero. Faust stopped his train of thought on that, though. Given Nero's behavior the night before, Faust had seriously underestimated how much Nero knew; he wondered if Nero was waiting for him to make a move to confirm that Faust was also a traitor. Everything was bluff and double bluff, and Faust was trying to understand whose bluff was whose.

Usually Faust would have quietly planted seeds of doubt and mayhem to manipulate people over months, but things were moving fast and there hadn't been time to do that. He needed to make a decision. He knew that if his next move was wrong, he would be watching Nero do horrible things to Alypia, if she could be found. Alypia was too valuable to his plans to be in the wind, but he didn't have the time or resources to find her when he had to focus on both Boatman and Nero.

It was time for the false emperor to be deposed, and Boatman was the key. It was time to see what happened when an unstoppable force met an unmovable object.

Chapter 37

Bella had her head on Alypia's stomach, and Alypia was stroking her hair. Bella was lying at a right angle to Alypia so they made a T shape.

"How old are you?"

"It's rude to ask a woman's age," said Bella. She tilted her head to look at Alypia. "I'm 31."

"By the gods, that makes me a cougar," said Alypia.

Bella stroked Alypia's leg. "A very sexy cougar."

"I can't work it out, why me?"

"Why you? Have you seen yourself?"

Alypia blushed. She wasn't used to such compliments. Well, she was used to compliments, but genuine compliments were another thing. Before being married to Faust, Alypia had resided in the elite community of Roman royalty. She was the daughter of a Grand Senator, a man who dealt with the politics the emperor had no time or interest in. The Grand Senator monitored the socio-economic impacts of the emperor's decisions and made policy accordingly. Unlike Jonas, who advised the morality of a Caesar, the Grand Senator analyzed the pragmatic consequences of domestic decisions. Essentially, the Grand Senator's motivation was to make sure the elite stayed wealthy and continued to get wealthier, himself included.

Alypia grew up in this lifestyle, so had never wanted for anything material. Even things she hadn't thought of were bestowed upon her. The jewelry she wore was worth than some countries' GDPs. And being the daughter of the Grand Senator meant everyone fawned over her, telling her she was the most beautiful girl in the entire Roman Empire. For years, Alypia enjoyed the adoration, but as time rumbled on hearing the same endless platitudes desensitized her to the emotion. It was as easy to become numb to deification as to Roman violence. Alypia barely heard it anymore when someone fell over themselves to praise her for her eternally youthful looks.

Until she met Bella.

Bella had caught her off guard. Alypia had never really found other women attractive. Yes, she appreciated the beauty of other women but had never felt it at an intimate level. When she first saw Bella, though, she was surprised at how Bella caught her eye. And Bella had been almost indifferent to her, which hardly ever happened. Being the daughter of a Grand Senator and married to Faust, one of the greatest Commanders in the Roman Empire, meant nobody was indifferent to her. Nobody but Bella.

Alypia had arrived at her favorite seafood restaurant, Kiss from the Sea, and been greeted by the owner, who always made the restaurant come to a standstill until Alypia had been seated at her favorite table. When Alypia entered a room, everyone stopped and stared. The evening she met Bella, the staff were waiting to greet her and diners had stopped eating to get a glimpse of Alypia Faust. Except Bella, who was eating on her own and paid no attention to the grand entrance. She just carried on cracking the claws of a lobster. After Alypia had sat down with her friend, Lucille, and the restaurant had resumed normal service, Alypia couldn't help but keep looking over at Bella. Bella never once even looked at or acknowledged Alypia. Lucille had asked Alypia if she was okay, as she seemed very distracted. Alypia had reassured her friend and drank even more Champagne. All it did was cause her to get more and more intrigued by the lone, indifferent woman.

When Lucille had excused herself to the bathroom, Alypia had called over Charles, the owner, and asked him who the woman was. Charles glanced over to Bella and said, "Her name's Bella. She eats here the same time every Friday night. Has done for two months now. Is everything okay?"

"Oh, fine, thank you Charles. I don't often see people eating alone in here."

"She's new to the city and said she could never get lobster where she grew up so wants to make the most of it."

"Would you see if she would like a drink? On me."

Charles raised his eyebrows momentarily. Alypia had never bought a drink for another diner. "Of course, madam."

Charles went to Bella's table, spoke to Bella, gesturing over to Alypia's table. After a short conversation, Bella got up from the table, ignored whatever Charles was saying and sat down next to Alypia. Lucille wasn't far behind and sat down with a quizzical look. Charles was hovering at the table, unsure what to do. "It's okay, Charles. Go get us another bottle for the table." Charles melted away like good maître d's do.

"Lucille, this is Bella. She's new to the city."

Lucille looked Bella up and down, the way super rich people do when looking at poorer versions of humanity. "I'm going for a cigarette," she said and left.

"Did I do something wrong?"

"Lucille is the wife of the emperor's cousin. She's visiting for a few weeks. She can smell whether you're rich. You clearly don't smell very rich, so you're of no interest to her."

Bella cocked her head at the now-empty space left by Lucille. "You might want to tell your friend that no matter how much money she may have, she's being cheated by whoever does her face lifts. She looks like she's constantly in a wind tunnel."

Alypia snorted on her Champagne. She wiped her nose with a napkin. "You did hear who she is, didn't you?"

"I don't think it's me who should be worried about who she is, it's her plastic surgeon. By the gods, I would crucify him if he did that to my face."

Alypia had never had anyone speak to her in the way Bella did, and she found it liberating. From that moment in that restaurant Alypia wanted to know Bella. She wanted to really know her, and now she was lying in Bella's bed, undressed and enamored with the woman. And now, the woman who had been indifferent to Alypia was showering her with words of affection. Alypia was transfixed by it all.

"Why would you take such a risk to be with me?" Alypia asked.

"I'm not really risking anything. I'm just a single nobody. It seems you're the one taking the risk."

"A year ago, it would have been a risk. I guess it isn't so much now."

Bella shifted her position so she could look at Alypia better. She carried on stroking her leg, "Why not?"

Alypia carried on playing with Bella's hair, without looking up, "I shouldn't really say. I'm not sure what's what anymore, but I'd probably be done for treason."

"We're both naked. I'm clearly not wearing a wire."

Alypia laughed. The laugh felt good. It was genuine. So many years of strained, fake laughter had made her wonder if she would ever genuinely laugh again. "That's true." She leaned forward and kissed Bella. "You can't tell anyone what I tell you. You have to promise."

"Who would I tell? I live alone in London and go out once a week to eat lobster. I'm tragic."

"Seriously, Bella, you can't tell a soul what I tell you."

"I promise," said Bella. "But before you tell me anything, I need to ask you something."

"What?"

"Why are you doing this with me? You could be the next emperor's wife."

Alypia laughed again. It was another genuine laugh. By the gods it felt nice to feel real joy at the little things again. Finding someone genuinely amusing. Being happy to be in someone's presence. Not feeling like things were forced. And that's what she told Bella. That's why she was taking the risk.

She also said, "I'm miserable, Bella. And afraid. Ironically, I'm not afraid of The Beast or Boatman. I'm not sure I'm of any interest to them. Even what happened to my house doesn't scare me. I hated the place anyway. I know they're scary, but for some reason I'm not scared of them. I'm afraid of the constant anxiety I feel. I'm afraid of the darkness I feel as the wife of Faust and the daughter of the Grand Senator. I'm just a trophy."

Alypia moved so that she could be alongside Bella. They were both on their sides, facing each other, foreheads touching. Alypia was whispering. As if she were still afraid of being listened to. "Faust has these two Ming vases, no idea how much they're worth. He adores these vases. They're a gift from Nero so he treats them like me. A trophy. The thing is, he seems to worry more about their welfare than he does about mine. A few months ago, The Beast and his partner in crime broke into our house like they were warning Faust because they didn't do anything apart from swap the vases around. It was weird. But even though Faust acted like he was really upset as my life was in danger, I know. *I know* he was more upset by them messing with his vases. I'm just another object in Faust's possession, and I'm not even the most important one." Alypia had started to cry and tears had formed in her eyes. "That's why I'm taking the risk with you."

Bella used her thumb to wipe a tear form Alypia's cheek, "You've been married for years though, surely there's more to how he feels than like you're an object?"

"I used to think so, but—", Alypia sniffled, "he's clever, Bella. And when I say clever, I mean his brain is beyond our mere mortal brains. I think he behaves like he thinks he should, but it's all an act. His while life and career is a game to him, I'm sure. I'm a part in that game, and I think my part is coming to an end." Alypia shivered, but she wasn't cold. Bella hugged her close.

"Which is why you've run away."

Alypia nodded.

"Will he know where you are?"

"No. I'm certain of that. I've been so careful. He picks up on the tiniest of details, so I have been normal. There's nothing of you in my life, digitally or emotionally at home."

"Thanks," said Bella.

"Honestly, you don't exist outside of our time alone at the restaurant. That's why it has always had to be there. I can be honest with him then when I say I have been there with my friend. I don't have to act and give something away. He would know."

"You make him sound like he's not human."

Alypia didn't respond to that, as if it didn't need answering.

"What about your friend? You said she's covering for you?"

"She's covering by saying I'm staying with her, but she has no idea where I am. Augustus won't harass her. He knows she's lying but won't have any idea of my whereabouts." She just stayed close to Bella until the emotional exhaustion of the day overwhelmed her and she fell asleep.

Bella pulled a blanket over her lover. When she was sure Alypia was in a deep sleep, she sent a message to Boatman.

Chapter 38

"He wants you to go there alone." It wasn't a question.

"It seems that way," said Boatman.

"And you're sure that's where he wants to meet?"

"Absolutely," said Maverick.

"Well he's definitely one for the theatrics then. What's wrong with an old-fashioned ambush down a dark alley?"

"It will be fine. If it goes right, it gets us to Nero."

"I mean, I hate to be the one to state the bloody obvious, but if there were neon signs everywhere flashing that this is a trap, I still don't think it would be obvious enough," said Tobias.

"It might not be a trap," said Maverick.

"Have you been smacked round the head and no-one had realized?"

"I'll smack you round the head in a minute."

"Please do. It might wake me up from the weird dream I'm having where you two have become gullible."

"He's taking a big risk contacting us."

"I doubt it. He's probably got Nero next to him as he's typing the messages." Tobias snorted and sat down. The three of them were in Boatman's conference room trying to plan a decent strategy for meeting with Faust. Maverick was concerned about protection. Faust had chosen an open space that had few places for Maverick and Tobias to observe from cover but close enough to act before it was too late. Tobias had said cover was pretty pointless because as soon as Boatman stepped into the open a Roman would probably blow his head off or spear him in preparation for crucifixion.

Boatman looked at Tobias. "I understand your concerns, Tobias."

"Concerns? I get concerned if I run out of coffee in the morning. Losing my shit is a more appropriate description of what I'm feeling."

"Tobias, remember Faust had the opportunity to get us killed only two days ago and yet he let us walk out of the HoC unscathed."

"For a former gladiator and a rebel leader against the Roman Empire, you guys are fucking naive or stupid."

"I'm definitely stupid. After all, I'm with you," said Maverick.

"That's the only clever thing you've done."

"Killing you in the gladiator arena would have been the smart choice."

"I would've kicked your ass."

Boatman butted in to yet another squabble. "You two need to see a therapist. Can we get back to the plan?"

"There's a plan?" Tobias looked genuinely puzzled. "I just thought we were going to let the only guy with a chance of overthrowing the Empire just walk to his death."

"Tobias, shut the hell up for a minute, would you?" said Boatman.

Tobias shut the hell up.

"Where's Bella?"

"She'll be here soon," said Boatman.

Boatman sat down next to Tobias and said, "Obviously I

know Faust wants to kill me. Obviously I know meeting him will give him that chance. But something has happened, which means he's desperate."

"I don't buy it." Boatman went to say something else but Tobias cut in, "I don't buy it, but I'll go with whatever you want. I know desperate men and Faust didn't seem that way the other night."

Bella walked into the room. "So, what's the plan?"

Maverick threw his phone to Bella and she read the message from Faust. "Seriously? This is where he wants to meet? It doesn't leave us much room for protection."

"We'll manage," said Maverick.

"So let's go over it, now Bella is here," said Boatman.

Tobias found a real-time image of where Boatman would be meeting Faust and projected it on the wall. No matter how they looked at it, the Britannia Colosseum was a perfect place to take someone out. If they wanted to meet an enemy, they would choose this place. Yes, Maverick, Tobias and Bella could hide in the stands, but Boatman would be dead before they even worked out where a sniper shot had come from.

The Britannia Colosseum was an almost perfect replica of its famous counterpart, situated in the heart of London, perched on the bank of the Thames River. The main difference from the one in Rome was that it had a retractable dome so that it could host events through all weathers and have its climate controlled for specific events. It was larger, too, with a capacity for 80,000 people. 30,000 more than the ancient original. Its design, though, paid homage to the Rome Colosseum. It was a truly beautiful construction.

Faust was able to choose it for meeting with Boatman because it was currently closed. It was undergoing expensive surveys because the foundations seemed to be shifting and on closer inspection

London's banks were built on millions of oyster shells. These shells, although robust, were not taking the weight and shape of the colosseum very well, so drastic action was needed. The venue had been closed for a few weeks while surveys were conducted and possible solutions were discussed.

Tobias gave his best ideas about where people should be posted to help Boatman as much as possible and discussed entry and exit strategies. They went over the strategy until afternoon had become evening. No-one was happy with the plan, but they agreed it seemed like the best one possible. Before parting ways and getting prepared mentally and physically for the next day and for any surprises Faust would have, Tobias said, "Let's hope he's on our side. Because if he's not, we're fucked."

"You should go into public speaking," said Maverick, "you're inspirational."

Chapter 39

Maverick and Tobias rose before dawn to reconnoiter the colosseum and surrounding area. If Faust were true to his word then he was meeting Boatman alone, but Boatman wasn't being true to his word, so why assume Faust was?

The couple wanted to not only understand the layout of the colosseum, they wanted to check the surrounding buildings for any agents of Faust who might be hiding. It was tricky, though. If they took out anyone working with Faust, then Faust might not show up. Alternatively, if they left accomplices, then Boatman was at higher risk of being assassinated. The task felt futile. Even so, there was a routine and due diligence needed for any operation; they weren't going to deviate from that.

The men split up and checked buildings separately to reduce the time needed. There were many abandoned buildings, deemed unsafe like the colosseum itself. The Romans were known for their robust architecture, so the problems were an embarrassment. The Romans didn't have much experience building on ground dominated by oyster shells. The Romans were known for loving oysters as a delicacy. For the Britons, oysters were a staple. Discarded shells dominating the Thames shoreline was as normal as soil and sand to the Britons. Faust had been astute in choosing to use this area to meet. If he assassinated Boatman, the body would be lost to all the oyster shells, never to be found again.

Maverick touched his earpiece and said, "Found anything?"

"Nothing. Maybe Faust is being genuine."

"Maybe. Let's rendezvous on the south side of the colosseum."

"Understood. See you in ten minutes."

At the Colosseum, Faust was standing on a VIP balcony that had an unparalleled view of London. He was wearing night-vision binoculars, watching Maverick and Tobias scurrying through various abandoned streets. He had assumed Boatman's lap dogs would be doing some pre-dawn raids on buildings trying to catch anyone. He would have done the same. He watched as they met up at the south side entrance to the Colosseum, exchanged a few words and broke into the building.

Faust watched them until they went out of view and then removed his binoculars. He had assumed Boatman wouldn't come alone because why would he? Faust hadn't come alone either. He had brought only one other with him though. He couldn't risk a fire fight or one of Bella's arrows taking the wrong person out and ruining it all. He needed Boatman to kill Nero. He needed to have a scapegoat. He sympathized with Boatman's cynicism though; this was the perfect opportunity for Rome to take out the rebel leader. "Not today, though," said Faust to himself.

Faust moved from his vantage point and made his way toward the arena where he would meet Boatman.

Maverick and Tobias made their way into the Colosseum and were working out best spots for concealing themselves.

On their earpieces, Boatman asked, "How are we looking?"

Tobias responded. "There's not a sign of a single soul."

"No-one?"

"No-one."

"Maybe Faust is telling the truth."

"It's like I'm listening to a scratched record," said Tobias. "Faust telling the truth is like Mav laughing at one of my jokes."

"I would laugh if you ever said something funny," Maverick said.

Boatman brought the conversation back to the important point. "You're sure there's no-one there?"

"Well, we haven't been able to sweep the whole place, but where we would expect to see soldiers waiting for us, there's no-one. The place seems deserted. I think he's hoping for a nice, intimate meeting with you."

"I'm honored," said Boatman. "I'll be there soon. Make sure you're where you should be."

"Will do," said Maverick.

"Tobias, you're okay with what you need to do?"

"All good."

"Okay, great," said Boatman, and contact was cut.

Faust watched as Maverick and Tobias said a few words to each other and then dispersed. He looked at his watch and saw it was almost time for Boatman to arrive. He made his way down to the arena, skirting the perimeter. Faust was known for his tactical expertise and for his leadership skills, but he was proud of his combat skills. He loved the raw brutality of combat. Today fired him up. Today was the kind of danger he loved most. He was pitted against The Beast and Boatman. It was rare to engage with such perfect fighters.

Faust made his way to the grand archway, where in normal shows fighters and entertainment would be revealed to cheers and applause. He remained in the dawn shadows, ensuring he wasn't visible. He was wearing all black and merged with the darkness of his surroundings. He crouched and waited. It was nearly time to meet Boatman.

He looked at his watch. When the timer hit zero, he pressed a button. From the end opposite the grand archway, a figure dressed like a centurion walked into the arena. As the figure got to the center of the arena, Faust felt the atmosphere change. A figure moved close by just ahead of him. Faust had hidden himself in the alcoves of the entrance so that no-one would detect he was there. His enemies were all focused on the arena.

"Is that Faust?" Tobias whispered into his mic, struggling to see who was walking across the arena floor. The light was dim in the early morning.

"It looks like him," said Maverick.

"Is the arena clear of anyone else?" asked Boatman.

"All clear," said Maverick.

"All clear," said Tobias.

"Bella? Have you got a clear shot at him?"

"He might as well be wearing a giant target," said Bella. She was in the stands, arrow loaded and bow drawn.

"Well, okay then. Let's go meet Faust."

The figure stepped forward, slightly tentative, and looked up and around, searching for potential threats in the stands of the arena. That's when Faust made his move. He stepped out of the shadows and was behind the figure. Silently, he drew a small blade and stabbed the figure in the side. The razor-sharp blade went in and out easily, and Faust was gone as quickly as he had appeared.

The figure took a moment to react. He touched his side as if he had been bitten by a bug. His hands were soaked in blood. He called out in pain he collapsed and his knees hit the ground.

Maverick heard the cry of pain through his earpiece, "Bella!"

Bella loosed her arrow at the Faust impersonator, a perfect shot, aimed for the heart. Bella gasped as the centurion anticipated the shot and batted the arrow away with his shield. His reactions were abnormal. Before she could draw another arrow he was gone from the arena.

Maverick rushed from his hiding spot and over to the collapsed figure and immediately saw the blood pouring out of a wound. He clamped his hand over the wound and said, "Tobias, can you hear me?"

Tobias didn't respond.

Maverick called his name again and again to try and keep and conscious. He looked up and saw the centurion had disappeared.

Boatman was now by Maverick's side. He saw Maverick's giant had clamped on Tobias's wound.

"If we move him, he could bleed out."

"If we don't move him, he will bleed out," said Boatman. "Bella, get down here, fast." Boatman looked at Maverick and saw him consumed with worry for his fiancé. "We'll save him, Mav."

Maverick didn't look up, he just stared at Tobias, not daring to look away, as if doing so would make things worse. Bella was with them and said, "What do you need?" She didn't even ask what'd happened.

"We need to seal the wound."

Bella pulled out an arrow and a mini blowtorch. She had a quiver full of various arrows, including fire arrows, which as ancient as they were, still provided effective destruction. Why improve on perfection? She sparked the blowtorch and started heating the arrow's head.

"Mav, when Bella says, you need to take your hand off the

wound. It's messy and not ideal, but it should be enough to be able to get him back to HQ."

Maverick still didn't look up.

"Maverick?"

Silence.

Boatman spoke louder, "Maverick!"

Maverick looked up. His eyes were glassy. "I heard you."

"Now's not the time to falter. We need to act fast. Bella, say when."

Bella gave the arrow's head a few more seconds under the torch and then signaled. Maverick moved his hand, and Bella placed the hot metal on Tobias's wound. The skin sizzled. Tobias went from barely conscious to screaming in pain. Maverick held his hand and pulled Tobias's head to his chest. The shock of the burn pumped adrenaline through Tobias, and he opened his eyes. Maverick sat him up and said, "Tobias, we need to get you to the medical wing. You've been stabbed. We don't know how bad it is. On the count of three, we will get you to your feet and get you out of here. Okay?" Tobias nodded.

They pulled the injured man to his feet and made their way out of the colosseum. Maverick's phone rang. "Boatman, my phone."

Boatman pulled Maverick's phone from his coat pocket and saw it was Faust. He answered, "You motherfucker."

"You didn't stick to the rules, Boatman. You're the motherfucker."

"If he dies, you die."

"No, that's not how it works."

"Now, you listen to me—"

"No!" Faust cut Boatman off. "You listen to me. I said to meet me alone. You and only you. You arrogantly ignored my request and got someone stabbed. I took one of your top soldiers out without breaking a sweat. Remember that."

"And we entered your home while you slept, without breaking a sweat. Remember that."

The line went silent for a few seconds. "Well now we're even."

"What do you want?"

"To stick to the original plan. Meet me alone and I'll help you sort the Nero problem. Try to deceive me again and see more blood on your hands."

Boatman stayed silent as he tried to weigh up his options. "Send me the details." He cut the line and gave the phone back to Maverick.

"If you're still meeting him, you had better kill him," said Maverick.

"It's not that simple."

"It is that simple."

"Let's get back to HQ."

Faust watched from a distance as the four rebels disappeared into the distance.

The fake centurion asked, "Are we not following them?"

Faust shook his head.

"You could have warned me an arrow might nearly take my head off."

"You handled it fine."

"No thanks to you."

"I trusted your skills."

"Or you wanted me dead," said the Faust impersonator.

"Of course not, I need you," said Faust.

"I'm sure you won't be offended if I think you're talking bullshit."

"I couldn't care less what you think," said Faust who turned on his heels and left.

Chapter 40

Tobias felt Phobos, the god of fear, breathing down his neck. The god was like a mixture of black smoke and tar swirling and oozing and congealing all over him. It was like having his brain smothered by fear and his lungs filled with anxiety so he couldn't think or breathe. He was trying to escape the horror but his legs wouldn't work properly.

It's just a dream.

He's not real.

It's just a dream.

He's not real.

It's just a dream.

But he couldn't wake up. He couldn't escape. He couldn't get away from the claws scratching at his brain, triggering fear and panic.

Tobias.

My Tobias.

My slave, Tobias.

Let the fear in.

Breathe it in.

Take big lungfuls of it.

Surrender to it.

My slave, Tobias.

My Tobias.

Tobias.

Tobias opened his mouth to scream but Phobos reached out and stuck his hand down Tobias's throat, his fingers searching and scraping down his windpipe. The god of fear reached down and down, making Tobias gag, and then his fingers turned to smoke and filled Tobias with fear from the inside.

Chapter 41

"Why's he choking?"

"Sir, could you please leave the room and let us help him?"

"He shouldn't be choking. What have you done?"

"Sir, please."

Bella put her hand on Maverick's arm. "Mav, let's wait outside and let them do their job." The doctors had managed to stabilize Tobias and get his heart rate down. "See, he's in safe hands."

At that moment, The Beast seemed to deflate and allowed Bella to guide him out of the room and to a sofa in the waiting room. "Why don't you try to get a bit of rest? You're exhausted."

"I need to be awake just in case Doctor Silverman needs to know anything about Tobias's medical history."

"Maverick, Silverman knows Tobias's history intimately. He's stitched him up enough times. Tobias is in the best care. You know the doctor. He'll come find you when he needs to. Tobias knows you love him and are close by."

Maverick was a stubborn man, a powerful man and a fearsome man, but when Bella said those words she was talking to a vulnerable man. Tobias was his world. Seeing his true love fight for breath broke him more than any gladiator arena could have. Hell, seeing Tobias so afraid was more torture than his time in the Slavic camp. Maverick nodded at Bella's words and slumped back on the sofa. He shifted his legs and lay down. His huge frame filled the sofa and his legs dangled off the end, but even so, the exhaustion, both physical and mental, wrapped themselves around him and he was sleep in seconds. Bella quietly exited the room and told a nurse that Maverick would want to be woken as soon as there was any new information on Tobias's condition.

She pulled out her phone and saw a message from Boatman to go see him in an hour. She hoped he had some idea on how to salvage the situation because, right now, it seemed like Faust was teaching them what warfare really was and exposing how amateur they were.

Bella had never considered herself amateur. She had been trained by her father, an expert huntsman from Ariaca. The Romans loved Indian spices and the Indo-Roman spice trade was still as strong now as when Augustus I built the trade routes two millennia ago. They also loved the exotic and people like Bella's father, Abdul, had established a rather lucrative business selling king cobra skin and Bengal tiger fur. Abdul was a skilled bowman and could kill an animal from afar without ruining the pelt by putting the arrow through its eye. Bengal Tigers were a precious commodity, so to be able to hunt them you needed a license and there were quotas on how many could be hunted per year. This made sure populations remained stable. Poachers who tried to hunt tigers and sell them on the black market were crucified and placed in the middle of Bengal tiger hunting grounds. Very few people ever took the risk of poaching.

Abdul had taught Bella how to hold a bow as soon as she was

able to walk. Every day, he put her on his back and trekked to areas where he would practice his skills. He only had a few days a year where he could actually hunt, but a quota of three tigers a year made home life very, very comfortable. It came through thousands of hours of practice. To kill a tiger was difficult. To kill a tiger through its eye was nearly impossible. Abdul was one of three people in India who could do it. With such skill, he wanted to ensure the family held onto the contract after he was gone and therefore taught Bella.

Bella abhorred hunting tigers. She abhorred that it was done to make Romans happy and themselves wealthy. She hated that her family relied on Roman gold. She loved learning how to shoot, though. She loved honing such a specialized skill. Training was bittersweet. She got so much pleasure learning from her father. He really was a master bowman. She hated that he trained her so that she could kill such beautiful creatures.

She had told her father this on one occasion. His response hadn't been sympathy but anger that she was considering throwing away the family's legacy. She had responded that having a legacy of killing tigers for Roman pleasure wasn't much of a legacy. He had declared that she was no longer welcome to go practicing with him.

As months went on, Abdul and Bella's relationship deteriorated to barely acknowledging each other. Bella went practicing and hunting in different areas than her father, selling what she could to prove she didn't need to hunt something as regal as a tiger. Abdul scoffed at her efforts; Bella dug her heels in even more.

She had eventually grown tired of living in such a toxic environment and decided it was time to move away and maybe put her skills to use in another country. She told her father that she wanted to see what else the world had to offer and to put her skills to the test elsewhere. Abdul struggled to wish his daughter well. When Bella had decided to see Britannia, she had hoped the new opportunity would build a bridge between her and her father. The morning she was due to leave though, Abdul had left the house before dawn without even a note to say goodbye. It almost broke Bella. For a moment she considered staying in Ariaca because of the guilt, but knew she would resent her father even more.

She did text her dad to say goodbye and she hoped he would be proud one day. He never responded.

Bella had been taught how to be an expert huntress but lost her family in the process. Maverick had been trained to be the greatest fighter and was at risk of losing the man he loved. Boatman had trained to be the most feared man in Britannia but nearly lost his wife. As she walked to Boatman's office, she wondered if they had angered the goddess Vesta, who watched over family. Boatman would have sneered at the thought; he didn't believe any of the gods existed. Bella wasn't superstitious but thought that maybe, just maybe, the death and destruction they had been causing had created an imbalance that the gods were no loner happy with. Maybe they were on the wrong side and the Romans were going to be favored.

Maybe they weren't the heroes they thought they were.

Chapter 42

Boatman poured himself and Olivia each a drink. She had a small glass of wine, her first in months. Boatman cracked open a bottle of beer. He always preferred what came from the Germanic region. It didn't matter what new stuff came around; the Germanics were famous for their beer because they were the best at brewing. He took a swig and contemplated finishing everything in the fridge to drown out how the past twenty-four hours had gone.

He slumped on the sofa next to his wife. Olivia ran her fingers through his hair. "What happened?"

"Tobias is in the medical wing."

"Will he be okay?"

Boatman made a fingers crossed sign and rubbed his eyes. He'd really messed up this time. Olivia turned to face her husband. "How's Maverick holding up?"

"Like Maverick always holds up."

"That's not an answer."

"He's obviously upset. To be honest, I've never seen him look so scared."

"Boatman, you need to abort whatever you have planned."

Boatman shook his head while he finished his beer. He got up from the sofa and retrieved another drink. "Not possible."

"You're a man down. Faust has the upper hand. You're exhausted."

"It doesn't matter about being a man down now." Boatman rubbed his face.

Olivia put her glass down on the table. "What have you done?"

"I haven't done anything. My hand's been forced."

"You're never forced to do anything."

"It looks like that's not true anymore."

Olivia asked again what he had done.

"Faust wants to meet me. He wants to take Nero down."

"If he wants to take Nero down, why doesn't he do it himself?"

"He can't be directly associated. He needs me."

"Does he?"

Boatman ignored the question. "He won't compromise. We thought we could hide our plans from him but he saw through it all. And now Tobias is fighting for his life."

"So what's his condition for meeting you that you didn't do before?"

"He wants to meet me alone."

Olivia snorted. "You're going to meet Centurion Faust alone and actually expect to come out of it alive? Have you been hit in the head?"

"Tobias said pretty much the same thing."

"By the gods, Boatman, Nero's probably behind the whole thing."

Boatman shook his head again. "I don't believe he is, Liv. If he was we would have been swamped by hundreds of soldiers this morning. I think this is the moment we've been fighting for. It was never going to come easy or in the way I hoped. But I think this is it."

Olivia stood up. "You're blinded by your obsession to kill Nero, and it may kill you."

"Liv, I'm trying to free this city, this country—shit, the whole world—of him."

"And then what? What's the plan for after? You're going to be emperor? You might get rid of a man, but what of the Empire? What of Max? What about those men clawing at the gates to replace Nero?"

"He's poison. You know he is. I thought you supported me? Surely you want to see him gone?"

"Fucking hell, Boatman, you're not listening. Of course he's poison, that's not my point." Olivia left the room but before she closed the bedroom door she said over her shoulder. "The whole world is poison."

Chapter 43

Doctor Silverman woke Maverick to inform him of Tobias's condition. He said that the wound was deep and, because of that, recovery would be painful. To Silverman's amazement, the blade hadn't punctured any organs, despite being close to Tobias's spleen and left kidney. It had torn through flesh and muscle, though, so it would take Tobias time to heal and the risk of infection was always present. They would keep him in the medical wing for a few days to monitor him and drip feed him antibiotics, but then he would be able to go home and have lots of bed rest. The doctor told Maverick to go home since Tobias was sleeping, to come visit him in the morning. Maverick didn't resist. He was shattered and knew Tobias was safe and cared for. Tobias would have probably told him to piss off anyway. The Beast thanked Silverman for all his efforts and made his way back to his quarters.

As he walked through the corridors, he pulled out his phone and saw a text message from Faust. It had instructions for where Boatman should meet him. Maverick resisted the urge to throw his phone against the wall. He texted Faust back asking why he would be so cowardly as to stab a man in the back. Faust replied instantly, calling it a perfect metaphor for the potential ambush. Maverick replied by writing that as common courtesy he would stab Faust in exactly the same place that Tobias had been. Faust read the message but didn't respond. Maverick reread the address for where Boatman was to meet the centurion and then set an alarm for just before dawn. He put his phone away and made a mental note to get his set of knives out of the safe.

Chapter 44

"We need a lot more information from her," said Boatman.

"I have to be careful. It takes time."

"We don't have the time."

"I'm not sure she'll have anything you could use tomorrow."

Boatman said, "Bella, she's been married to him for twenty years, she'll know something I can use. He'll have a weakness, a chink. There's something she knows that I can use. You need to press her."

"If I press too hard she'll get suspicious and clam up."

"It's not a request," said Boatman. "Go, press her. Find a way." Boatman dismissed Bella, not willing to discuss it any longer. "And Bella," she paused at the door, "I need you back here at oh-four-hundred-hours with something useful." Bella nodded and closed the door behind her.

Bella made her way out of the labyrinth of the HQ. Her usual exit was now a pile of rubble since the disaster with Kevin. She had been to see Sam and Molly to check in on them and see if they needed anything. Sam had gone to a dark place, mentally, and Bella was worried she wouldn't come back from it. Bella wasn't an expert in mental health, by any means, but she recognized when depression was taking hold. She saw herself in Sam.

After she had left India and arrived in Britannia, Bella had been consumed by loneliness and grief. She didn't know she was grieving at the time, but losing her relationship with her father was like someone had died. She felt consumed by the grief, as if it had drained her of all energy and all she could do was sustain the grief. She had found a job hunting wild fowl for a local estate owner who then sold them on to butchers around London. He liked that she used arrows as it meant the meat wasn't riddled with shotgun pellets. He was also amazed at how many she could bring down in a day. Better than his previous gamekeeper by a mile. The thing was, her depression was causing her to perform far below her skill with her bow. Her boss had paid for her to have some sessions with a therapist. That therapist turned out to be Olivia. Olivia had helped her navigate through her grief at losing the relationship with her father. Bella believed Olivia could do the same for Sam. She would go see Olivia and ask if she had the energy to at least talk with Sam. If Sam wanted to talk, that was.

Bella lived underground in quarters, but Boatman had set up an apartment for her to use since making contact with Alypia. Before Olivia had been abducted by Max, she had spent hours profiling Alypia. Being such a prominent woman in the Empire, Alypia was constantly on the news and posted thousands of pictures and messages online for her adoring fans. Like the God-Carpenter once said, *the fruit of a person's heart is expressed through their words,* and Alypia's heart was regularly expressed through her words. Only subtly, but Olivia picked up on it. Olivia could tell that Alypia was miserable and her life was as a trophy to Faust. Olivia could tell the woman was lonely, too. She spent hours analyzing Alypia's habits and routines, which was easy through scrolling through her online presence, and built a profile.

Olivia was disturbed by how easy it was to get to know a person and their habits through what they posted online. It also raised the question of how lax security was when it came to Faust's wife. She was vulnerable. Bella would prove this in the coming months.

Once Olivia had compiled information on Alypia, she took it to Boatman and agreed that Bella would be the perfect person to try and get close. Based on her profile, Alypia had become suspicious of men. Wary, even. Being an object, paraded around first by her father and now by Faust meant she had become disillusioned by men. Her posts barely mentioned Faust or her father and Olivia suggested that for anyone to get close, it would need to be someone not in a position of power and most likely a woman. It was a ruthless tactic, using Alypia to get information, but they believed not only could they get vital information, they might even be able to turn Alypia and get her to join the rebel effort. Her knowledge could propel the entire effort.

Bella had taken little convincing to try and engage with Alypia. First, because she hated the Empire. Her father had become very rich from trading with the Empire, but she saw the brutality of it when walking past crucified corpses each day on London Bridge. It made her sick. Yes, she had killed, but out of protection and preservation; the Romans enjoyed killing. They had fun doing it, and she couldn't stomach that. Second, she thought Alypia was fascinating. If she could get to know such an intriguing woman, she would happily do that.

Months later, and now they were lovers. Bella's stomach knotted. She had grown to love Alypia. She truly had, but duty to Boatman and the greater cause meant she had been deceiving Alypia for all this time. The anxiety of the lies was becoming too much.

She got to the apartment and let herself in. Alypia was cooking. Onions and garlic wafted through the place. It smelled delicious and made Bella's stomach rumble. "I hope you like mussels."

"Have you been out of the apartment?"

"Don't worry, in this weather I had a scarf around my face and sunglasses on. Even my biggest fans wouldn't have recognized me."

"You double checked no-one was following you back here, though?"

"What are you, a spy? No-one even gave me a second glance, Bella." Alypia gave the mussels a stir, the shells rattling against the saucepan. "So?"

Bella hesitated, "Of course not."

Alypia's face dropped. "Oh. Okay. I was sure you said you liked them." She turned the stove off. Bella realized what Alypia was referring to and stepped forward and put her hand on Alypia's. "Sorry, I misheard you. Of course I like mussels. I love them and whatever you have done with them smells amazing." She kissed Alypia and pulled her in close. "Sorry, work was a bit stressful, and I wasn't listening."

"You know, you've never really told me what you do."

"Clear up other people's messes, it seems." Bella stepped away from Alypia and poured herself a drink. She tipped the bottle at Alypia, and Alypia held out her glass.

"It will be ready in moments, why don't you take a seat?"

Bella sat down, still trying to figure out how to navigate the conversation. Boatman wanted information and having nothing for him wasn't going to be good enough with him walking into the unknown tomorrow. Alypia scooped the mussels into a bowl, the cooked molluscs steaming. She poured Provencal sauce on the top, the smell of tomato, chilli and garlic intoxicating both women. They dug in without ceremony, the mussel shells rattling against the bowl. Bella was plucking a mussel out of the shell when she spoke. "Where does Faust go for drinks when he's not working?"

"I wouldn't worry, you won't bump into him. Besides, he wouldn't have a clue who you are."

"That's not what I'm worried about," said Bella.

"Why do you want to know where he goes then?" Alypia had paused eating.

Bella had also stopped eating, "It's difficult to explain, but knowing where Faust goes when he's not working would really help me out."

"Why? You won't be able to hurt him. Bella, you shouldn't go near him, it's dangerous to know Faust. Trust me."

"Alypia, it's so hard to describe, but knowing something about your husband's habits would be good for my job."

"'Your husband?'" Alypia did air quotes with her fingers. "Why are you speaking to me like we're in an interrogation room? Who are you?"

Alypia felt so naive. Growing up as the Grand Senator's daughter meant she was regularly used as a political pawn. Whether it was to sweeten a deal with another senator by having her serving drinks as a distraction or her father making false promises of marriage to every important figure in Rome. She had grown close to someone before only to find out they were trying to get information about an upcoming trade deal and whether they could get rich out of it. Being with Faust was no different. At first he had been charming and almost telepathic in his understanding of her. Later, she realized that his photographic memory and deep psychological understanding meant he could read people like a book. Really, he had played her and exploited her vulnerabilities. He knew the power he could have by being her husband.

Now she was sitting here, with her new lover, thinking that maybe there was a chance at something normal and yet again she was just a pawn in someone else's fucked-up game. She couldn't remember the last time she had cooked a meal and felt the tinge of excitement about serving up something freshly prepared. She had felt a bit giddy with joy when she did the mundane task of shopping for ingredients. Just nonchalantly picking out a bulb of garlic was one of the most joyful things she had done in years. Being in the buzz of the Fish borough was exhilarating. Romans moaned about the smell of the fish market, but she adored it. It smelled of something genuine. It was busy and vibrant and people paid no notice to her. Someone even bumped into her as they walked past and didn't apologize. She wanted to laugh out loud. If that had happened at the Castrum or HoC they would have been on their knees in repentance. Being a nobody made her feel like a somebody.

"Is this the moment you want to shatter my trust? I cooked for you. I don't think you understand what that means to me. To cook for someone. Doing this," she waved her hand at the meal in front of them, "felt more intimate than us making love, Bella." She went to say something else but the words caught in her throat. She felt so stupid.

Bella felt her throat tighten too. "Darling, I…"

"Don't." Alypia clenched her fist. "Don't you dare 'Darling' me. Tell me who you are."

Bella had been caught out. She had thought the assignment to get close to Alypia was going to be easy. Yes, she found Alypia attractive, but her disdain for Roman aristocracy made her believe deceiving and plying information was going to be rather satisfying.

She didn't expect to find Alypia so utterly compelling. The night they first met had been predictable to Bella. Her aloofness had been like a drug to Alypia, and Bella initially assumed this Roman was just like the others.

She had been wrong. So very wrong.

Bella found herself falling fast and hard and wanted to build a life with Alypia. Tonight though, tonight highlighted how that was probably never possible because their relationship had been built on a foundation of lies. And lies crumble. So now she was sitting across the table from a woman who had let herself believe in something better to have it torn away in seconds. Bella hated herself.

"So?"

"Alypia, I swear my feelings for you are true. I was just trying to find the right time to talk to you about what I do."

Alypia slammed her fist on the table. "Stop avoiding the question."

"I work for Boatman."

The laugh was a resigned laugh, lacking in humor. "Of course you do. So you're lying when you say your feelings are real."

"No." Bella reached out her hand, hoping Alypia would take it. "No. I'm telling the truth." Alypia didn't respond to the gesture.

"Well either you're lying or you're stupid because as soon as *my husband* finds out about us and who you really are, I will be crucified on London Bridge like the rest of you rebel scum."

Bella stretched her hand out to Alypia again. "Come join us. Be a part of what we do."

There was that hollow laugh again. "You don't get it, do you? I don't want to be a part of what you do. I don't want to be associated with your leader and his barbarian followers."

Bella felt like she had been punched in the throat and only

managed a whisper. "But you said you're so unhappy in the roles you have in life."

"I am. I'm just a pawn. That doesn't mean I don't love Rome. By the gods, my life may be so completely unfulfilled, but Rome is so much more than me." She laughed again, this time with humor. "I was going to ask you to come back to Rome with me. My father would have given us protection from whatever retribution Faust might have planned. He won't protect me knowing I'm a traitor."

"Boatman can protect you."

"Like he protected his wife?"

Bella had no answer to that. Everything was collapsing, and Bella was struggling to see how she could save it. "He is a good man. He wants what's best for this country."

"Don't waste your breath with your propaganda, Bella. I'm immune."

"You would actually choose Nero over the change Boatman can bring?"

"What change, Bella? What change? If you managed to kill Nero, what difference would that make? Seriously? My father would call the Senate together and they would bring forth another emperor as bad as, or possibly worse than, Nero. Imagine a world with Bjorn Åska as emperor."

"We have to try."

"Try what? Futuo you're ignorant. Your little gang of merry rebels thinking you will make a blind bit of difference. It's pathetic."

Alypia stood up.

"Where are you going?"

"Home," said Alypia.

"I can't let you leave. You know too much."

"So kill me," said Alypia. She turned and walked away, saying,

"Faust drinks at The Victory if you're stupid enough to go there." She left leaving Bella sitting unmoving but for the tears falling onto her discarded mussel shells.

Chapter 45

Bella walked into Boatman's office at 4am exactly. Before Boatman could ask a question, Bella said, "She knows who I am."

"I thought the assignment was easy for you?"

"No assignment is easy."

"Clearly," said Boatman. "How compromised are we?"

"I'm not sure."

"Will she tell Faust about you?"

"I doubt it. It could put her life at risk."

Boatman stared hard at Bella. Bella tried to maintain eye contact but failed. "Are you compromised?"

Bella swallowed. It was weird with Boatman. He made people feel so at ease as a mentor and leader, but when something went wrong, he switched with complete ease. It was unnerving. "What do you mean?" Bella asked.

"Are you still focused on what we need to do?"

Bella looked Boatman in the eyes, "Always. I still think Alypia will turn to us," she lied.

Boatman didn't give any indication whether he believed that statement. "Does she know about the meeting."

"No, the conversation never got there. But she told me he drinks at The Victory. She didn't specify which one in the city. I assume there are a few pubs with that name."

"I need you to find out which Victory he drinks at," said Boatman. He looked at his watch and stood up. The meeting was over. "Bella, if your love for this woman has caused our mission to collapse, you know you can't be with us anymore," said Boatman.

Bella nodded.

"It would be exactly the same with Maverick or Tobias."

Bella nodded again and was dismissed. She went looking for Faust's drinking haunt, thinking she might kill the bastard herself if Boatman didn't today.

Boatman pondered Bella and whether Alypia could cause any damage. Any more damage, that is. He didn't feel confident that Alypia would somehow breeze back to Faust and fail to mention she had a brief affair with a member of the rebel effort. But then again, confessing to Faust might mean facing execution. Yes, she was the daughter of one of the most powerful men in the world, but Nero wasn't known for rational thought. If he were to be enraged by her treachery, he doubted the Grand Senator or Faust would be able to save her. Boatman mentally added yet another unknown to the pile of scenarios he was dealing with and left his office to face the major unknown of whether Faust was planning assassination or genuinely needed his help.

Faust had specified to meet at the Church of Constantine, which was a replica of the Church of Santa Costanza in Rome. Constantine had been a convert to the religion of the God-Carpenter and tried to convert the Empire to his beliefs. Many in Rome and beyond resisted, though, refusing to abandon the Roman gods who had provided so much prosperity for the Empire for so many years. He had fought a hard battle against those wishing to overthrow him and was going to radically overhaul Roman law and culture to officially make Christianity the Empire's main religion. A contender for the throne, Galerius, found this idea an abomination and met with Constantine, supposedly to try and dissuade him from angering the gods. In fact, Galerius had no intentions of diplomacy and stabbed the emperor to death. Galerius himself died soon after, executed by Constantine's bodyguards.

Even so, Constantine was revered for the achievements of his short life, and the church in London reflected that adoration for the young emperor. When Boatman arrived at the church, he thought it was just another tacky addition to the city. The Empire had hastily built various replicas of Roman architecture. From a distance it seemed to Boatman that a Roman god had vomited buildings on London. They didn't suit their surroundings.

It was only 6am, so it was dark and damp and quiet outside the church. Boatman had considered trying to scale a wall or enter through the back, but stealth seemed redundant. If he was walking to his death, he would do it bold as brass and enter through the front door. Which is what he did.

The doors were already unlocked and automatically opened as he stepped near them. The word *tacky* went through his mind again. The building was circular (to represent eternity) with an altar at the far end. There was a statue behind the altar of the God-Carpenter holding a hammer and chisel, arms outstretched. The hammer and chisel represented how this Jesus could mold you into someone new, just as he was able to create beauty out of wood. Tobias worshipped the God-Carpenter and went to church regularly. He had tried to convince Boatman to go, but Boatman saw enough darkness in himself to know a path of redemption wasn't meant for him.

The chairs were set out so that they followed the shape of the building. It meant the focal point of the room was the center. Tobias had said that was so that anyone and everyone in the room had the opportunity to take center stage, because the God-Carpenter saw no hierarchy in people. No wonder Constantine was murdered, Boatman had thought when he heard this.

On this November, morning the person taking center stage was Faust. He stood, waiting. Unmoving. Like the statue silhouetted behind him. Boatman glanced around the room to see if anyone lurked in the balcony. It was too dark to tell. Boatman stepped to the center of the room and stopped a few meters away from the centurion.

"Good morning," said Faust.

"Morning," said Boatman.

"You know, I've always loved that greeting. It's so very Britannic to wish someone a *good* morning. It's very polite. I love it. When I go back to Rome I make a point of saying it and am always met with strange looks." Faust laughed, "Romans are much more pragmatic with their greetings."

"I remember killing a former bodyguard of yours who had been sent to assassinate me. When I captured him after his poor attempt to kill me, I pressed him for information about you. The only thing he gave up was that to disarm people you share quirky little anecdotes. You think it makes people feel at ease and therefore they let their guard down."

"He was a good bodyguard."

"But poor assassin." Boatman smiled. Faust smiled back.

"I wasn't actually trying to disarm you. My anecdotes feel like a habit I can't shake off anymore."

"Normal people smoke as a habit."

"I do that, too."

"Maybe you need a therapist with all these habits," said Boatman.

"I don't think a therapist would enjoy time with me."

"I think that applies to most people," said Boatman.

Faust laughed. "You know, when we met briefly, those years ago, you were very serious. No humor. Being with The Beast and Tobias has given you a bit of a lighter side."

"And you being a patronizing asshole hasn't changed," said Boatman. "Incidentally, don't mention Tobias again or I will rip your throat out."

"Fair enough," said Faust.

"You have me alone. What do you want? Or do you need your drones to give you the all clear?"

Faust absently stroked his beard and looked up to the balcony. "I kept to my word about being alone. Unlike you."

"I'm alone."

"This morning you are, I assume. Yesterday you weren't. You lied."

Boatman laughed this time. "A Roman centurion outraged by lying. I seem to recall you stabbing one of my men in the back." Boatman stepped forward. "Like a coward."

"We're all cowards, Boatman, it's just how we cover the cowardice up. That's why I wanted to meet you alone. Face my fears and all that."

Boatman scoffed. "You're not afraid of me."

"Oh, I am. I really am. You occupy a place in my mind, and whenever I visit you I am terrified as I have no idea how I would physically defeat you."

"Take a risk now," said Boatman. Faust went to laugh but before even a snigger could come out of his mouth, Boatman was on him and had a knife at his throat. Boatman's speed was almost mystical and one of the reasons he was feared so much by Roman soldiers. Faust had thought he understood Boatman's skill and speed, but the almost undetectable movement was more than impressive. Faust wasn't even able to reach for *his* hidden knife before feeling the blade against his throat. Boatman had moved his way behind Faust, his right arm around his throat and his left hand holding a knife near Faust's eye.

"I stand corrected," said Faust.

"What?"

"You're still just as serious as when I first met you."

Boatman pressed the knife against the Roman's skin and said, "I've wanted Nero dead for as long as I can remember, but my wife said something quite jarring last night. She asked me what would happen after Nero is killed? Who would be emperor? I may kill him, but that wouldn't kill the Empire. So really, why should I bother with him when I can pick off parts of the Empire with people like you?"

Boatman pressed the knife harder. Faust winced.

"Wait." Faust was breathing hard. He had been caught out by Boatman's speed. He had wandered through his memory palace the night before and analyzed Boatman's behaviors. The thing he had discovered was that Boatman was pragmatic. Yes, he had been ferocious many, many times. Yes, there were plenty of bodies, killed by Boatman's hands, whose blood had stained the streets, but Boatman killed almost objectively. He did it because it was necessary. He was rarely impulsive because being impulsive usually meant mistakes. But right now, Faust found himself subject to Boatman's impulsiveness and had not predicted it.

"Wait," Faust said again.

"I have a good friend in my medical wing and here's a chance to be done with you and your fucking anecdotes," said Boatman. He positioned the knife between Faust's ribs.

"Nero isn't Augustus's son."

Boatman eased the pressure on the knife. "What?"

"Nero," Faust said, trying to stay calm, "he's not Augustus's biological son."

"You're talking shit because you're about to die," said Boatman.

Just as Boatman went to plunge the knife into Faust's side, Faust said, "I have evidence! In my jacket. Nero isn't the rightful emperor! I have proof!"

Boatman hesitated.

"Just think about it for a moment. If he's basically an imposter, killing him tears the Empire apart. Which is what you want."

"What do you get out of it."

"Freedom," said Faust. "I want to get out of your shitty country." Faust held his hands up, "No offense."

Boatman lowered the knife but didn't loosen his grip on the Roman's neck. "If you have the evidence on your person then I don't need you." Boatman raised his knife again.

"That's only half of what you need," said Faust quickly.

Boatman paused again. "What do you mean?"

"Just ease the pressure a bit would you?"

"Not a chance," said Boatman.

"No harm in asking," said Faust.

Boatman pressed the knife. "Stop stalling."

Faust raised his hand in submission. "The evidence I have on Nero proves it's worth killing him, but you won't be able to unless I give you the information on how to get to him."

"I'll storm the HoC," said Boatman.

"Well, you won't. As we speak there's going to be an emergency alert relating to the safety of the emperor. A credible threat to life. He will be bundled into a bunker that is practically impenetrable. There's no way you would be able to get in."

"But you can."

The knife was making rivets of blood on Faust's cheek. He gritted his teeth. "Yes."

"Show me what you have. Slowly." Boatman moved away.

Faust carefully reached into his jacket and pulled out an envelope. He held it out to Boatman. Boatman took it and examined the contents. He looked up at Faust. "There's been plenty of emperors who weren't biologically connected, which the Senate approved."

"Do you think the Senate will accept a bastard whose real father was so depraved? After what Nero did to Jonas, the Senate would welcome Nero's demise."

Boatman read through the papers again. "Why not just take this to the Grand Senator?"

"And what would they do?"

Boatman didn't respond. He knew the answer. Even if Nero's legitimacy were questioned, the Senate wouldn't be able to do anything. They were too afraid. Nero would come for them in the night. A dead man couldn't, though. Boatman felt a tingle of hope. He put the evidence in his own pocket. "What do I need to know?"

Faust proceeded to go through everything with the rebel leader.

Chapter 46

Olivia woke up at around the same time Boatman was meeting Faust. She didn't wake gently, though, she woke with a terrible pain in her head. Well, not so much like pain as like someone else's pain was intruding in her mind. Olivia had been to see a local priestess when she was a teenager because the noises in her head caused her to think she was possessed. The priestess prayed over her and revealed Olivia had been bestowed with the gift of necromancy. She was blessed with the powers of the goddess Diana. Olivia's father instantly dismissed these claims as superstitious nonsense and refused to engage with any talk of it. Because of her father's derision for what the priestess had said, Olivia made every effort to conceal the extreme empathy she felt on a regular basis.

She too wasn't convinced she had the powers of a goddess, but she did know that she felt people's pain and that made life difficult. Which is why she became a psychiatrist. She hoped that by almost traveling in other pain she would be able to help them navigate out of it. Sometimes it worked and sometimes it didn't.

This particular morning though, she felt overwhelming terror. It wasn't a terror of someone or something else, it was a terror from within. It was like being afraid of herself.

I can't cope with this fire in my head.

I can't deal with this pain.

I'm scared of what I will do.

I'm scared of myself.

I'm scared of Sam.

Sam.

Olivia got out of bed, dressed and made her way to Sam and Molly's apartment. She knocked on the door until it opened. Molly stood there, tired eyes, hair messy from sleep. Olivia got down on one knee to be more at Molly's level.

"Hey, is your mom at home? My name's Olivia."

"She doesn't like people seeing her when she has her bedroom door closed."

"Do you think it would be okay if I saw her? I just want to make sure she's okay." Olivia held out her right hand and made the 'pinky promise' sign. "I promise not to bother her for too long."

Molly stared at Olivia's hand and didn't reciprocate the gesture. "She might get mad at me."

"I promise to tell her you've done nothing wrong. I only want to have a quick chat with her."

"She won't be happy that it's so early."

"I know, sweetie. I will be really quick." She held out her hand again. This time Molly entertained the gesture.

"She's in her room." Molly guided Olivia through the generic apartment. Sam's bedroom was at the back, past the kitchen. Olivia felt a pang of unease as she went through the kitchen and saw a pile of plates and dishes. The surfaces were cluttered and the sink was full of dirty utensils and crockery.

They got to Sam's room and Olivia said. "If it's okay with you,

Sweetie, can you just go and watch one of your favorite shows in your room? I need to have a bit of a grownup chat with your mommy."

"Has Boatman hurt her too?"

Olivia faltered. "Why would you say that? Of course he hasn't."

"I have bad dreams about him," said Molly.

Olivia pulled Molly in close. "You don't need to worry about Boatman. He's a nice man. He would never hurt your mommy."

Molly sighed, as if she wanted to say something but hugged into Olivia instead. "Mommy's not very well."

"Okay, Sweetie, I won't bother her for too long."

Molly let go of Olivia and made her way back to her room.

Olivia took a deep breath and turned the handle of Sam's door. She felt such a darkness that it scared her. When she opened the door and walked in, she saw Sam on the bed. She was on her back, arms in a crucifix position and her body pale. Olivia had learned to deal with dead bodies; being Boatman's wife, she was never going to avoid them. There was something brutal and unnecessary about suicide, though. Olivia knew it was suicide straight away. Her gut told her before her logic kicked in. On closer inspection, Olivia saw empty pill packets on the floor and on the bed. There was an empty bottle of wine cast aside on the bed and, amazingly, a cigarette butt still in-between Sam's fingers. The shock of a dead body overwhelmed her, but days later she would muse on how it was a miracle the apartment hadn't burned down.

Olivia carefully removed the cigarette butt from Sam's fingers. She looked around for a bin but then felt disrespectful for putting the butt in a bin, as if it was a sacred object, and slid the butt into her jeans instead. She did nothing else to Sam's body but pulled the duvet over the body to make sure it was hidden from Molly.

She thought about the anguish that had ripped through her mind last night and how Sam had been crying out. She felt guilty because if only she had been sooner. If only she had been more aware. She couldn't help think about what Molly had said only moments before Olivia had opened the bedroom door: *Has Boatman hurt her too?*

A little girl had been in contact with Boatman and all she had seen in a very short time was death and destruction. Olivia felt Molly was right; Boatman had hurt Sam too.

She left the room and closed the door. Molly appeared again. Olivia had spent years helping adults to process grief, but standing front of this little girl, knowing her mother was dead in the room next door, well, that was a different kind of grief. Olivia didn't know how she was going to explain things to Molly so just pulled her in close.

Molly didn't resist or stiffen. She allowed the hug to envelope her, and that told Olivia a lot about the little girl's understanding of her mother's demise.

Chapter 47

Faust watched Boatman leave the church and breathed out. He had never seen Boatman as an impulsive killer but, for a moment, he'd thought he was wrong. He waited for Boatman to be out of sight and then made his way out the back of the church. He opened the back door and stepped out. A hand grabbed his scruff and a knife went against his throat.

"Futuo," said Faust. "I thought I saw you leave. I swear the information I gave is real."

"I couldn't give a fuck about the information."

Faust paused. "I assume saying sorry isn't enough?"

"Like I said, I'll repay you with the wound you gave Tobias. Professional courtesy."

"Hello, Maverick. By the gods, don't you all take a break?"

"Tobias isn't taking break from the knife you shoved in him."

"He brought that on himself."

"Just like you've brought this moment on yourself."

Faust was impressed. He thought the attack on Tobias had scared the rebels enough to not push their luck by going against conditions a second time around.

"I would have thought Boatman would have been more intelligent than to kill me, considering our conversation a few moments ago."

"I wouldn't know, I haven't spoken to Boatman."

"So you're rebelling against the rebel leader. And people say the Empire is dysfunctional."

"Dysfunctional or not, at least I can put another one of you motherfuckers in the grave."

A voice came from behind Maverick. "This is not the time, Mav."

"Seems a good a time as any, I should have blown his face off in the HoC. We're being treated like mugs, Boatman."

"Think of your brother."

Maverick pushed Faust to the ground and punched him hard in the face. A six-foot-five behemoth like Maverick bringing his fist down on anyone would cause instant unconsciousness. And it did. Faust went out like a light.

He turned to Boatman, Faust crumpled on the floor, no longer a threat. "Fuck you. Seriously, fuck you. Don't bring Damba into this. He's dead."

"You don't know that."

"He might as well be if Max had his way with him." Maverick kicked the unconscious body of Faust and growled in frustration and anger. "This motherfucker almost killed Tobias. The fucking Roman who almost killed your wife has my brother hostage. How can you deal with them?"

It was Boatman's turn to show frustration. He shoved his sword into the dirt. He ran his hands through his hair and paced like a lion ready to pounce. Maverick felt himself tense; Boatman moved so fast if was impossible to anticipate. "Don't be so naive, Maverick. Of course we have to do a deal with them. If we kill him," Boatman pointed at Faust, "then we step backwards in trying to get rid of Nero." Boatman was still pacing, "Why am I having to explain this all the time?" Boatman stopped pacing and sighed. "You came to me, remember? You chose Britannia over Rome in order to save your brother. You chose the long game."

Shit. Boatman's words stung. They stung in their truth. He had chosen finding Boatman's help in order to save Damba over storming Rome in rage, and Boatman was right, there was a long game that needed to be followed. If Damba was valuable to the Romans' mission of flushing out Maverick, then he wasn't going to be disposed of anytime soon. Having a fiancé in hospital and a good friend lucky to be alive though meant it was hard to understand the long game at times. For Maverick, as a gladiator and as a warrior, long games usually meant death. He saw a threat and removed it before damage was done. Seeing Faust sprawled on the floor made his instincts flare with the need for survival. Faust needed to die in the short term to remove yet another danger. In the long term though, Faust provided a gateway to maybe saving Damba. Objectively, it was so obvious. Emotionally, though, nothing was obvious.

Boatman walked over to Faust and checked his pulse. He looked up at Maverick, "You nearly knocked his head clean off."

"I'm happy to have another go."

"I'd rather you didn't. He has some vital information so I need his head still attached." Boatman looked at the unconscious centurion. "Although it doesn't look like I'll get anything out of him for a few hours." Boatman stood up. "Probably best to put him somewhere a bit more comfortable until he wakes up."

Maverick obliged and grabbed the scruff of Faust's jacket and dragged him back into the church. He pulled Faust like a rag doll through the rear hallway and into the main hall. As he walked into the hall with the Roman an almost comical extension to him, he nearly bumped into a priest who was preparing the church for the day ahead. The priest nearly jumped backward in fright of the giant man in front of him. Maverick, not unused to people's fearful reactions to him said, "Apologies. I didn't mean to scare you."

The priest, who clearly knew how to compose himself quickly, said, "Not at all. I don't usually see anyone here this early seeking to worship."

"Well, we won't get in your way," said Maverick.

The priest looked quizzical. "We?"

Maverick sometimes forgot about his presence. Being with Tobias, Bella and Boatman for so long made him forget about his size. They never acted intimidated by him or even impressed by his utter hugeness, so when people paused or gasped when they saw him it took him a moment to realize why. Also, those confronted by a six-foot-five muscle mountain tended to focus on the mountain's face. Which is what the priest was doing, so he hadn't noticed that Maverick wasn't alone and had the body of a Roman centurion by his right leg. Maverick glanced down as a hint and the priest followed his gaze. "Oh!"

"I think he has been overwhelmed by the power of the Holy Spirit," said Maverick. Maverick let go of Faust's jacket, and the Roman collapsed on the floor. "When he wakes he will be on fire with God's power," said Maverick. Maverick stepped over Faust and left the church.

The priest stared at the now empty doorway wondering if he had actually seen The Beast. He looked down at the unconscious man and it kickstarted his protectiveness, and he quickly knelt beside the body to check he was still alive. The priest then realized who he was looking at. He knew Faust. Hell, most of London knew Faust. Faust wasn't a centurion; he was a celebrity. His wife was an idol. They were the power couple of Britannia. A priest wouldn't ordinarily worry about such terms as 'power couple' but this couple brought huge numbers to his church. He adored Faust and Alypia because they only worshipped at the church every couple of months but it was enough to make people attend every week in hope of seeing them.

He slapped Faust's face to rouse him, but the Roman didn't wake. The priest shrugged. He'd had far worse dumped at the doors of his church. An unconscious centurion and staring into the eyes of The Beast, though, that made great material inspiration for his preach. He slapped Faust again, just to be sure and then made his way to his office to start scribbling notes.

Chapter 48

Boatman and Maverick got back to Boatman's office and started to read through the information Faust had passed over. It appeared that Augustus kept a diary and somehow Faust was privy to its details. Maverick raised his eyebrows when he read it. According to DNA results, which Faust had obtained too, Nero wasn't the biological son of Augustus. In fact, it appeared he was the biological son of Augustus's sister, Claudia.

It was 1981, and one of the hottest summers in Rome's history. The heat had made some people behave strangely. Heat always did that. It made people want to fight and fuck. Augustus's bodyguard had burst into Augustus's residence without warning. He was carrying the limp figure of Claudia. She was bloodied and unconscious. The bodyguard explained he had found her on the steps at the gated entrance to the emperor's palace. Augustus adored his sister. He worshipped her. She ensured he stayed human. As an emperor, it was easy for him to forget the humanity of the world he ruled and become detached from the core reasons for being a person. As a child looks through a magnifying glass and scorches ants, so too does an emperor scorch his conquered peoples if he's not careful. Augustus wanted to be revered the way his namesake of two millennia ago had been, and Claudia brought empathy to his table when he needed it. Jonas brought pragmatic criticism, and Claudia brought emotional stability.

When Augustus saw his sister had been raped and beaten, he flew out of his residence to call his entire protective legion to go find the animal who had done this to her. The thing was, standing at his residence entrance was Centurion Ira. Centurion Ira was Augustus's blunt instrument. He did the dirty work no-one else wanted to do. And that was very dirty work considering Rome was famous for not being concerned about morally repulsive tactics.

Ira enjoyed being the blunt instrument of the emperor. His violence kept dissenters quiet. Augustus liked to believe he was like his namesake from two millennia ago, who was known as a prince of peace. He believed that the combination of making his supporters rich and being seen to be an advocate of peace and prosperity would mean the history books would be kind to him. There was a dark underbelly to his reign, though. He wasn't like Nero, who openly adored the fear he created. Nero relished in terror. No, not Augustus. He wanted to be loved and revered after his death. He was desperate for that adulation, so anything or anyone who created a counter to that narrative made him angry. He couldn't be seen as openly angry about those admonished him, though. He had to be angry behind the scenes.

Centurion Ira allowed Augustus to be the personification of his anger, but in the shadows. Ira made people disappear or have an unfortunate accident. He was good at what he did. Ira's role as the emperor's assassin was never public, but a loud whisper through the Empire named Ira 'the Rage of Caesar.' Of course, it worked wonderfully for Augustus while he lived. To be publicly abhorred at

Ira's actions could potentially mean you would find Ira standing at the foot of your bed one night. It was better to not talk about him.

Augustus saw Ira like a son. Ira's allegiance and willingness to do anything for his Caesar meant Augustus had a deep affection for the man. It helped Augustus to love his young centurion too by not being told any details of what had become of anyone unfortunate enough to cross paths with the Rage of Caesar. So this was the problem, when Augustus found his not-so-secret assassin standing at the entrance to his palace, covered in blood.

Augustus knew immediately that it was Ira who had raped Claudia. He just knew. If he had been honest with himself, he would have sought to protect Claudia. He had seen the way Ira moved his eyes over every inch of her body. Augustus had seen the primal look in Ira's eyes and chosen to ignore what that meant. He relied on Ira to keep his opponents silent and, therefore, his profile pristine. Even if he didn't admit it, that had been more important than Claudia's safety. Now that desire for adoration proved he had been negligent in protecting his sister.

Augustus and Ira stared at each other for a few moments, both men unsure of what the next few moments would mean. Augustus's initial rage at the treatment of his sister had dispersed. He knew it had dispersed because, essentially, he felt a closer bond to his personal assassin. He *knew* he should be calling his guards to detain Ira, drag him off and beat him within an inch of his life, but he found his mouth was dry and his words empty. He didn't want to do that. He wanted to pretend Ira had done nothing and this incident could be ignored. But his sister was beaten and traumatized. His sister had trusted the way, he imagined, a number of people he had ordered to be killed had. Claudia was the representation of all of Augustus's orders. And he should have felt shame.

Ira was the first to speak. "Things got out of hand."

"That's the emperor's sister. My sister." Augustus felt exposed. His protective legion were at the main entrance of his estate, guarding it just in case anyone who had hurt Claudia tried to gain access to hurt the emperor. No-one thought to question Ira as he walked in all bloody. Most soldiers who knew Ira assumed him being covered in blood was normal. Augustus knew Ira wouldn't kill him because he would die within minutes of the act, but that didn't comfort him as much as he would have liked. "How could you?"

Ira laughed. "How could I? The fuck is wrong with you? All I do, week after week, is kill people." Ira laughed again, he was pacing. "How could I?" He said it more to himself this time. "If you breed a monster, Caesar, then sometimes that monster slides out from underneath where you've been trying to hide him and he does horrible things."

Augustus had a panic button in his jacket and had pressed it. His bodyguard and a portion of the protective legion were now surrounding Ira. Caesar held up his hand to indicate that no-one hurt Ira. "You're finished, you understand?"

"Crucifixion will be a relief."

"Crucifixion?" Augustus felt his eyes prick with tears. "You've been like a son to me, Ira, I can't kill you."

Ira laughed again. "Then why are you being a sentimental fool by crying?"

Augustus was sad, genuinely sad. He knew Ira was damaged, but he loved him. He loved him because he would do what Augustus could never do. "Because I'm going to miss you. Because I won't ever see you again once you are in the Aestii province."

Ira's face went white. There wasn't much that scared a psychopath like Ira, but the Aestii province was certainly one of them.

"Caesar," Ira was stuttering, "You can't send me there."

Augustus took one last look at his adopted son, turned his back and walked back into his palace. The soldiers closed the doors to muffle the shouts and cries of a desperate man realizing that he was being sent to a place even demons would be afraid of.

Augustus had shed a tear for Ira, because the torment of Aestii would cause Ira to pray for an early death. His sister though, she needed the emperor to look after her and the baby. He had no choice. Claudia resented her pregnancy and resented her baby because of the trauma she had endured to give birth to him. Augustus quickly stepped in and treated that baby like his son. In the end, he decided that baby should be his son. Only he seemed able to form a relationship and the boy's mother appeared happy that maybe the boy would disappear from her life. When the boy was born, Claudia recoiled from the infant, remarking that he was grotesque. Augustus scolded his sister for such a comment about her own child, but Claudia said, "It's not my child, it's a tumor that has been removed."

In private, Augustus agreed the boy was ugly, with his overhanging brow, large nose and ears and small mouth. In fact, Augustus thought he was the reincarnation of another emperor and therefore named him Nero. The biggest problem for Augustus was that in the fourth Century, after Constantine's son and grandson became rightful heirs to the throne, a dynasty of rulers appeared not by birthright but by coup. Generals and senators claiming the throne through deceit and treachery. Emperor Nepotianus put a stop to that by forging an alliance with Western and Eastern armies. He was seen as naive because of his belief in his right to the throne, being the nephew of Constantine, but he had his uncle's intelligence. He quickly drew together the East and West and, in turn, quashed those seeking to usurp Nepotianus.

When the emperor had shown his strength and, for some, proof of his god-given right to be ruler, he introduced a law, passed through the Senate, that only those in a genetic line, directly from the emperor, could be declared Caesar. That law had remained engrained in Rome up until the present day. This is where Augustus had a problem. Even though Claudia's son was technically connected to Augustus, he would be viewed as an imposter because he wasn't a direct descendant. A bastard nephew. He had to pretend he had a biological son to keep the dynasty going.

Augustus lived to see Nero have a son and lived long enough to see that Max was a magnified version of Nero. He was an abomination. Near his death, Augustus lamented that his legacy would not be one of peace and prosperity but seeing a lineage of men each more corrupt in their souls than the last.

He died wondering he had destroyed an Empire that had lasted for over two millennia.

When Boatman and Maverick finished reading the material, they both found themselves surprised by Augustus. He hadn't raised a monster, he had simply been the caretaker of a monster. A monster who produced a bigger monster. That was some legacy.

"So technically the Empire died with Augustus," said Maverick.

"It seems that way." Boatman thought about it for a moment. "So Nero and his armies have actually been imposters. We're not the rebels at all." Boatman laughed.

"Do you think if we make an announcement about this the Romans might all bugger off?"

"If we can at least put Nero and Faust in the ground, I'd settle for that."

Maverick wasn't sure whether to say anything, but his boyfriend in critical care meant he had lost any sense of diplomacy (if he'd had any in the first place), "That's quite a climb down from wanting to expel the Romans from Britannia."

"Your partner was nearly in the ground. My wife was nearly in the ground. A soldier I thought I could save is now in the ground. Olivia has texted me to say Kevin's wife is dead from suicide. At this rate, there won't be anyone left to expel the Romans." Boatman slumped on his chair behind his desk. "I just want one win now."

"We got Max."

"He's under twenty-four hour security, so we didn't get him. You said you did, but you didn't."

"He must have a head made of iron."

"I must have a head made of iron because this is all futile. It always has been." Boatman closed his eyes and leaned his head back against his chair. "Remember when I said we would get Damba back to you?"

Maverick nodded. "That's what keeps me going."

"I think I lied." Boatman continued. "Not in a deliberate way." Boatman opened his eyes, sat up and looked at Maverick. "Believe me, I have always wanted to get your brother back to you." He sighed and rubbed his eyes. By the gods he was tired. "I just think I was lying to myself. How am I going to bring down an Empire?"

"By burning down their house," said Maverick. Maverick thought for a moment, choosing his words, thinking of Tobias in his hospital bed. "I need to finish the job with Max. I need to go to Rome. I need to destroy the house of Nero."

"But Faust has shown us that information so that I can kill Nero, here in London."

"Faust might be lying. He lied about the last meeting and now look at Tobias."

Boatman rubbed his face. "But I need you here. If Faust is telling the truth, then we have the moment we've been waiting for."

"You've been waiting for," corrected Maverick. "Faust is a liar. Tobias can vouch for that. I'm not playing his games anymore."

Boatman ruffled. "It's not a request. You're not going anywhere. You're staying and seeing this through."

"You have Bella, she's the best there is."

"I can't have any of my team scattered across the globe. We need to stick together, take Nero out and then we can move in on Max. We stick to the plan."

Maverick laughed. "What plan? Come on, Boatman, I thought you were a master strategist? *If* you kill the emperor, then the chances of getting to Max will be near zero. They're vulnerable and distracted by what we're doing in London. They're also arrogant pricks. Who would be stupid enough to try and kill Max in Rome?"

"You would be."

"Exactly. But they don't know that."

Boatman needed to think, but he knew there wasn't time for thinking. And as much as he thought he could control Maverick, he knew Maverick needed to be allowed to be Maverick. Maverick had been Roman property since he was a child, managed to escape and was now being told he belonged to someone else. If Boatman really was fighting for people's freedom then he was a hypocrite for trying to stop Maverick by flexing his own power. Maverick knew what Boatman was capable of but he also knew that Boatman was pragmatic enough to know the fights worth contesting. Maverick was right about Bella, too. She was the best of the best and this was going to be an assassination. If you wanted anyone by your side to perform such a task you would be lucky to have someone even half as skilled and deadly as Bella.

"When are you leaving?"

"Now," said Maverick. "I need to get out of Britannia before you do what you need to do and they close all the borders. I'll get smuggled out via the Fish borough."

Boatman nodded and Maverick left.

Chapter 49

Bella met with Boatman, and she looked at all the evidence Faust had passed over. To Bella, it seemed clear cut that in the event of Nero's death, the evidence she was reading about him would send a fissure through the Empire. A bastard son of a rapist centurion (although that seemed tenuous to Bella considering how many Roman centurions had bastard children) whose child was now comatose made it appear there wasn't much legitimacy to the line of emperors anymore.

In Bella's mind, there had never been much legitimacy. Somehow, Caesar after Caesar survived and ruled and expanded the Empire. She never understood how. Maybe it was the gods.

As she read the information about Nero, there was a footnote written by Faust with a question about where Nero's father would be now, '*Dead?*' Seeing Faust's handwriting made her think of Alypia and something caught in her throat.

"You okay?"

Bella coughed and cleared her throat. "Yeah, fine."

"What happened?"

"Nothing, it's fine."

"Shall we go through everything?"

Bella nodded. "Where's Maverick?"

"Separate mission," said Boatman.

Bella didn't push on the details so spent the next few hours going through what seemed like a suicide mission.

Chapter 50

Faust woke up with a blanket over him. He was in a back room of the Church of Constantine. He tried to work out why the hell he was still in the church and couldn't remember anything beyond speaking with Boatman in the main hall. He sat up and felt inside his jacket. Well he'd given Boatman the information about Nero, so that was good. Why he was still at the church though? That worried him. His head was pounding like he'd drunk a gallon of English wine. He felt the right side of his face and his cheek was swollen to hell. Either he'd fallen from a great height or someone had decided to smash him in the face with a sledgehammer.

Wait.

Faust closed his eyes and went into his memory palace. It was a bit trickier walking up its stairs and through the doors because of the blinding headache, but he made it. He traversed the black and white tiled floor in the entrance hall, skirted past the marble staircase to more important memories and went to a door underneath the stairs. He opened the door and a smell of regret invaded his nostrils. In the waking world, he guessed the smell would be similar to sweat from a seedy encounter. Like his wife had done, but that was for another time.

He descended the stairs, wrinkling his mind palace nose. He got to the bottom of the stairs and walked over to a tatty boxing ring. He climbed in and looked at a framed picture of Cassisus Clay hanging above the ring. Clay was, arguably, the greatest fighter of all time. He was an African fighter, specifically from Ghana, and was hated by the Empire because he annihilated every Roman boxer they put forward. The Romans had tried to make Clay a gladiator but his boxing prowess made them much more money. The portrait of Clay began to change and merged in to that of Maverick.

Maverick.

That was it.

Maverick's image then floated from the frame and descended upon the boxing ring. Within moments there was a dreamlike figure of Maverick standing before Faust. Before Faust could react Maverick swung his fist to punch Faust in the face. Just as Maverick's fist was about to connect, his image froze. Faust stepped away from the frozen fist and tilted his head.

That was it.

Faust opened his eyes, taking himself out of his mind palace. Maverick had almost punched his head off. It wasn't exactly the truce he thought he had been assured. Maybe in using Boatman to kill Nero, he could slip in a way to have Maverick killed too. Faust got off the sofa and slipped out of the back entrance of the church. He needed to get ready. If they were going to kill the emperor of the world, they needed to be organized. And killing someone out of ego wasn't going to help the situation. Also, killing Maverick meant he had fewer options for a decoy.

He made his way home, walking slowly with each step making

his head pound, and tried to formulate how he would succeed in killing both the emperor of the world and also the leader of the rebel world. However he was going to pull it off, he needed to get his head down for a few hours so his brain stopped rattling around his skull from being punched by the personification of a hurricane. Clay may have floated like a butterfly and stung like a bee, but Faust needed to sting like a nuclear blast.

Chapter 51

Nero pressed the connect button on his laptop and it dialed Rome. Grand Senator Frigus appeared on the screen. "Hail, Caesar."

"Good evening Frigus."

"Good evening, Lord."

"How's my son?"

Frigus shifted in his seat. "There's not much change to his condition, unfortunately. He's responding to certain sensory cues but he isn't able to verbalize anything. Yet. There's optimism he will recover."

"I'm optimistic I will get a hard-on after five quarts of wine, but that doesn't mean it will happen, Frigus. I don't need optimism from a doctor, I need pragmatism. I need to know if the sole heir to the Empire will recover or was Max being born about as useful as that fucking Senate I seem to allow to operate each year?"

"I recall your grandfather found the Senate to be a good source of balance for his decisions, which is why we're still here today. *My Lord.* Democracy keeps us all in safe play. And, with all due respect, you don't allow us to operate, the Constitution of Rome ensures we operate."

"Frigus, don't bore me with your deluded idea of a democracy. I'll stamp on your neck if you dare try to stand in my way. Our relationship remains magnanimous because you handle the boredom of policy detail. Don't step outside of that or your body will be dumped in the same spot as Jonas's was."

"You can't threaten me."

"Shut the fuck up. I will take your whore of a daughter and nail her to a cross on live stream and then send her body back to Rome and have it strung up outside your Senate Palace, you piece of shit." Spittle had formed round the edges of Nero's mouth. "You fucking hear me?"

Frigus remained silent and nodded.

Nero was breathing hard. What the hell was wrong with these morons? Everywhere he went, he was confronted by arrogance and disrespect. He was appointed by the gods to rule this god-forsaken planet. He was ordained by powers beyond this earth to drag these plebs to a place of worthiness. His son was possibly a vegetable and therefore cursed by the gods and created a chance the rule of the Caesars would come to an end after his death. He had the literal weight of the world on him, and he was being distracted by imbeciles like Frigus.

"I want to hear that my son is getting better, you understand me? When we next speak you will have news that Maximus is improving. By the gods, if those words aren't coming out of your mouth, then I will come for you." Nero cut the connection to a rather pale-looking Grand Senator.

He got up from his desk and walked over to his drinks cabinet. The cabinet had a mirror on one of the doors and Nero stared at his reflection. His black eyes stared back. When Nero was born, his mother wasn't surprised the child had eyes as black as coal.

Claudia believed Nero was the son of the devil and his eyes only confirmed her fears. Augustus, at first, was horrified by those eyes as it seemed like baby Nero had no soul, but he believed he could show Nero how to be a leader with compassion and maybe it would bring color to those eyes. That never happened, and in his final months before the shadows of death overwhelmed him, Augustus saw only evil in Nero. Nero though, he loved his black eyes. He loved the reactions of people he met for the first time and how they tried to hide their shock. They always failed. Fear and shock were his tools to maintaining power, and his eyes helped keep those tools sharp.

He pulled a bottle of red wine from the cabinet, poured a drink and went and sat on the sofa. He thought about getting a hooker to torment, to try and take his mind off the fact that he was still in London, but before he could do it there was knock at his door. He told whoever it was to enter. It was Faust.

"My Lord, there is another credible and imminent threat to your life, we need to move you to the safety of the bunker."

Nero barely reacted to Faust's warning and took a drink of his wine. He smacked his lips, overdoing the enjoyment he was getting.

"My Lord?"

After another swig of his wine, Nero spoke, "Tell me, Faust, where are your ancestors from?"

Another game, thought Faust. He had to play it. "Germanica, mainly."

"That makes sense," said Nero

"It does?"

"Of course," Nero necked the rest of his wine and got up from the sofa to pour a refill. "There were a bunch of Germanic schemers, ready to take over the Empire but my father stamped them out before they could." Nero clicked his fingers, "What were they called?"

"Nazis," said Faust.

"Ah, yes, that's it. Cute name. That Hitler had delusions of grandeur, didn't he? A real schemer that one, from what my father said. You know what his mistake was?"

Faust slightly shook his head.

"He thought he was cleverer than he really was." Nero eyed Faust. "Schemers are like that."

"I'm sure they are," said Faust.

Nero burst into laughter, like a rabid animal. "Oh dear Faust, you're very hard to read. Would you like some wine?"

"No, my Lord, we need to get to the bunker. You're not safe here."

"I'm not going anywhere."

"Lord, you need to."

"I don't need to do anything. I'm staying here. I'm in the HoC with hundreds of soldiers, if you can't protect me here then I should strip you of your rank, *Centurion* Faust."

"But we know what Boatman is capable of, keeping you here puts the odds of him getting to you much higher."

"Schemers, schemers, schemers. They're everywhere. Are you like your Germanic ancestors, Herr Faust?"

Faust knew he had to shut this conversation down before booze and rage dominated Nero's mindset. Nero was unstable at the best of times. Adding paranoia, red wine and the thought of confinement to that instability made it impossible to know what would happen. "Of course not, my Lord, you're absolutely correct, I need to keep you protected here. I will post soldiers on every floor."

Nero waved his hand to dismiss Faust, bored of him. Faust left and Nero heard the centurion barking orders to form a protective detail around the emperor's office. Nero was happy to remain in his office. He had wine and sofas to lounge on. He wasn't worried about Boatman getting into the building. A part of him was hoping for it, because if Boatman was going to be here then that meant The Beast would be too and, by the gods, he really wanted to look The Beast in the eye. And then pluck those eyes out. The fear Boatman and The Beast caused in the soldiers was pathetic. Yes, he had seen the carnage these men had wrought on the Roman occupation of London and he had seen the destruction they had brought to Maximus, but, at the end of the day, they were just men. They were men who weren't worthy of even licking the mud off his boots. He was god-made man. He was the foundation that held the Empire together. These two men were an inconvenience, a blip in his grand designs for the Empire. Britannia was his, and would remain his. Britannia was a gray, miserable stepping stone to getting his forces to the RIA. Boatman and The Beast were bugs who scuttered around on his stepping stone. It was time to look at these bugs close up and squash them.

Nero wandered over to one of the windows of his office that looked out over the River Thames. It was lunchtime, and the river was busy with half a dozen fishing boats steaming back and forth catching the first salmon of the season. Long fishing lines were strung out over the stern of each boat. Each boat would catch up to one thousand salmon per trip which would provide a very healthy salary for the skipper and their crew. There were limited days on which they could hook salmon, but despite the short season it was still lucrative. Nero watched as one boat hauled its lines, silver flashes of flapping salmon being brought aboard. He felt an odd sensation of jealousy watching the fishermen go about their work. It was simple for them. No politics. No house of cards ready to fall. Just cast your line and wait for something to bite. He smiled. Maybe being an emperor wasn't so different.

He walked away from the window and over to a small table where he had a bottle of wine. As he started to pour another glass, he felt a breath of air on his neck. Strange, he hadn't opened a window. Before he could turn around to see where the breeze originated from, he felt the chill of a blade on his throat and a powerful hand gripping the back of his neck, manipulating the pressure points there. "Hail Caesar," said the voice.

"I assume it would be futile to call out for help."

"You'll be gurgling blood before you manage to utter the first word."

"Not to be to presumptive, but you're not very tall so I'm not being blessed with the presence of the Beast. Do I finally get to meet the legendary Boatman?"

The blade pressed a bit harder. "Maybe. Or maybe you'll die in a second without ever having seen my face."

Nero allowed himself to laugh. "Your giant African counterpart hit my son with a crucifixion hammer and he didn't die. You know why?"

Boatman hated how relaxed Nero was. People feared him. Nero seemed amused by him. But he couldn't kill him, just yet, because he needed answers. He needed vital information about not removing just Nero but somehow removing the Empire. "I'll play along. Why?"

"Because my son is a god-made man like his father is. The gods would not let him die because he is the rightful heir to the Empire."

It was Boatman's turn to laugh. He kept the knife to Nero's throat but guided the emperor to an armchair. He sat Nero down and put his blade away. If Nero tried anything, Boatman would snap his neck in a matter of seconds. "You think you're a god?"

Nero ruffled, "I am a god. I don't *think* I am."

"You're deluded, I know that."

Nero reacted and went to lunge for Boatman, but Boatman punched Nero in the side of his right knee. It was like a hammer blow and caused Nero to crumple on the chair, the pain tearing through his body. Boatman knew exactly where a human body's vulnerabilities were and that a swift blow to someone's knee caps caused agony. Nero cried out in pain but no-one came through the door.

"Okay, this is how it's going to work, *my Lord*. I'm going to ask you some questions and you're going to answer them. If you don't provide an answer, then that knee that is in a lot of pain will be in even more pain. Clear enough for a god to understand?"

Nero nodded, trying to keep the bile down. He leant forward, breathing hard.

Boatman proceeded to ask Nero key questions about the Empire and, specifically, how Nero fit in the system. Nero didn't resist. He saw no reason to. Boatman was deluded to think any of this information would change anything. Once Boatman left, Nero would employ the entire might of the Empire to come to Britannia and not only kill Boatman but kill every single person with any association with him. Boatman's third cousins who had never met him would be crucified. As Nero dutifully answered, he imagined seeing Boatman's sister (if there was one) hanging from a cross.

Boatman finished the interrogation and wasn't surprised that Nero spilled so much without any real resistance. For an Emperor who was an incarnation of a god, he was quite the pussy. Boatman knelt down in front of the emperor and squeezed the injured knee in case there were any thoughts of trying to get a cheap shot in. "I have one final question for you, Caesar."

"You know, when I find you and your scum family, I will make sure I return the favor on your knee, but you'll be hanging from a cross when I hit it with a hammer."

"I doubt that, because no-one will be willing to listen to you."

"And why would that be?"

"Because the bastard son of an outcast centurion doesn't hold much sway over an empire."

Nero laughed again. "You think you can scare me with shitty rumors about my birthright? I've heard them my entire life."

"Oh, they're not rumors," said Boatman and he pulled out the DNA results Faust had given him. He handed them to Nero, and Nero went white. "That's right, the apple doesn't fall far from the tree. And your tree is far away from the emperor's palace."

Nero just kept rereading the DNA results proving he wasn't heir to the Empire and that Augustus had lied to him. He needed to destroy any evidence and lurched for Boatman. Boatman was too quick, and Nero felt a sting in his chest. He looked down and saw the hilt of a blade protruding from his chest. He didn't feel any pain but could feel life oozing out of his body.

Now he knew he wasn't a god. He wanted to lift his hands to pull the blade out but everything felt weak and distant. He no longer felt connected to his body and as his life slipped away, he thought he had been wrong about the fishermen he was watching earlier. He wasn't like them at all, waiting to hook something. He was actually like the salmon, waiting to be hooked. He was just another pawn in the game of the gods and now was his time to reach out, like a salmon, be snagged and die with no-one around to care.

And indeed, as Nero breathed his last, no-one in that room did care. As silently as Boatman entered the room, he briefly glanced back at the dying emperor, felt no remorse, and left with only a slight puff of breeze tickling the dying man's face.

Chapter 52

Faust decided to roll the dice. He wasn't going to get Nero into the bunker where Boatman would pounce, so he needed to find another time to depose the emperor. He had to be patient and play the long game. He was fed up with appeasing Boatman, too. He wanted to use Boatman to get rid of the emperor and try to forge a new era for the Empire, and Boatman was a pawn in that, but now it was getting tiresome. He thought he was going to be able to manipulate Boatman to do what was needed and he almost had managed that, but now Nero had put a damper on that. Faust was unable to manipulate him. He was trying to play too many pieces, and it wasn't working, so it was time to go back to basics and remove a complication. He found a room and radioed Boatman. "Are you in position?"

"Yes. Is he inside the bunker?"

"He's inside and alone. For his safety, I told him."

"Good. We're directly below the bunker and will let let you know when it's done. Speak soon." Boatman cut contact.

Faust left the room and found four soldiers. He instructed them that they were to go to the emperor's bunker and without hesitation open fire into the room. There were to be no survivors and to be no mercy. The soldiers nodded and made their way to the bunker. Faust told the soldiers to keep their helmet cameras on so he could see the situation play out. He walked back toward Nero's office and passed dozens of soldiers guarding every doorway and hallway. There was no way Boatman or one his his acolytes would get through this wall of Roman might.

Faust looked around and asked a soldier, "Where's Aloysius? He should be guarding the emperor." The soldier shrugged and said he hadn't seen Nero's bodyguard, who wasn't in the office. That had been locked as soon as Faust had left earlier. Faust tried to reach Aloysius but couldn't connect. Opposite Nero's office door was an armchair that Faust sat on. He would watch as the soldiers stormed the bunker and killed Boatman, and then he would please the emperor with the news. Hopefully that would deflect Nero's suspicions about loyalty, and then Faust would be able to focus on a more efficient plan.

Faust pulled out his phone and linked to the live stream of the soldiers entering the bunker. They opened the bunker door and immediately opened fire. No words of warning. The live stream went blank as the gun fire blasts overwhelmed the screen. Faust waited for the soldiers to give feedback about confirmed kills. Gunfire ceased and Faust's phone caught up with what was happening. Two bodies were sprawled on the bunker floor. The solider with the helmet camera walked over to one of the bodies. It was a man and looked like Boatman's physique. Faust needed to be sure. "Turn the body over so I can see his face. I need to be sure that's Boatman."

The solider acknowledged Faust's request and bent down and heaved the body over. He stood up and allowed the camera to focus again. "Get in closer. I can't make out his face," said Faust.

The soldier knelt down so Faust could see the body's face. Faust squinted and held his phone closer to his face, 'What the fuck?" He pulled the screen closer to be sure of what he was seeing. The body, riddled with bullets wasn't Boatman, but Nero's bodyguard Aloysius. Faust leapt from his chair and rushed into Nero's office. Nero wasn't at his desk. Faust turned around to see Nero sat serenely in an armchair against the wall. Faust walked over, knowing Nero was dead but finding it hard to believe.

Nero was ginger-haired and pale-skinned, so even being dead with a knife through his heart hadn't change his complexion much, but Faust was stunned to see Caesar Nero dead through murder. He scoffed at the idea of emperors as gods, but cultural indoctrination meant he still, deep down, thought there was no way you could truly kill an emperor. He had tried to employ the services of Boatman, if he was honest, because he was actually unsure a Caesar could die. Faust had a photographic memory. He found superstition primitive but yet, these men had been ruling the world for thousands of years. That surely wasn't a fluke.

So he stared at the body of Nero and felt frozen. What would happen? Max being barely able to blink meant there was a vacuum waiting to be filled. The thing was, he was aiming to fill the vacuum without anyone able to reveal his intentions of how he got to that point. But Boatman wasn't dead and would be able to reveal their collusion. As he thought of Boatman, his phone rang. It was Boatman. "Let's cut to the chase. I've done you a favor and killed the emperor. Meet me at your local and we'll settle things." The call ended.

Faust didn't think anyone knew about his local. He always went in secret. Anyhow, Boatman had managed to kill Emperor Nero II.

It wasn't time to get weird about watering hole knowledge. Faust left the office and locked the door. He called two soldiers and told them to guard the door. No-one in and no-one out. And if either of them disturbed the emperor, they would be crucified. Faust made his way to the Victory.

Chapter 53

Boatman was sitting at a long table at the far end of the pub. He was just sitting there, nonchalantly, like a normal guy, having a casual beer on a weekend afternoon. Faust admired him for that. Before Faust arrived, he had instructed soldiers to evacuate the pub, telling them there was a genuine terrorist threat. He had also said that if Boatman was in there, then they were to go nowhere near him. It appeared a couple of soldiers saw their chance for glory and ignored orders and went to apprehend Boatman. One soldier looked like a rag doll with his neck facing the wrong way to his body and the other soldier appeared to have died clutching his chest hoping to stop the flow of blood coming from what Faust assumed was a ruptured heart. Faust stepped over the bodies and remained a safe distance from the still sitting Boatman.

"Well done," said Faust. He looked down at the soldiers' bodies. "You've taken down an emperor and, possibly, an empire. I'm impressed."

Boatman didn't say anything, but got up from his stool and smashed the bottle he was drinking from on the table so the neck was now a weapon. He stepped round the long table. Faust didn't step back. "What, no comment on the history you've made?" Boatman took another step. "You need to learn from your right-hand men. They at least have something pithy to say in these situations."

Boatman ignored the comment. With speed that made the motion almost imperceptible, he thrust the bottle at Faust. Faust was a bit of a mystery within the Empire. It was well-known that he was an intellectual behemoth, but he was a mystery as a centurion, who were known to be fighters. Few living had really seen Faust fight.

Faust's defense was as rapid as Boatman's thrust. Two lightning-fast forces colliding made things appear to be in slow motion. As Boatman went to plunge the bottle into Faust's neck, Faust grabbed Boatman's wrist, twisted it and released the bottle from his grasp. Before the bottle even hit the floor, Boatman allowed the momentum of his lunge and his wrist being gripped to carry him forward and spun anti-clockwise. It almost looked as if the two men were doing a dance routine. But as they drew parallel, Boatman dropped to one knee and punched Fuast in the groin. Boatman always knew that when you meet an equal you play dirty. Faust let out a gasp but instinctively brought his elbow down on Boatman's head and both men collapsed on the pub floor.

Boatman felt like he had been smashed on the top of the head with a hammer, and his head was spinning. He tried to get to his feet but collapsed, the power of the blow dazing him. It was also surprising; he rarely found anyone able to inflict any damage on him. Faust seemed almost prescient. Boatman got to one knee and raised his head to see Faust bringing a punch square at his face. Boatman brought up both arms and blocked the punches. He was in an awkward position, so used Faust's momentum against him. As Faust rained down more punches, Boatman rolled backwards, grabbed Faust's shirt and threw the Roman over his head with his left leg on his chest. A classic Judo move. Faust went scrambling, and it gave Boatman time to get to his feet and make the fight even again.

Faust was unperturbed and moved like lightning at Boatman again. Boatman barely saw the punch and just managed to deflect it before it connected with his throat. Honed instinct kicked in, and Boatman relaxed his body. As Faust went for a second attempt at Boatman's throat, Boatman stepped forward. This meant the Roman's strike hit Boatman's ear, which was painful as hell, but far less damaging. As soon as Faust's punch connected Boatman, whipped his left arm up and throttled Faust, squeezing his throat. Even Faust was unable to handle the sudden loss of power and breath and collapsed.

Boatman pinned Faust down. Boatman saw the opportunity to rid London of all its diseases and carried on squeezing the Roman's throat.

Faust managed to rasp a few words under the pressure of Boatman's grip, "You have a choice."

"A choice?"

"Save your own life or save the lives of your loved ones."

"I don't think you're in a position to threaten me." Boatman squeezed harder to prove his point. As he did that though, he felt pressure at his left side. He looked down and saw a red stain pooling on his shirt. His grip loosened on Faust."

"That's your choice, get to hospital to save yourself or get to your HQ to save your loved ones. If you're at your HQ when my soldiers arrive, they will execute you as payment and let your loved ones go free."

Boatman felt his strength falter. The wound was deep but not deep enough to be instantly fatal. He let go of Faust's throat and staggered to his feet. "Bullshit, you don't know where our HQ is."

"Don't I? Can you take that chance?"

Boatman touched his ear and radioed Bella, "Bella, you hearing this?"

"I'm on my way. I'll get them out," she said.

"Ah yes, your right-hand lady, Bella. There to save the day. You think she will get to them on time? If you leave now, I'll delay the soldiers by a few minutes. Call it sacrificial courtesy."

"Fuck you," said Boatman. He dropped to one knee. He wasn't sure he would make it out of the room, let alone manage to make it back to HQ.

Faust eyed Boatman. He didn't think he had wounded the rebel leader that badly. Maybe he had overestimated this man again. The legend of Boatman seemed to be much more formidable than the reality. But wasn't that always the case? Myths, legends and realities. After all, only moments ago he had looked at the murdered body of Nero. Something seemingly impossible based on Nero's belief in his god status. Then Boatman had shown why he had been the thorn in the side of the Empire for so many years, moving with such speed that Faust barely had time to register it. "If I'm going down, then you're going down with me," said Boatman and with his own blade wounded Faust in the same spot. Faust dropped to the floor.

"Now you have a choice," said Boatman. "Get us both to a hospital, or we both die." As Faust pulled out his phone, Boatman took it from him and said, "And call off your soldiers or I will let us both die here."

Faust obliged and radioed for soldiers to urgently take him and another to hospital for stab wound treatment. As soon as Boatman was sure the attack dogs had been called off, he got to his feet, walked over to Faust and kicked him hard in the head. Faust was badly injured and couldn't even lift his hands to stop the blow.

Faust's world went black. He had, in fact, underestimated Boatman as the rebel leader exaggerated how injured was and staggered out of the pub through the back door and made his way home.

On his way, he got in touch with Bella who confirmed she had evacuated Olivia, Tobias and Molly and they were moving through the tunnels to the Fish borough. Boatman said he would meet them there and, like the phantom he was renowned to be, disappeared through a secret entrance to the tunnel network. The only indication of his presence was the trail of blood droplets marking his every footstep.

Chapter 54

Two weeks later, Faust was in Nero's former office. The knife wound from Boatman had almost killed him, so he was on light duties and certainly not going to be visiting any front-line incidents. Since Nero's death, the Empire had been thrown into chaos. The Senate thought this was their opportunity to create a true republic. Caesar cultists threatened insurrection if the Senate attempted a coup against the rightful heir to the Empire, Maximus. Faust saw his opportunity to manipulate the political chaos and said to the Grand Senator that he would, temporarily, install himself as the Grand Protector of Britannia. He said that in his temporary role he would limit immigration into the country, so as not to allow new terror groups to rise up, and he would also use the time to formulate how to start a dialogue with the RIA.

Boatman and his followers were in the wind and had seemingly disappeared. It was all quiet on the Britannia front. For now. Faust was looking at a document on his desk. It was similar to the DNA test results that revealed Nero was the biological son of a centurion called Ira. A nasty son of a bitch. Faust wasn't there when Nero died at the hands of Boatman and wondered whether Nero had been told the truth of his origins. Did he die knowing he wasn't the god he thought he was? That realization would have been more painful than the knife wound to his heart.

This DNA test result did still involve centurion Ira but instead of it showing Nero as the biological son, it read Boatman. Boatman King was Nero's half-brother and uncle to Maximus. Faust was struggling to understand the information or how to use it. He was still struggling to negotiate the knowledge he had that Max wasn't a true heir to the Empire, but to reveal that truth wouldn't necessarily change Max's ascension if he ever woke up. Max's injuries had made him a martyr and the fact that he survived an attack from The Beast meant an increasing number of citizens thought Max was chosen by the gods.

Indeed, the information about Max's ancestry could even cause a change to how the Empire decided its Caesars, which could technically make Boatman a contender to the throne. No, Faust concluded, he would keep that information close to him until there was a time or place to use it to his advantage.

His phone rang. When he answered, a familiar voice said, "How's your side?"

"If you were trying to hit an organ, you missed."

"Call it professional courtesy."

"There seems to be a lot of that going around. How about you drop by the office and just admit defeat?"

"Defeat? From where I'm sitting, I see an Empire with a dead emperor, a comatose heir and an isolated Britannia. I'd say mission accomplished."

"I'm sure you would. By the way, how's that shitty cave you're hiding in?"

There was a pause and then Boatman said, "At least I'm not

sitting on the cum-stained seat of a dead emperor." The line went dead and Faust turned around to the window behind him, got up and looked out. The Thames was its usual busy self, with fishing boats lining for salmon. He watched as the salmon frantically flapped, unaware that the more they fought, the deeper the hook went. It reminded him of Boatman, who was unaware of the Empire's hook. The more Boatman fought the system he despised, the closer and deeper it would take him to that very system.

Faust wanted to feel a sense of superiority that he was the Grand Protector of Britannia and Boatman had been exiled, but all that kept going through his mind were Boatman's recent words on the phone. It struck Faust hard that, essentially, all he was doing was carrying on the stained legacy of a deluded emperor. All he was doing was overseeing a smutty mess but trying to pretend it was all new. Really, he was just chaotically flapping around and the Empire's hook was digging in deeper.

Faust walked over to his desk and picked up his phone. He called back the last number and, to his surprise, it rang. Boatman answered, "Phoning to surrender?"

"I'm coming for you."

"I'm looking forward to it."

The line went dead.

Epilogue

Max opened his eyes, and the light made his head scream. He managed to make the scream inside his brain turn into a scream via his mouth. The doctors came running into his room. Shouts were hollered to each other that the emperor's son was awake and to quickly administer pain relief.

As the pain relief was given, Max felt the brain scream die down and his eyes adjusted to fluorescent light that was offensive to even the healthiest person. As his mind settled, images of Maverick standing over him with a bloodied hammer flashed in and out of focus like a sadistic flip book. Max allowed the images to come into focus, though, embracing the pain of the man who had caved his skull in. He would relive that moment again and again and again. He would use it as his visual mantra to recovery. He would use it as his motivator to get out of this dump. So he focused on the image of Maverick and mumbled his name. He ignored the banal presence of the doctors and nurses and, each hour, each day continued to mumble Maverick's name. He would mumble The Beast's name until he was released from the hospital and was able to hunt him down and mumble his name in his enemy's ear as he caved his skull with Tobias helplessly watching.

Milton Keynes UK
Ingram Content Group UK Ltd.
UKHW032325070824
1193UKWH00003B/152